DOCTOR WHO

THE TAKING OF PLANET 5
SIMON BUCHER-JONES AND MARK CLAPHAM

Published by BBC Worldwide Ltd,
Woodlands, 80 Wood Lane
London W12 0TT

First published 1999
Copyright © Simon Bucher-Jones and Mark Clapham 1999
The moral right of the authors has been asserted

Original series broadcast on the BBC

Format © BBC 1963

Doctor Who and TARDIS are trademarks of the BBC

ISBN 0 563 55585 8

Imaging by Black Sheep, copyright © BBC 1999

Printed and bound in Great Britain by Mackays of Chatham

Cover printed by Belmont Press Ltd, Northampton

I don't normally do these Oscar speech things. However, thanks are due to:

Sarah for putting up with nocturnal typing and daily zombification; Lawrence Miles for letting me loose on his creations from *Alien Bodies* (yes, I *know* he'd signed away the rights and couldn't stop me but it's nice to feel trusted by an author I admire); everyone at the Tavern who invites me to parties I never go to; my other friends for repeatedly asking when I'm going to write a proper book (I didn't say I listened to them); and (of course) Mark for being a nifty writer and helping me out when it was clear that a more important project – my second daughter, Rhianna Linnea Bucher-Jones, who was born in April – wouldn't let me do a solo book this year.

– SB-J

Dedicated to my fellow sufferers:

Marianna Adams, Rosie Hawes, Vanessa Hill, Emma McCarthy, Mike Redman, Sam Sanders and Jess Thomas. It's been an experience.

Thanks to Simon for letting me loose on his book; the Bloomsbury Local Group (Jon Miller, Jim Smith and Tat Wood) for advice and whatnot; Lance Parkin for 'being my Yoda'; Peter Siani-Davies for realising where my priorities lay; Rebecca Kneale for the Stacy anecdote; and all the rest of the author mafia (especially Jon Blum, Kate Orman and Lawrence Miles) for continuity discussions. May our critics soon sleep with the fishes. Thanks also to Mum, Dad, Sarah, Orlando, Emily Coles and Andrew Plummer.

– MC

Some things are true everywhere. One of them is this. No society can endure for ever without at least one outsider.

There are reasons for this. One is essentially pragmatic. No ruling body can ever comprehend the most likely causes of its own destruction. Power ossifies even before it corrupts. For the powerful too many things are both arbitrary and contingent. To be told that something is beyond control becomes unthinkable. Rulers need outcasts to tell them what they can no longer see. Even if they kill the outcasts afterwards: they need them. Not that that's any consolation to the outsiders, I expect, even if they get baked into a pie – as is the custom among the Androgums.

Then there are the forces of snobbery. These are not to be underestimated. The singing squids of Anagonia nudge each other furtively when a tone-deaf sidles by banging its six muted gongs. The sessile stalagbats of Marinus affect not to notice the echo soundings of their cave-mouth-dwelling cousins. There are even stranger examples, but naturally I wouldn't discuss them with people of your sort.

– Extract from Captain Cook's *Letters from Golobus*

Prologue

There was a place in Hell where skulls were the only ornaments, and the servants had no faces. Even from there he had been cast out. As a shadow of a shade he came to dwell at the edge of a certain abyss, in a tower built out of the bodies of those he had personally marked when he had been allowed in the dark councils of Mictlan. This happened soon after the masters of the Celestial Intervention Agency, the Celestis, had pulled the doors of perception closed behind themselves lest their histories be unravelled in the war with the Time Lords' future enemy, in the battles they had foreseen. They had put reality behind them like a bad dream and turned themselves into creatures built out of mythemes and the working of nanoscopic machine-demons. They had poisoned the walls of reality itself, until Mictlan had bubbled up into existence on its far side, a cyst of galled space-time cut off from the time winds. It was their glorious world of the dead.

The outcast had been young. In his opening speech to the Last Parliament – the grey and stifling government of Mictlan – he had, in passing, described the achievements of its building as 'parasitic' in operation. While accurate, it was perhaps that infelicity of expression that began his fall.

It may have been something else. He may have committed a social *faux pas* or perhaps a crime or a breach of some protocol or ruling. He never knew. The Celestis do not explain. They do not apologise. They turned their shadowy backs to him like cases of mummified beetles and drew away. He never heard another voice. The servants alone did not scorn him, but their husklike regard was worse than their master's indifference. He realised he had already become less even than they.

Even so he found something to occupy him.

He watched what was on the other side of Mictlan.

He watched the endless sea of nothingness where universes pass and repass.

He did not remain alone for ever.

Of all the secrets, the child knew, the sea was the most hidden. It was hidden by custom rather than by walls or invisibility shields and the child had learned early that custom hid a multitude of sins. The sea had had no name and was shown on no maps. In whispers the damned called it the Invisible – or the Outer – Ocean.

When the exams and the cull were over, and the doors of the orphanage had creaked open the width of a thin man to allow the blood of the unworthy to flow into the grey gunmetal gutters, the child, still aching from the pain of delivering the killing blows, would creep out, alone. It – no gender had yet been selected for it from the Wardrobes – had earned the privacy with the fury with which it had dealt out the fatal wounds. No one would stay to talk with such a one after the sluices had activated. Without companions then, it stalked, hunched over, into the night, up on to the promontory of spars and flotsam that edged the unacknowledged sea.

It was a serious crime. The Teachers in their hooded robes pretended not to know of the Invisible Ocean. Although their whole curriculum was dependent on the understanding of the Inland Sea – which some call the universe – and the exploitation of its inhabitants, the Other Sea, looking outward to the unknown, was beyond their claustrophobic world with its narrow universal walls.

The servants also ignored it. That did not surprise the child. The young of Hell, no less than their peers, viewed their servants in the same way as they might view a chair or a table. Servants were furniture: each a thing valuable only for its usefulness, or – perhaps – its beauty, whose only danger might lie in its deployment by others in some lethal or obscene practical joke. The other pupils, male and female, neuter and unformed, affected also to give it no mind, although it was clear that some at least knew of it. Once, a drawing of the Ocean had been found pinned to a submonitor (through the eye, killing the nasty little beast stone dead) and the whole scholarum had been put to the Kindly Question, but even then the reality of the Ocean had not been officially conceded. It was as if it simply were not there to the Masters, although its waves beat with persistence more terrible for its very mindlessness on the outermost walls of the orphanage itself. One day, the child thought, one day soon all this will be washed away. It was as near to a prayer as any thought can be in Hell.

A hermit lived by the Invisible Ocean, if living described his broken existence. He had somehow transgressed the strict rules that governed the doings of the Masters. What his crime had been, the child could barely imagine: speaking in Council with his face visible perhaps, or intoning without irony the Principles of Rassilon. The Masters were unforgiving. All praise to the Masters!

The hermit had been broken. Yet still some knowledge remained in him, and he alone – outside taboo, allowed to exist perhaps because his sundering from the Masters gave him a sacred status beyond damnation – had studied the Invisible Ocean. Gradually he told the child all he knew about the things he had seen on the other side of that burning, bruise-dark sea.

One cold midnight, they watched together as one of the orbs that hung like phantom fruit high on the tree boughs of the night was devoured by something vast and strange. The old man had held a thin finger to his lips. 'The Swimmers come and go,' he said. 'The Swimmers eat.'

The child's eyes had been large with wonder, fear and darkness. 'What do they eat, Master?'

The hermit shuddered. 'Everythings,' he whispered. 'They eat Everythings. I will show you universes in a bowl of gruel.'

Chapter One

The City is of Night; perchance of Death,
But certainly of Night; for never there
Can come the lucid morning's fragrant breath
After the dewy dawning's cold grey air;
The moon and stars may shine with scorn or pity;
The sun has never visited that city,
For it dissolveth in the daylight fair.

– The City of Dreadful Night
James Thomson 1874

Painstakingly, gloved hand over gloved hand, Thomas Jessup climbed down the rope ladder into the cavern under the partly dismembered mountain range. It was perilous work. The ladder swung free of any wall, attached to the rim of a ten-foot hole in the ceiling, thirty feet up from the cavern floor. Don't think about that, Jessup told himself. Don't think about slick grapples coming loose, or snow boots failing to grip steel rungs. With some relief he found his boots making contact with solid rock.

There was no one around. The generator whirred away to itself, a deep self-satisfied whirr like a fat bee, surrounded by half-empty equipment cases. A series of linked sodium bulbs stretched away from the generator and down the tunnel, strung out like fairy lights.

'So, start without me, why don't you?' Jessup muttered to himself. Twenty minutes on the surface wrestling with the sat-phone, doing the bureaucracy no one else on this team bothered with, and they ran off without him. Pausing only to give one of the crates a childish kick, Jessup proceeded to follow the trail of lights, around the tunnel corner to the site they had located only an hour before. Here he found Ferdinand, already hard at work examining the walls of Site B. Site A had proved to be a dead end, a ragged pit – apparently bottomless – that appeared to have been torn out under the subterranean ruins, whole levels of possible discoveries tumbling down into darkness. Schneider insisted that the damage had been done from below. It had given Jessup the creeps, but now he thought that Site B, with its promise of finds intact, may be worse.

The electric light illuminated only a small area, but the vastness of the structure was clear: an odd, rounded entranceway, artificially carved from local rock and inscribed with seemingly endless spirals of signs and pictograms. Ferdinand was concentrating on a ground-level strip of symbols, the old Venezuelan scribbling in a notebook, a wizened figure swamped by his bulky environment suit.

'Cold out,' said Jessup by way of conversation.

'It's Antarctica,' Ferdinand replied eventually, too engrossed to notice any irony. 'What do you expect?'

'I expect the ice above our heads to crush us to death any time now,' replied Jessup. 'But that's hardly the point. How're things going there?'

Ferdinand shrugged, scraped his fingernails through his wispy grey beard.

'Disturbing,' he eventually replied. 'The way these symbols are organised, the whole five-pointedness of the arrays, seems to represent a radical approach to language structure, a whole different mindset to ours.'

'To translators?' asked Jessup facetiously.

'To humans,' replied Ferdinand, turning to fix Jessup with

his pinprick black eyes.

'Oh,' replied Jessup quietly. The UN had been expecting something like this, ever since the images from the orbital X-ray observatory, whose Earthward-pointing end-of-life calibration checks had been passed on by the Max Planck Institute for Extraterrestrial Physics, confirmed that there was something there under the ice. Something large. Possibly something alien. Project Icepack had been sent in, hoping to find a nice little geological anomaly, perhaps evidence of an advanced form of igloo, then head straight back home.

Instead, within an hour of cracking through the ice and lowering themselves into the tunnel system, they had come across the ludicrously ornate entranceway. An entrance obviously not designed for five- to six-foot-tall bipeds.

'I hate all this Lara Croft bullshit,' said Jessup.

'Huh,' snapped Ferdinand. 'At least exploration's your field. Most of my colleagues get to do their translations in their nice warm offices. Speaking of which...'

'Yeah, yeah, I'm off,' replied Jessup. 'Any idea where my fellow grave robber has got to?'

Ferdinand shrugged. 'God's gift to archaeology? Miss McCarthy does as she pleases, as well you should know. Schneider's with the artefact, though.'

Jessup blinked. 'The what?'

Following Ferdinand's directions, Jessup wandered down a few corridors. Air shafts and crawl spaces twisted off from the larger tunnels, the wind whistling through them in disconcerting fashion. The lesser passages weren't built to the same scale as the massive corridors and Jessup wondered if they had been used by a different type of creature: to judge from the insane twirlings and grooved toing and fro-ing of the side tunnels, anything that had found them comfortable would have been very odd indeed. Sickeningly odd.

Jessup tried to ignore the noise of the wind. Above their heads it was subtracting a hellish ten degrees from the baseline minus eighty-seven degrees of the Antarctic winter. By night it may be minus a hundred degrees Fahrenheit out there.

The eye-bending friezes carved into most of the walls seemed to mock his frailty. According to initial tests on the microfractures in the material, they had to be between ten and twenty million years old. They were going to last for ever. He felt he might just see out the week.

He found Schneider at the centre of a rounded, delicately tiled chamber examining the 'artefact'. To his surprise, Jessup realised he couldn't find a better word for it himself. He sure as hell had never seen anything like it before.

It stood on an obviously custom-built stone plinth. Its base was an intricately patterned box made from some unearthly, blue-tinged metal. Oily pink flashes occasionally drifted across its polished surfaces. Sprouting from the top was an ovoid, glassy black object – a lens? – in which amorphous shapes seemed to reside. The ovoid was attached to the box by what seemed like fingers of bone, reaching up to clasp the ovoid in place. In all, it must have been five foot tall. The globe itself was about the diameter of an American football helmet.

'Don't even ask,' said Schneider, the group's Valkyrie-esque leader. She had been with EDICT for years, working on the potential threat from millennial death cults. Rumour had it her work was so impressive she had been offered the chance to come across and play with the big toys. She was currently setting up a digital camera, adjusting the light to get the best perspective on the artefact. No matter how she adjusted the lamps, the damn thing seemed to absorb it, swathed in gloom.

'What's the latest from the geosat guys?' Schneider asked, frowning at the artefact as if it were a wriggling child refusing to co-operate with a school photographer.

Jessup shrugged. 'Not much. They're still thinking the unthinkable, that there was some kind of mountain range here once, and it was levelled by a –'

He was cut off by McCarthy bursting into the room. The plump American's face was even redder than usual as she grabbed Jessup's hand. Her blue eyes were tripped-out wide. Her head jiggled, simultaneously trying to address both him and Schneider.

'You gotta see this,' she croaked, short of breath. 'You just gotta see it.'

Before he could complain, Jessup found McCarthy's grip on his hand tightening, and she was dragging him down the corridor. They were moving away from Site A, deeper into the outlying 'city'. There were no lights here, so McCarthy led them by torchlight. Jessup could hear Schneider muttering to herself as she followed close behind, stumbling as she tried to keep pace with McCarthy. As they proceeded through the dark, only the wildly swinging beam of McCarthy's torch to give any indication of their surroundings, Jessup found himself feeling the urge to turn back, to run. He tried to ignore it as he was dragged onward through a zigzag of similar tunnels.

DESPAIR. *Kittens scrabbling at the black sack interior as the water rises, blood and fur clogging in the pitch-dark waters under the ice. The taste of blood, iron-strong.*

What was that? Jessup found himself trying to break McCarthy's grip, but the American was nothing if not a sturdy country gal.

DESPAIR. ENDLESS AGONY. *The rack, the iron maiden, the re-sensitisation of nerves worn down with pain. The anti-endorphins in the sealed laboratory. Room 101. Room 101.2. The fact that radiation is measured in Grays. The false memories of a thousand abductees.*

Thomas Jessup had always been sensitive to these things. That was why UNIT chose him. That was why he wanted to run, while neither of his companions noticed a thing out of place. Trapped between McCarthy and Schneider in the narrowing tunnels – surely they couldn't be claustrophobic: hadn't they been built for things larger than humans? – he couldn't escape. The images themselves did not make any sense, or possibly they made too much. Things he had seen done, things he had been forced to confront or imagine on other missions. His own prepackaged frozen albatrosses.

DESPAIR. LONELINESS. ABANDONED. *The door closing. Mother's face angry and pinched in the final narrowing gap of light. The sounds from the other room. Over and over and over. A bamboo cane striking flesh.*

Christ, that wasn't his memory. Someone had had a rough childhood.

Round the corner now, into its presence. The chamber was similar to the room with the artefact, similar swirls of coloured tiles covering rounded walls, all surfaces focused on the mass residing in an alcove opposite. They didn't need the torches: the very walls crackled with energy from the thing, lightning flickers licking bare stone. All radiating from the creature whose despair Jessup could feel, the creature whose presence McCarthy had dragged him into. Fifteen feet wide, a creature of raw stuff, pitch-black flesh impenetrable to the rough sodium light. A maw, a void. The mouth that eats itself for ever. The word for agony made flesh. Jessup keeled over in its presence, the thing's eternal pain flooding his mind. This time he got a taste of its images. *The tormentors. The stiff-necked, narrow ones. The war between the aeons. The sundering between the moments, seconds eating away like mouths.*

For want of something better to do, they had been reading the literature while they waited: Fitz slouched against a giant cactuslike pillar that seemed to have been designed as a yak's back-scratcher, and Compassion constantly pacing. Fitz wasn't sure what he had expected; the Wallachians were humanoid – not like the human colonists he'd met on the other future worlds the Doctor had taken him to, but not like monsters either. *Real* aliens. And they looked like men with slightly dodgy make-up. Blue eye shadow and warty heads aside, they had been as unhelpful as anyone when the Doctor had turned out to want to see everything on a budget of only thirty walloons a day. A walloon was the smallest Wallachian coin in existence – worth about a farthing, Fitz thought.

Waiting rooms were alike everywhere. True, the leaflets were self-sustaining patterns of 3-D light that the Doctor called holograms, and the wire racks looked like fountains or orchids, but that didn't stop it being basically a room dedicated to getting people out and about to fertilise the local economy with big spadefuls of cash.

Compassion had swept the room once with her most disdainful gaze, before picking at the holograms as if she were picking the petals off flowers, or legs off spiders. She waved one vaguely in Fitz's direction. 'Can you see the sense in this?'

Fitz watched the holofield reshape itself, and felt an entirely unwanted blush creeping up around his collar. He grabbed the flickering floating handkerchief of light and shoved it in a pocket. 'I think I'd better study that properly back in the TARDIS.' He managed a sardonic shrug. 'From their pose it's probably an advert for Vick's vapour rub, but I'm going to have fun finding out if it's audience participation. If we're going to be at the Second Wallachian Exhibition, as long as the Doctor wants we may as well start stocking up on things to see.'

Compassion shrugged. No small talk, that was her problem. Remote in every sense of the word. Fitz absently stroked the side of his nose with a finger. He was itching for a cigarette – the urge seemed to have picked up again – but the stylised syringe on the wall, shot through with a threatening purple lightning bolt, suggested that the Wallachians frowned on stimulants. Unless they sold them, of course.

He wished he had had time to change. True, they hadn't seen anyone yet in anything but basic bureaucratic gear – all pinstriped tabards and chrome bowlers – but, judging by the scarlet and silver décor, any second the cast of *Flash Gordon's Trip to Mars* were going to saunter by and he was going to look like a fool still wearing the faded sixties outfit he had reverted to for comfort before the Doctor had pulled this unexpected pit stop. He had been pillaging the TARDIS wardrobes for a while, as if dress sense were the only sense he could make of things, but finally the familiar had overwhelmed him as if it were a kind of uniform. Mr Out-Of-Place First Class.

By contrast, Compassion looked – as always – as if she owned the place, or as if she might be heading a consortium dedicated to tearing it down and putting up something else. Something from elsewhere. Something alien. In a sense she was as human as he was, but it was at least a sixth sense. She was on the edge of human. She was attractive; hair dark red, well-built in a muscular rather than a sexy way, but still with enough curvature to make an archimandrite kick a hole in a stained-glass window. Particularly in the black cocktail dress she had found somewhere in the TARDIS wardrobes. Fitz smiled. Maybe one day. If he was very drunk. And if she'd had a personality transplant.

She tossed another hologram his way. 'Another for your collection.' A smile quirked her lips. 'Call it the Library of Congress.' He glanced at it. A caption, indented in semi-raised type, read: ANGELIC COURTING RITUALS CAPTURED ON VIDEO. He tried to gauge her reaction. Tone alone wasn't always a good guide with Her Majesty. She wasn't angry or upset, he decided. She wasn't peeved, or displeased, or put upon – all of which might well describe his feelings. She just honestly didn't care – or perhaps she cared in ways he couldn't fathom. So lacking, as usual, any key to turn, any path to follow, any way to reach her, he shrugged and took refuge inside his own thoughts. Her dark eyes watched and her lips moved, and someone very strong was at home inside her head, but Fitz increasingly didn't know who. It made it worse that he had once, in a sense, known her extremely well. Once he had taken her orders, but that had been another him. He had been separated from the Doctor.

Lost on her remote world, which, while it had been of Earth origin, had also been raised to a pattern set by Faction Paradox, the militant voodoo hippies from beyond time. There he had died and been remembered by Compassion's people. As he had been remembered, so he had been reborn by their technologies. Not once, but many times, and the end result of that chain of memories had worked with her, until the Doctor had caught up with the program, and the TARDIS had remembered Fitz back the way he had been originally.

He didn't remember much of their time as the Doctor's – there was no nice way to say it – enemies. Not that the Doctor had ever referred to it again of course, but he guessed that Compassion understood things in him that he didn't know himself any more: possibly just distorted things, maybe true ones. It made her creepy. Creepier. Did she resent losing authority over him? Did she resent losing him? Had she had him? Had he had her? God, it was complicated.

He hadn't seen much of her during that business with the Enclave and the fit Time Lady, hadn't been sure he'd wanted to, and the pace of events had swept them apart anyway. Now they were back together and he didn't know how to talk to her. He missed Sam; either Sam, any Sam.

Compassion's silence was getting on his nerves. He gestured. A grand wave of his arms like a mad guitar player, taking in the luminous statues, the hologram-bearing orchids, the giant plaster ducks fixed in midair by, he guessed, the appliance of science.

'Who can say, my pretty one?' he leered. It wasn't a serious leer – hell, he'd run a mile – but it never hurt to get some practice in. 'Perhaps the artists are followers of the Dadaist movement. Perhaps they're flinging paint in the faces not of their audience but of reality itself. Surely not even the sinister paintings of Pickman or Martinique himself ever held so sublime a shudder!' He wondered where he had got the name Pickman from – it had just popped on to his tongue.

'And more than their eyes followed you round the room,' the Doctor added stepping round from the other side of the row of black monolithic autotenders that ran along the chamber's far wall like displaced dominoes. He was carrying three 99s. Ice cream had dribbled on his bottle-green velvet sleeves. 'Get Fitz to tell you about the Vega Affair properly sometime. It was a singularly gruesome business.'

'No doubt you intervened at some moment of planetary calamity,' Compassion said, raising dark eyes to the false heavens of the ceiling. Ordinarily, with anyone ordinary, Fitz would have been inclined to pick up on that. To answer that yes, the Doctor and in all modesty Fitz himself had done their bit, and that the peoples of several worlds had owed their continued sleep and well-being to their masterly grasp of interstellar diplomacy, poker, shove-ha'penny and basic art criticism. He didn't do that often with Compassion, though. What would have been the point?

'It is almost certain that everyone involved would have solved their own problems without your assistance,' Compassion continued, 'and if they did not it is certain that it would not have mattered. Still, if it amused you...'

The Doctor looked stung. He leaned closer to Compassion and thrust an ice cream at her, flipping Fitz one at the same time. Fitz fumbled the catch, and it fell on the floor. The Doctor offered his, but Compassion got in first and closed Fitz's hand round her cornet, a small, possibly relieved, smile flitting over her – currently – bee-stung lips. Oblivious to this possible by-play, the Doctor had meanwhile taken a mouthful of chocolate, and having fished in his breast pocket was brandishing three golden tickets with his other hand. His hair bounced like something from a shampoo commercial.

Much as he admired the Doctor – and it was a jolt to his self-image to realise how much he was coming to depend on him – Fitz could have done without his being such a blatant bird-puller. And the horror and the shame of that was even greater when he confronted the evident fact that the Doctor didn't even seem to notice. Still, he was pleased to see it didn't work on Compassion. Not obviously anyway. If she was turned on to the Doctor's proximity she wasn't showing it.

'Now this is what I call amusing.' The Doctor beamed. 'Professor Mildeo Twisknadine's Wandering Museum of the Verifiably Phantasmagoric. Also known as the Museum of Things That Don't Exist. I've been trying to catch up with these people for some time. They've made a special study of the mythic, the outre and the rum. With the Enclave up in smoke, if anyone can suggest a backway into the Obverse, they should be able to.'

'You really want to go back?' Fitz asked, remembering the icy terror of the plains, and the ruined shards of glass that had rained down when war came to that peculiar little crystal city.

'He doesn't like to be thwarted,' Compassion said. 'You must see how it would annoy him to have to bow to destiny.' Her voice was slightly too cold for humour.

'Destiny, my dear Compassion, is the art of throwing darts at random and claiming that anything you hit was the target all along,' the Doctor said. 'I suppose I just can't bear to leave a story unfinished, still less a universe unexplored.'

'Gnomic,' Fitz muttered, 'brilliant.' But his spirits lifted as he imagined other reasons for the Doctor's interest. 'They're up to something then. A crime.' He stared round at the neonlike walls of the chamber as if expecting a bunch of ruffians to jump out of them, and lowered his voice. 'Smuggling dope, or gun-running.' His face brightened. 'White slavery!'

The Doctor combined shock and disapproval in one thunderous but brief expression, before reverting to his normal state of twice human enthusiasm.

'Oh no, nothing like that. At least, I don't think so. Honestly, anyone would think I spent all my time looking for trouble. There's quite enough mistrust in any universe without going around suspecting people of things. Sufficient unto the day

12

is the burden thereof, Fitz.'

Fitz sighed. 'So what is this Mildew Twistknacker's Museum about, when it's at home? We can't make any sense of these leaflets.'

'Why, my boy,' a strange voice boomed, and, as if by magic, a man appeared behind them. 'It is quite simply the plenum's premier peripatetic plenitude of potentially possible parafactology, and I have the honour to be none other than –' the plump little man's eyes gleamed – 'Mildew Twistknacker himself, so I ought to know.'

Turning, Fitz saw a rotund bear of a man, flashing tortoiseshell shirt split open to show chest hair braided into a thousand pleats. The man's face, too, was covered in hair, so that he resembled a botanist looking through foliage, but his eyes were icy circles of scarlet, piercingly, frighteningly alert and interested. Fitz felt an all too familiar embarrassment threatening. He opted for bluff and manly certitude.

'No offence, Professor: probably a common enough name where you hail from, but sadly a tongue-twister to my humble language translator.' He had seen such things in use a few times – to complete his gambit he made a burbling sound between his teeth, and poked at his pocket, deliberately mumbling a few random verbs. Right, sorted.

Sadly, his explanation fell on deaf ears, for the professor and the Doctor were too busy clapping each other on the back, and name-dropping third parties. They were, Fitz gathered, both friends (possibly, in the case of Mildeo, a rival) of someone called Vorg the Magnificent. Professor Mildeo claimed to have known him when he went by the name of Vorg the Adequate – 'and that was a gross extension of his capacities into the realm of hyperbole' – while the Doctor confided that he had last encountered the other showman trying to sell crustacoid pornography to the bemused unicellular life forms of Van Madden's Star.

'What', Compassion asked, 'is parafactology?'

The Doctor opened his mouth to explain, but glanced sideways at the self-proclaimed professor first and, as if in acknowledgment of his evident eagerness, waved a hand for the man to continue.

'Parafactology is the science of the untruth, my dear. The study of mistakes, misapprehensions, hoaxes, bamboozles, misconceptions (both common and rare), and the twelve catalogued kinds of bafflegap. We also have a small department dealing solely with technobabble, but that is rather new and will not be a serious discipline until another thousand years or so have passed. By studying the limits of the possible, by examining the things people choose to believe in the face of the absence of disproof, we can map the domain of the real, and –' he bowed as if expecting applause, 'thereby transcend it!'

The Doctor grinned. 'Splendid. I couldn't have put it half so well. I'm ever so pleased to have caught you. My friends and I would love a tour, and I have one or two special fakes and oddments aboard my ship so I've been meaning to drop in to see your collection ever since I first heard about it. Tell me, have you got a South American Missing Link? I have a bund forgery somewhere.'

'No, but I've got nine types of Yeti, including the robotic and the fungi varieties – perhaps we could swap!'

Fitz looked at Compassion. Compassion looked at Fitz. Perhaps some things did transcend all cultural barriers, bind together the divergent strata of the mind's metaphorical tectonics. It looked like being a long tour. A very long, boring tour.

* * *

14

Actually the museum was a surprise. It was serious, even imposing, from the outside, a hymn in marble and gold – although Mildeo's mannerisms had led Fitz to expect a cross between a gypsy caravan and the nine boxes of knick-knacks he had kept at the back of his flat, waiting for his mum to get better. Presumably they were still there, if the landlord hadn't tipped them out for the bin men.

The museum also looked utterly immobile and about as peripatetic as the Empire State Building. Fitz stopped himself asking how it got from world to world. He knew from experience that the Doctor would say something like, 'Well it emfoozles via the ephasmotic metahedron' – and he'd just have to nod as if he had understood. Sod it! He'd just take it as read for once.

Mildeo saw his look, but mistook it for architectural interest. 'It's modelled on the temple of Zeus, one of the seven wonders of Ancient Earth. Specifically chosen because the best reconstructions made up to the mid-twenty-ninth century were conclusively proved by zigma-photography to be completely wrong.'

'So this is based on the latest findings,' Compassion said.

'Oh no. The earlier ones, naturally. All the worst bits. We're very interested in certainty. Particularly when it's mistaken.'

After that Fitz really started enjoying himself, and it may have been his imagination, but he thought Compassion was unbending just a little. Perhaps she went for hairy men.

The planetarium was an especial hit.

'Here', Mildeo intoned proudly, 'we have the entirety of the Solar system. Vulcan of course, nearest to the sun – as detected wrongly in 1880, disproved by Einstein, and then deliciously discovered again in 2003, only to vanish by 2130.' He waved his plump, hairy fists around like an excited

Homo habilis. 'Mercury,' he continued, 'one side always facing the sun, onward through jungled Venus – note the stuffed *Venusaurus erectus* – Mars with its canals, and stilt cities.'

'The tyrannical natives of North Polar Jupiter,' the Doctor joined in excitedly, 'the caroming worlds of Velikowsky, and the Black Star Nemesis. The Five Outer Worlds named after the lowest circles of Dante's Hell.' The Doctor, Fitz thought, had forgotten all about the Obverse in his sudden surge of boyish enthusiasm.

Compassion was peering at the model of Earth. 'Hyperborea, Mu, Atlantis, Hy-Brasilica, Antilles.' She shook her head. 'Meaningless, I'm afraid.'

'Ah, no. Wrong, perhaps, but meaningful, I must insist. Press the red button, my dear,' Mildeo added, 'and the interior of Pellucidar-Symlandia will unfold itself.' It did, and they were able to see the minute mysteries of the interior. Someone on Mildeo's staff was an excellent model maker. One of the minuscule dinosaurs waved cheerfully. Fitz started pointing out the volcanoes but the Doctor had bounded on to another exhibit.

'Oh dear.' The Doctor sounded disappointed by something. He was examining a planet between Mars and the verdant Jupiter.

Even Fitz had heard of that one. He remembered Patrick Moore, an imposing man in early middle age, talking about it on *The Sky at Night*. The planets seemed roughly to follow a law that meant each successive world was about twice as far out as its predecessor from the sun. Except that between Mars and Jupiter the gap was more like six times, as if a world had gone astray. For a while there had been a theory that a world had shattered there, making up the asteroid belt, but in time it had been disproved. The perturbing gravity of Jupiter had simply prevented anything forming there beyond the size of the largest of the asteroids, Ceres.

'Is something the matter, Doctor?' Mildeo asked. 'I acknowledge that our Thyrop-Minerva is less detailed than the other worlds but we simply have less to go on. It wasn't believable for as long. The mythology lacked time to accrete.'

'I'm sorry, Mildeo,' the Doctor said heavily. 'Perhaps you ought to sit down. I know this will be a blow, but there really was a planet between Mars and Jupiter. This isn't untrue – not in the essentials anyway.'

Mildeo winced. 'Don't tell me. *Another* real item. It's such an embarrassment when that happens. I'm only allowed to include Vulcan because it wasn't real when people thought it was, and one of our sponsors thinks it was invented by *Star Trek*.' He took in Fitz's and Compassion's bemused expressions. 'I take it your friends aren't into the classics. Still, who is?' A glum expression made a brief attempt to machete its way out of his beard. 'I'll have to call a staff meeting. They won't like it. That makes the second case of our displaying a "real" item this year. We do our best but it's very difficult to authoritatively inauthenticate a display.'

'I can see it must be,' Fitz said lightly. 'What was the other one? Merlin turn up, did he, to verify the Once and Future King?'

Mildeo sniffed. 'Worse. It was one of our best exhibits. See the Antarctic Elder Things – truer than life, and twice as eldritch.'

Before Fitz or even Compassion could react, the Doctor's face was inches from Mildeo's, and his hands were fixed in the professor's tortoiseshell lapels.

'Someone verified what?' he shouted.

* * *

17

Change was good, Xenaria repeated to herself, as she waited for the pain to rip through her body. They had been taught that mantra at the Academy, she and the rest of the strike force. They had been taught it with techniques that embossed it directly on to the brain like the most annoying tune in the world, like the bit of doggerel poetry that never dislodges.

Change was good, was one slogan. *Local situations needed local measures* was another. That didn't make it any easier. Their last mission had been a sabotage run in an aquatic environment, and they had gone in as armour-plated, crablike creatures. Xenaria had grown used to walking sideways and breathing water, but there was little point in nostalgia. Soon she would be altered into a new battle form, her flesh glowing white as the crusty plating gave way to a new, more appropriate shape.

Change is good, they had told her. Any soldier curses when they hear that.

Change can kill you. So can suicide missions.

The mission target was located at one of the planet's poles – an isolated community, possibly a scientific base; the briefing had been imprecise on that point. Command had arranged for the site to be surveyed by a cloaked orbital satellite, and for its data to be diagrammed directly into the strike force's hindbrains. When Xenaria blinked she could see colour-coded corridors printed like bruises on her retina. The maps were blood-vessel blurry, and floaters of loose optic tissue drifted along them like clouds in the orange skies of her dreams. It would not be long now before she was blind in that eye. It was a necessary side effect.

The walls of the generator surrounded her, as they did the other twelve members of the team. They were bare metal walls, dull and pitted with tiny flaws. She wished she could reach out to them, clean them, but the impulses racking her body were too strong now. She hated this indignity, hated the playpen technology her unit was forced to deploy, but her orders were clear. Local appropriate instrumentalities only – this was to be a deep-cover mission with all that that implied.

A pain – fierce as a fire – shot through her, as the drugs and devices that were resculpting her body forced her towards the point of death. As it approached she wondered if this was how the current inhabitants of the base would feel, facing a force they could not hope to understand, even if it had been inclined to give them time to try.

So be it. It was war. The moment had been prepared for.

Chapter Two

He was there when the office was due to open – 9.15 a.m., 1 October 1999 – an early start for Buenos Aires. A tall lean man, whose frayed nerves looked to be nearly outside his skin. At 9.17 he had hunched in his black worn coat against the sky-blue wall of the barrio and smoked three cigarillos in succession. By 9.20 he had paced the narrow street a good dozen times. The office's entrance was nothing special to look at: a brass plate in Flemish (a language deliberately chosen for its lack of local use) on a thick wood door identified it as a part of the United Nations Pantographic Survey (South American Section). Actually it was a front for the Intelligence task-force section of the organisation; the door was an MDF laminate over reinforced armour, and a dozen pinhead cameras covered the street outside from sufficient angles to cover any avenue of attack.

Frances Muerte, the duty receptionist, had been watching the man since he came within range of the monitors. She had put off any action in the hope that one of the field agents – preferably one of the more muscular ones – would have reported in early. She even considered paging security, even though she was still angry with Capitano Esparza after last night. She wondered if the marks of her slap still showed on his fat silly face.

By 9.25, the man's face was showing on all the monitors – as if, impossibly, he were somehow in front of every pinhead camera at the same time. His long sallow face with its thin-lipped mouth opened out on the video screens as if he were a fish gasping for air. Frances leaned over to key in the lip-reading software originally developed to augment voice-type programs but long co-opted by the espionage community, but the mouth had ceased its twitching, and she found her gaze drawn up into his. As her dazed eyes rolled up, seeking safety in unconsciousness, he was already dumping data into the computer terminal on her desk.

Capitano Julian Esparza had regarded the posting to Buenos Aires as a welcome chance to exercise authority in his own country, a small reward for faithful service across the global theatre. He had been sickened to find that so much had changed. Buenos Aires was a sick city in these latter days, he felt, a city obsessed with psychoanalysis and drunk on caffeine. The Italianate streets of La Boca that he had grown up in were full of fags and yuppies these days.

The waiting was setting his nerves on edge, but he was damned if he would go out into the city to sip designer coffee in the stainless-steel bars that had sucked the life out of La Boca. He was waiting for the police, his own agents and anyone else he had managed to get hold of to report back in. His station covered Latin America, but, with the current focus on the Middle East and the Balkans drawing resources from around the world, he was working backup down to the bottom of the world. He was running errands for Geneva.

Geneva had demanded that he look after an academic on a lecture tour of South America who should just have commenced the first of two projected weeks at the Universidad Nacional de Buenos Aires. He was an occasional UNIT adviser, and Geneva liked to keep track of such people. For Esparza it was a babysitting job, dull but easy. Except, of course, the man had gone missing. Abducted, possibly, by aliens with no taste. Now half the city was out looking for him, and if they failed, Geneva would want to know why.

He clicked through the video footage he had pulled from the net for the third time that hour. Surely the professor had been fatter than that, the last time? Perhaps coffee was a good idea. The close-ups were blurring before his eyes like acid spilled on negatives. The text was like islands of certainty in the haze. Credentials good, but nothing special, a typical academic – by all accounts a respectable, even worthy individual. So far, the only sighting that could be relied upon had put the man in the heart of the red-light district, cadging beer and telling fortunes. At one in the morning, under the neon glare of a sign shaped like a woman, he had reportedly been shouting abuse at the sky in classical Spanish. Something in the line of planets, Neptune, Uranus, Jupiter and Saturn, slung like cheap lights in a bar across the north, had upset him. Sober, his listeners had been unable to say what it was. One had called him possessed.

A notation on the file showed a delta-class psionic rating. Esparza didn't remember seeing that before – perhaps it explained the carry-on. Slamming his chair against the desk with almost vicious intensity, Esparza strode out of his office and into the main reception area. Surely the field agents would have reported something to the Muerte bitch.

He found a man, laying her head down tenderly on her desk, a long finger pressed to his lips. As Esparza entered, his hand falling on the butt of his service revolver, the man straightened up and said, without turning round, 'Good morning, El Capitano Julian. You may call me Professor Nathaniel Hume. I believe you wanted to see me. I'm afraid we don't have long – I expect you'll be getting a message in about twenty minutes. Project Icepack will be requiring my services.' The man, whose midnight-blue, staring eyes Esparza recognised from the files, sat down on the edge of the desk. To his own surprise Esparza found himself adopting a similar position, waiting for the message to come.

Twitching, slightly – couldn't the others see the impact the thing had had on him? – Jessup leaned in closer. Were the other team members sensitive at all? Were they even alive? Did anything insensitive to this kind of pain even deserve to be alive? Were they zombies, the people round him? The walking dead at the End of the World? Then he saw the sweat on Schneider's brow, the tremor in her hands. Thank God. If she felt it, then there was hope.

The creature pulsated before them, unearthly whispers coming from within its shifting mass. 'What is it?' Schneider asked, her voice strained.

'An alien!' exclaimed McCarthy excitedly. Jessup winced. Maybe he was ultrasensitive, but there was something about McCarthy that suggested she was hard-wired for chronic *in*sensitivity. Show her a headless corpse, she'd see a problem in the use of dental records for identification. Still, he had a better handle on it now. Now that he'd seen that Schneider too was afraid.

'Abused, subservient,' said Jessup, carelessly wiping vomit from his mouth with the back of one gloved hand. 'Good and faithful servant.' His entire body still shook from the waves of despair radiating from the creature. 'Lost, deserted and betrayed. Left alone, endless torture. The last shall be first and the first last.'

'Yes, yes, we've been through that ourselves.' Schneider sighed. 'I can feel it too, though thankfully not as strongly as you seem to. Anything else?'

Jessup frowned, puzzlement briefly overtaking unease. 'A new feeling,' he said tentatively. 'Communion, loss of control, a feeling of losing hold of someone close –'

Jessup was cut off in mid-sentence by a vast convulsion

rippling through the creature. All three humans jumped back, alarmed. The thing expanded wildly, amorphous limbs thrashing outward, inner flesh curving and swirling, forming some kind of orifice. Beyond that could be seen eternity, endless space and an infinity of colours. Colours wild and impossible: colours out of space.

'Losing hold,' barked Jessup, stumbling away from the thing.

A shape was flung out of the creature's exposed inner spaces, hitting the ground and rolling limply across the tiled floor. The sodium bulbs exploded, leaving the creature's weird innards the only source of light. Then the creature folded back in on itself, closing the opening.

Jessup felt the creature's thoughts calm slightly, as if it was, for the moment at least, emotionally exhausted. The hollow emptiness left when its fear faded from his mind was almost as bad as the despair had been. There was a power to the feelings that might be addictive. He would have to watch that.

They flicked their torches on, and Jessup saw Schneider running across to the dark, huddled shape on the floor, while visibly trying to keep a safe distance from the dormant creature. McCarthy ran across to join her, but Jessup didn't really have the energy. He heard Schneider swear, all harsh Nordic consonants. McCarthy gasped.

'A girl,' said Schneider, seemingly to convince herself. 'Bruised, unconscious, but still breathing. McCarthy, get back to the surface ASAP. Get on the sat-phone and tell base we need backup.'

Jessup saw McCarthy's torch beam jiggle around as she ran out of the room. He staggered over to Schneider, who was absently stroking the girl's head. Schneider's impassive eyes were narrow in the dim light as she looked at the unconscious figure.

'How the hell did you get here?' she asked.

The message had come, of course, Geneva demanding the services of the man Esparza hoped they never realised had been missing. His relief stopped him from even caring how Hume had known in advance.

'I don't regret the lectures, of course,' Hume said waspishly as Esparza struggled to slam the door of the military transport plane against the wind. 'No matter how much I'd have tried to keep them essentially philological in nature. They would have to have been couched at the level of the audience.'

'Yeah, right,' Esparza said, adding, 'as the Americans say' under his breath. Thank God he wasn't going. He didn't know what Hume would make of the things the team had found under the ice, or what the team would make of him, but he wished them all the very best of each other. The liver and the lights. The soft muscle tissue and the hot red blood. God that was a gruesome thought. What pit of the unconscious did that crawl out of? He needed sleep. Everyone's thoughts seemed on edge these days.

When the plane had lifted off from the end of the runway he watched it dwindle away heading south along the coast, and cursed under his breath.

After what Fitz thought was his rather extreme reaction to the reported verification of the Elder Things' existence, the Doctor had insisted Mildeo show him the relevant evidence. Mildeo, understandably flustered after the Doctor's outburst, had agreed, and now led the way through the museum's private areas. Fitz noticed wryly that even in the far future, the areas not open to the paying public were still several grades of décor downmarket from the museum's classy front end. Chipped plaster and yellowed paintwork were still the order of the day for staff.

They passed through a room where a line of scholarly, wide-eyed creatures were restoring ancient parchments.

'Correspondence sent to 221B Baker Street,' explained Mildeo. 'The nonexistent address of the entirely fictional Sherlock Holmes. A fine example of the powerful reality of the utterly unreal.'

The Doctor stared at his shoes, hands stuffed in his pockets as if trying to bottle in some vital revelation. 'Could we be getting to the point, please?' he asked uneasily.

'Of course, my dear fellow, of course,' replied Mildeo, bustling them through a pair of cracked double doors. 'Always such a hurry with you, isn't it? These creatures have not been with us for millions of years. I hardly see the need to rush now.'

The Doctor grimaced sulkily. 'I had enough problems with unspeakable and ancient whatsits from the dawn of forever in my last incarnation,' he said wearily. 'I rather hoped to have put all that behind me. Got them all tucked up safe again, poor dears.'

They turned a corner.

'Well, Doctor,' Mildeo said, a semblance of pride creeping back into his voice. 'What do you think?'

The statue stood about eleven feet high and was made of a dull lead-coloured material. Fitz prodded it surreptitiously. He was right. It was the same lead alloy they used for model soldiers, no doubt supported on an internal armature. So that was all OK. All reasonable. Now all he had to deal with was what it looked like. Its central body was basically an upright cylinder, but ridged and distorted so that it looked organic and alive. Why on Earth it should be so disturbing for a statue of a living thing to *look* living Fitz couldn't imagine, but the feeling was there. The cylinder rested on five long tentacles, which ended in flat five-veined triangular feet. Its 'head' was a smaller five-pointed star, all eyes and smaller tentacles and sucking mouths. Five arms, ropy, limp things hung from the middle of its body each dividing and subdividing into finer fibres, and from its 'sides' black batlike wings were furled like tight umbrellas.

The Doctor grabbed some boxes from around the exhibit and stacked them quickly, climbing up for a better look. He pulled one of the wings out and stared down the end of its central support structure, which looked as hollow as bamboo. 'Good model work. The prothallus spore-cases are clearly visible.'

'That's a vegetable?' Compassion said. 'Its world must have had some seriously tough vegetarians to evolve that.'

'It isn't the product of evolution,' the Doctor snapped. 'That's the problem.' He pointed at a metal scroll on the base of the statue. '"Old One, a.k.a. Elder Thing. Source: H.P. Lovecraft's *At the Mountains of Madness*, first pub. *Astounding Stories*, February–April 1936. Widely regarded as real by twenty-fifth-century fringe archaeologists, particularly Bendecker, Vildson and Urnst." It.' Space of a heartbeat. 'Isn't.' Space of a second heartbeat 'Real.'

Fitz wondered why it mattered so much, but he wasn't about to ask, not with the Doctor in one of his energetic moods. It would be like getting in the way of a tornado. It could wait.

'So,' said the Doctor, fixing Mildeo with his glittering eye. 'What have you got that says different?'

Ten minutes later they arrived in an archive of some kind, shelves stretching out into the distance, all stacked high with diverse manners of tapes, reels, discs and other methods of data storage. The room was overstocked and a little cramped, so Fitz found himself nose to nose with a pickled alien foetus in a jar. Its almond-shaped eyes stared blankly into his.

'Yeurgh!' he exclaimed, backing away hastily and bumping into Mildeo.

Mildeo sighed, picking up the jar gently. 'There was a time when people believed things like this were hidden everywhere,' he explained. 'We haven't displayed this fellow since the Archaic Paranoia exhibition a few years back.'

The Doctor coughed meaningfully, and Mildeo rolled his eyes.

'On the shelf behind you are ten flat-image digital video recordings, Doctor,' said Mildeo patiently. 'Quite a find, really, dating back to the Humanian Era. The first four are a little disappointing but believe me, the other six are well worth your attention.'

The Doctor balanced the tapes in one hand. They were only a few inches long, of a kind Fitz had seen tourists use in San Francisco.

'So,' said the Doctor, 'any chance of popcorn?'

Mildeo hadn't provided any popcorn, but he had found them a quiet corner in which to sit and examine the evidence. The Doctor, Fitz and Compassion crowded around a simple data screen as Mildeo struggled to get his equipment to accept the first tape. Fitz noticed Compassion's demeanour change as they waited for the show to start, her attention fixed on the screen, and her usual indifferent manner giving way to a quiet intensity.

Waiting for the signals, thought Fitz.

'Gotcha!' exclaimed Mildeo, and the screen crackled into life. The recordings were of surprisingly high quality, considering their great age. The date – '10.1.99' – flickered in the corner of the picture. The initial images were a blurry mess of what seemed like cave walls.

The camera spun around – it was clearly hand-held – to shakily point at a rather fierce looking blonde woman.

'Professor Mary Schneider reporting for Project Icepack,' she said in a European accent Fitz couldn't quite place. 'We are proceeding to Site B, after concluding that Site A has been too badly damaged to yield primary data.'

A map held up by another parka'd figure showed that the central area of the map had been cross-hatched out and marked with an A. B was round the edge. Something had rubbed out the heart of their find before they could even get to it. Fitz guessed they felt gutted.

They watched on as Schneider and her team examined an entranceway clearly not built for human use. The Doctor peered intently at the screen, muttering as he tried to read the inscriptions on the walls.

'Boring,' said Compassion flatly. 'Boring, and uninformative. Time to fast-forward.'

Reluctantly, the Doctor agreed. Mildeo skimmed through the material until something caught the Doctor's eye.

'Stop!' he exclaimed, bouncing on his seat. 'Yes, back a bit. There.'

They were looking at what seemed, to Fitz's eyes, like an unremarkable *objet d'art*, a big black Easter egg stuck to a metal box. Perhaps it was more impressive in real life; Schneider's team certainly seemed taken aback by it.

'I've seen that thing before,' said the Doctor, stroking his top lip meditatively. 'And I'm sure it has got nothing to do with Elder Things, real or fictional. You're an expert on these oddities, Mildeo. What can you tell me about it?'

Mildeo peered at the screen with academic scrutiny, and

stroked his lavish beard. 'It's ugly,' he announced authoritatively, 'and I don't think it's in the book.'

The Doctor sighed. 'Play on. I'm sure it will come back to me.'

Mildeo fast-forwarded some more. 'This is where the merriment really begins.'

'We're about to enter the creature's chamber now,' said Schneider's voice from off screen. The camera seemed to be pointing at a grey wall until they rounded a corner.

'Here it is,' said Schneider flatly.

'Oh my!' said the Doctor, examining the creature on the screen. 'A Shoggoth.'

Mildeo coughed. 'As you can see, we have substantial filmic evidence here of the Elder Things' existence: their city under the Antarctic ice, the Elder Runes on the walls, even footage of one of their servitors, the uncanny, nay eldritch, Shoggoths. Protoplasmic masses capable of taking on any form.'

'Yes yes yes,' said the Doctor, jumping to his feet and rubbing his brow. 'All very persuasive, if it wasn't entirely impossible. I'm very much afraid we'll have to go and see that city for ourselves.'

'What, join the expedition?' asked Fitz, visions of the great explorers he read about as a boy flitting through his mind. Scott, Amundsen, Howberry and now Kreiner.

'No no no,' replied the Doctor, eyes burning with a perplexing excitement. 'That would be boring, and require the wearing of mittens. No, better to go back to when the place was inhabited. We'll just pop in for tea and currant buns.'

Hume tapped a samba beat on the metal struts of the helicopter. It was even more cramped than the plane had been five hours before. Cold metal and burning engines, a machine of war. It was like coming home.

Machholtz's and Encke's comets hung in the sky like flaming embers. One alone would have sufficed to foretell the death of princes. He really couldn't remember now above the scream of the rotor blades whether either of them ever had.

They had flown from Cape Horn across the South Shetland Islands and up the Antarctic Peninsula towards the heart of the British Territory. Over the peninsula it had drizzled, the last liquid water this side of the Pole. Ninety per cent of the world's ice lay ahead of them: seventy per cent of the world's fresh water, locked down solid. Along the way they had collected a squad of soldiers and a small group of scientists, enough to fill two medium-sized helicopters. Hume – the name was as good as any other – wasn't sufficiently well versed in contemporary avionics to recognise the type straight off, but some of the internal controls were labelled in the Russian alphabet. Cramped together, the scientists shoehorned into 'his' 'copter had seemed friendly enough, and one, an attractive dark-haired girl who looked barely a graduate, had pressed her leg gently against his. A gesture that he had enjoyed for a moment as a purely accidental human contact, before he had moved away.

Her face had quirked to a tiny smile at that. He had wondered what they had been told about him. Probably just the usual cover stories. First-contact specialist. High-IQ loner, good agent, on a long leash, quirky but efficient, often blessed with remarkable hunches. Talented with languages. The half of it. The quarter of it, all things considered.

For a time he had watched the relatively ice-free browns and greys of the peninsula give way to ice sheets, and the rain turn to sleet, until the peaks of the Vinson Massif, black and ragged, rising naked above the ice line on the horizon, had made him long for the comforts of backstreet Buenos Aires.

He must have been dozing when it happened.

Jessup sat, cross-legged, before the creature. The medics had come to take the dark-eyed girl away, averting their gaze from the beast that had given her to them. Apparently UNIT had plucked one of their experts out of retirement and sent him on his way. That had been hours ago.

Schneider had recommended Jessup stay the hell away from the creature, and he had spent most of the last few hours in other parts of the complex, doing the standard archaeological stuff. Now he'd come back, to taste the creature's pain again. He hoped it wasn't a case of him developing a taste for S and M, this desire to commune with such agony.

He could feel tendrils of emotion touching his mind, the same feelings of betrayal and despair. Then there was something new. Recognition. Fear.

Jessup grimaced at the feelings. Something was coming, the creature could feel it. Something familiar, something hated.

Jessup could swear he heard the sound of distant thunder. He saw tendrils of greenish energy shoot out of the creature, flowing through the ceiling, presumably heading towards the surface. Jessup felt the creature's desire for vengeance. He pitied who or what was on the other end of that attack.

The forward 'copter bought it as the motors cut out heading dead south over the foothills of the Massif, in a wash of green flame. Hume imagined faces cold-sealed to the glass, reflecting the sickly aurora in their eyes as their corpses froze on impact, shards of rotor blades scything into powdered static.

The thought stabbed him awake and – for him – averagely aware. Caught in the fringes of the effect, magnetos fused in their casings, the second 'copter twisted. Hume flung himself forward, knocking the pilot to one side. The man swore in dialectic Russian. It was either one of the southern or the central dialects; both were distinguished by the so-called *akan'je*, coalescence of certain vowels outside of stress. Hume wasn't minded to ask which. He had about thirty seconds before they were all dead.

Ten seconds later, they had spiralled down, gliding with the rotors turning free like an autogyro. Hume knew he had a hero-worshipper on his hands. The pilot was nearly drooling over the flying, muttering that he hadn't even known that manoeuvre was possible with a troop transport. That was unfortunate. Out of the corner of his eye Hume thought he saw a string of domes on the ground below. Damn, they were near. Then the impact crushed his ribcage against the controls and everything went up in the magnesium flare of the crash. His last thought was that the landing hadn't been worthy of him after all.

Chapter Three

Neither now nor then, neither up nor down. Breezily unaware of any possible hostility in its environment, a blue wooden box tumbled unscathed through the endless chaos of the space-time vortex. It was a box made from numbers, complex equations forming its wooden slats and glass panels, the sign on the top which read POLICE PUBLIC CALL BOX.

Inside the box lay a small universe – opinions differed as to the meaning of 'small' in such a context – a microcosm block-transferred from mathematics itself. A living beast of time calculations and transdimensional equations, designed to relate to its pilot via a symbiotic bond woven into that pilot's very being. This was how the Time Lords of Gallifrey commanded their ships – TARDISes like this blue box.

However, the person who had engineered this TARDIS had fitted some subtle amendments to the basic design. Several sections of the ship were not block transfers at all but were built from actual materials from the real universe rather than dreamed out of the minds of Gallifrey's mathematicians. These areas could bypass the symbiotic relationship, allowing a physical, nuts-and-bolts approach to controlling the ship. Why a Time Lord should do such a thing, equipping such an exotic and sophisticated machine with crude manual controls, who could tell? Perhaps the ship's owner had become wary of overreliance on super-technologies. Perhaps he wished the TARDIS to be usable by a non-Gallifreyan, though such egalitarian thoughts rarely occurred to the Time Lords in their arrogant solitude.

Perhaps he just liked to drive occasionally to give the

TARDIS a chance to take in the view.

Whatever the reason, in one such area of the TARDIS the ship's current pilot and crew were gathered.

The Doctor slapped his forehead. 'Mictlan!' he exclaimed. He leaned against the wooden panels of the central console, shaking his head at the sluggishness of his own thought processes.

'Pardon?' asked Fitz, slumped in a wicker chair.

'Mictlan,' repeated the Doctor. 'Home of the Celestis, a rather unpleasant offshoot of my own civilisation. I knew I'd seen a device like that somewhere before. Unearthly materials, fingers of bone; Mictlan was full of that kind of tacky ornamentation. Biomechanical DIY is one of the first signs of a paranoid megalomaniac culture. The natural body being despised and feared is projected externally as other than the self, thereby justifying the abuse of it in others. At least that's what Adler thought when he wasn't playing the mouth organ.'

'What?' Fitz said.

'The Doctor is purporting to confuse one of the three founders of Earthly psychology with a fourth-rate musician,' Compassion explained cattily. 'I suppose it is intended to be amusing, which implies –'

'Trouble,' Fitz said moodily.

'The Celestis left this universe to avoid a war in my people's own future,' said the Doctor. 'They built themselves their own mini-universe, Mictlan, as a new home. Making a fictional species like the Elder Things would be child's play by comparison. What worries me is why. Why come out of seclusion and start throwing their technology around, interfering in the timelines of a fragile temporal focus like Earth? The Celestis expended a lot of effort putting the universe behind them, and whatever caused them to renew their involvement must be very big.'

'How big?' asked Compassion.

The Doctor sucked a finger. 'Oh, pretty big. For the Celestis, the death of galaxies would be a trivial distraction.'

Three minutes to impact.

The art of distraction is that of hiding a small detail in a big mess. The infiltration capsule did this, skimming the surface of space-time, leaving confusing ripples and patterns across the continua. Its indistinct, ghostly presence streaked across billions of miles and hundreds of years as it approached its destination. Its point of impact would indistinguishable from any other part of the time spectrum.

Two minutes and thirty seconds to impact.

Xenaria dragged herself upright, feeling the strength and breadth of her new form. The walls of the infiltration capsule seemed insubstantial now as they approached their destination, unnecessary equipment being shed and discarded in the vortex. The strike force would be spat out naked into real-space, no evidence of their method of arrival remaining.

Xenaria staggered, unsteady on her five base tentacles. Her long ribbed form stretched, tubular veined wings unfolding almost ecstatically along her sides. Tricky, but not unlike the crab legs of her previous form. The twelve members of her strike force were also flexing their new limbs, fitting appropriately customised weapons and equipment to their bodies. Although they all looked roughly the same, Xenaria's natural instinct to recognise members of her species regardless of appearance allowed her to tell them apart.

One was instantly recognisable just by the meticulous manner in which he examined the weapons pod attached beneath one wing, which he inspected with studious intensity. Such dedication ought to have been admirable, but somehow it wasn't.

'Allopta,' Xenaria addressed him, her own voice strange to her as it boomed out on a deep bass level below human speech. Allopta heard her nonetheless, and glided towards her.

Two minutes to impact.

'Commander,' Allopta replied. The capsule was juddering now, ready for break-up.

The excitement of imminent battle rippled through the older members of the strike force, the veterans. There was tension among the handful of newborns drafted in after the heavy losses of the Third Zone fiasco. Best not to waste them.

'Take those five,' Xenaria said, indicating the newborns. 'Approach the secondary assault point, monitoring our primary attack. Let them see how it's done before they have to join the fray.'

Allopta nodded, a strange dipping of his tendrilled head – crap body language, signalling poor control of his new form – then turned to the newborns. 'Recruits, with me,' he barked.

Xenaria turned to the other five, who were better at disguising any nerves. Fully equipped, flexing their bodies in measured motions, they were veterans of a dozen campaigns against the most implacable and deadly opponents. All the conscript species the enemy had co-opted.

They would have to do.

One minute and thirty seconds to impact.

Xenaria mentally ran through the inventory of the forthcoming mission. The first step was infiltration: eliminating the target species and slipping into their timelines, thereby disguising the rest of the operation from enemy detection. The second step was information retrieval: obtaining the target species' records concerning Planet 5, preparing strategies for the final stage. The subcommittee who had authorised the mission had briefly considered Mars as a suitable platform for the attack on Planet 5, but its advantages in terms of proximity were outweighed by the difficulties inherent in trying to hide a strike force in a devastated wasteland inhabited by a few bunches of reptiles. Earth offered more.

One minute to impact.

The final stage of the operation would be the hardest.

The recovery mission to Planet 5, itself.

It was a suicide mission. They had joined knowing the chances of their return, of survival, were unimaginably low. They were dealing with something beyond death. So be it.

Thirty seconds to impact.

The capsule was translucent now, slowing down both its geographical and temporal approach. Outside, thick jungle whipped past them, the flora of a planet in its primeval stages.

'Brace yourselves,' Xenaria bellowed over the cacophony of the impending real-world interface.

Impact.

The capsule was gone and they were in the real world. There was no sense of landing, just a crunching inertia, the internal lurch of gravity exerting itself as they materialised in a verdant forest, sending various bugs scurrying for shelter. Xenaria filtered the air through her breathing clusters – clean, unpolluted, so different from the thick black smoke of her own world. A pre-industrial air that didn't know the environmental horrors of weapon construction. The sky above was a blazing fire, and she swivelled her five red eyes looking for a source. The energy seemed to come from everywhere. She dismissed the point as an irrelevance, shaking the thought from her tendrilled head. This was a staging point, nothing more.

'Tachon?' she barked.

Her navigation expert tried a salute with his tentacles and failed abysmally, settling for a faint flutter of their fractal endings, as he compared incoming data to the mission briefing. 'Drop zone as instructed,' Tachon intoned. 'We're here. Target base only a couple of clicks ahead.'

'Very well,' said Xenaria, raising herself up. 'Primary team, prepare to attack.'

Xenaria and her primary team intercepted members of the target species close to their base; it was as if the Elder Things were expecting them. Nevertheless, the targets didn't attack first. Paltek fired the first shot, a thick beam of plasma ripping through the body of one of the targets. It split open without a sound, fleshy body exploding in a rain of tendrils and ichor. Its companions remained impassive, retreating slightly, but showing no evident concern at the death of one of their own kind.

Then the battle began in earnest. Two of the other targets raised their tentacles aloft, drawing down lilac-tinged fire from the sky. Some kind of neurally activated gravity disruption, Xenaria guessed. The clouds opened up, and as Paltek, one of Xenaria's longest-serving lieutenants, was torn to pieces by unnatural fires, Xenaria felt the rain drip down her alien body like heavy tears.

Her response was immediate and violent.

The Watcher turned slowly, the tendrils of its star-shaped head flashing their colour-coded pulses of microwave radiation. Organic computers on infrared and ultraviolet triggers responded smoothly within their iron cages, mouths gnashing mindlessly. Occasionally one of the computers' vestigial limbs touched a restraint symbol and triggered the genetic blocks. The screams went unheeded. The Watcher, having no concept of sound, maintained its scrutiny of the newcomers. Although one had fallen, the others only advanced with greater determination. The Watcher's companions had exhausted their powers. Soon they would be lost to the newcomers.

It had been an even million years since war had touched this land. The Others, the Interlopers, the octopoids had come, their war engines fighting with bolts of parallel matter, tearing through ordinary mass like the engineering Shoggoths through rock.

The Ubbo-Sathla had been used; the alien city of the Interlopers had drowned on the sinking land as the Engine had moved its vast bulk within the planet's crust. Such tactics would not work against a strike force with no home base. Perhaps the outpost was lost, to be usurped by the newcomers as they had usurped the Watcher's shape.

The Watcher did not care. Like all its kind, it knew its duty, knew – deep within – what it was for.

It was there to die.

Details of the battle were relayed directly into the minds of the secondary strike team. Allopta and the newborns watched aghast as Paltek died, then gained some satisfaction as Xenaria's force easily took out his two assailants.

'Observe,' said Allopta to the newborns as they flitted between the trees approaching the secondary assault point. 'The Elder Things' weapons are powerful, but their use leaves them drained and vulnerable to attack. Their bodies lack the speed and efficiency of our forms modelled on an earlier, less decadent phase of their own evolution. These creatures are dulled and infirm.'

'Then the base will soon be ours,' said one of the newborns steadily. Allopta could only agree, but deep inside he repressed his despair at the banality of the discussion. The war had made his people's conversation as interesting as dispatches.

Not far from where Xenaria and her team had emerged from the vortex, another group of space-time travellers made a more graceful entrance. Even over the storm and the noise of battle, a pained, groaning noise rang out across the primeval jungle, the sound of several basic laws of physics being elbowed repeatedly in the ribs. It was the sound of the fabric of reality being temporarily torn, to allow a blue box to solidify in a previously empty space, the light on top pulsing in time with the mechanical noise of the box's arrival. Rain hammered against the old police box's painted exterior, as if trying to repel the anachronism from this overcast Eden.

The door opened and the Doctor emerged, extending an umbrella into the sky. It was a futile gesture beneath such an onslaught, as the wind whipped the raindrops underneath the umbrella and into the Doctor's face. Nevertheless, Fitz and Compassion tried to join him beneath his feeble shelter, screwing their faces up against the rain.

'Looks like we might need those mittens after all,' shouted Fitz over a rumble of thunder. 'I always thought prehistoric times would be a bit... drier.' He tailed off, aware of how feeble the statement must have been.

'A tropical storm,' the Doctor replied breezily. 'Nothing unusual.'

'In Antarctica?' Fitz muttered.

As he spoke a great wave of unearthly energy exploded across the sky, accompanied by an unnatural mechanical screeching.

'Perfectly normal,' said Compassion, her voice the driest thing around.

Xenaria's force skimmed over the fern tops. The bodies were strange, their senses overwhelming, and Xenaria guessed that they had at most three weeks of usable time in them before the alien brain-sensory configurations began to disable their inherited perceptions. Time enough.

She sent a signal to the adjutant bearing the medium weaponry.

He shifted a black glass spike in his tentacles.

The parallel cannon.

In our universe, neutrinos fill most solar systems, pouring out of suns in a never-ending flux. They pass like invisible rain, harmlessly through worlds and space travellers alike. Only in nova concentrations do they pose a danger. The parallel cannon was a point hole into another part of the universe, into the nova of an anti-sun. Into a killing density of neutrinos. When the hole opened they poured through like rain. Like a deluge. Physics worked differently there: those neutrinos killed. It was an antique weapon – the Third Zoners had been on the verge of Parallel Weaponry before the closure of that front, in the Fifth Time Assault, and apparently a temporarily indigenous rival species to the Elder Things also used something similar. It added to the verisimilitude that was a prime factor in avoiding the attention of the Enemy. In the stream of right-handed neutrinos, normal matter just came apart, its chirality: the underlying principle of quantum-handedness shattering. Organic matter lasted a fraction of a second longer as it twisted, sugars and amino acids turning and churning before disintegrating. Thin dust fell for miles around as the beam chewed into the outpost's outer armour, the plant life and the atmosphere. The air started to fall in on itself. Leave a parallel-matter beam on, and you could eat through a world in three hours, use up its atmosphere in nine.

Crude stuff.

In the distance, the sky turned purple, and the Doctor shoved Compassion and Fitz into a pile of what Fitz sincerely hoped was mud. He got as far as 'Par–'

Then the shockwave hit. Something sizzled.

Fitz's eyes stung.

In the cold future, Hume opened his eyes, orientating himself swiftly with a few basic sweeps of his surroundings. The back of his head was on something flat and uncomfortable, and a git in a bulky anorak was leaning over him. He tried to say something rude, but could manage only a croaking noise.

'Well you've bruised your left side, and picked up a case of incipient frostbite.' The medical officer's voice was muffled by the parka, which hid his face, but a few grey hairs that had caught in the hood's thermal edging suggested that he was past middle age. 'Not bad for a dive on to the ice when a 'copter ruptures like a tin can in a microwave. How are you feeling?'

Hume remembered the hurried briefing he'd been given in a Nissen hut by an airfield on Cape Horn. The forward base was a collection of old SNOW-CAP geodesics, dug into the snow. Like six white mushrooms, they surrounded the great slice that led into the heart of the anomaly. Down there under the black rock, perhaps as deep as the Bentley subglacial trench, lay the thing that had drawn UNIT into this desert built of water.

He shivered. The doc's question seemed oddly emphasised, considering his injuries, but he opted for honesty. His voice was working again. 'Pretty fine.' He guessed that the doctor expected him to ask after other survivors. 'Did anyone else make it?'

'No.' The medic's voice was drained of any sympathy.

Fatigue alone? Hume wondered. He tried to grin and his face felt raw and tight. 'OK, bad start. Never mind. My name's Nathanial Hume, I'm from UNIT. I'm here to help you. Obviously it's going to take longer than we expected, but if I can use the radio we'll get the airlift under way as soon as possible. We'll have to set the 'copters down further out. What's the current radius of the tesla effects?' He was betting the strike had been deliberately hostile, but it might not serve to admit that he knew that just yet. Possibly it would only panic everybody. Better to blame the crash on electromagnetic flux.

Despite everything, he was starting to feel nauseous. The deaths of the science team – including that of the dark-haired girl whose name he had never learned – hadn't hit him, not properly. Perhaps they never would. He wasn't familiar with grief; although he knew it was expected of a sole survivor, even one who had done everything possible to save the dead.

'Airlift?' The doctor's voice was still toneless.

Hell, hadn't they been briefed? 'Yes, we can't expect you to remain in the proximity of the effects your leader reported. We'll get you to the South American mainland, and under observation, and get a proper team in here. No offence, but

45

you must see that the immediate investigation of the discovery will require something more than your skills.'

The medic's roar, harsh and distorted – 'No we must stay; we must not leave; she must not leave me!' – caught Hume off guard, as the hands in the heavy thermal gloves clutched at his throat. More grey hair spilled from the hood as the medic exerted his full strength. How could he be so old, and so strong? Hume tried to strike upward. Tried to break the grip. He remembered a detail from the briefing: none of the scientists who had made the discovery were over thirty-five. The team's cover story had been sponsorship by the Prince's Trust for Heaven's sake. An image of a file flipped past, committed to a memory that would have been amazing if it hadn't been mostly artificial. The medic had had blond-bleached hair and blue eyes, he was called Dennis, he had come from Manchester. He had been given a gamma psychic rating on the old Rhine tests. This had been a good career opportunity for him, his teachers had thought. See the world, build character, go mad.

Hume tried to reason with the man but his voice choked away, and his legs refused to obey him. The hands tightened.

The sound of thunder filled his ears.

In Hell. The Lord of the Smoked Mirror awoke in the dull night and smelled the subtle tang of woodland burning. On the shore a hundred miles below his manse, the Lava Sea crashed against the screaming forest of suicides. The air was misty with vaporised blood. He stretched on the vampiric silks of his no-longer-virgin bed, and yawned the yawn of an amused cat. His eyes were of different colours: red and green and gold. He had changed species in his sleep. He recognised his reflection in the endless mirrors. Urmungstandra: the devil god of the Silurians. It would do for now. It was, perhaps, overelaborate. He would have to check the latest styles before venturing among his peers.

Even so, despite the pure familiarity of his domain, something was wrong.

What was it? All that first day it eluded him.

The next day was worse. He knew something was wrong. Although it was just a feeling, he had experienced feelings like it before. When the war had first been hinted at in the projections he had felt somewhat similar, and, even though they were beyond its effects now, the feeling had never entirely gone away. This was like that, but new.

It was the feeling of the absence of certainty. It was a feeling like an unspecified yet fatal loss of control. It was the sort of feeling he had hoped to leave behind with the flesh. It carried another taste also, a bitter, coppery, twisting feeling, the name of which he had forgotten. It was not especially convivial.

The third day, his dresser attended him without speech, its hands dead but firm. His robes woven around him, he walked out of the bedchamber and down the forty-seven ivory stairs to the balcony and looked westward towards the sea. The sky was a mass of boiling fire. The sea was a stinking flat and endless plain of mud. The perspective of the pseudo space-time that was Mictlan stretched out to infinity. At his back a faceless servant twittered in dull oblivion, carrying the morning's first data-sacrifice. All seemed as it should be.

The feeling stayed with him. He walked round his private corner of Hell, testing its mathematical boundaries, watching. He saw the ghostly faces of the servants, their timelines distorted by the process used to excise them from real space-time. He understood that the process killed most of what could loosely be called personality in the underclass but that, somehow, a core of anxiety and suffering remained.

It was occasionally visible in the eyes. Some Lords looked away, but Smoked Mirror did not. To do so would have been to suggest that a servant mattered in some way. It would never even have occurred to him.

In that part of the grey hours of Mictlan that felt like the time of debate, he attended the Last Parliament. He saw the minute and ceaseless interplay of the squabbles of his fellow Lords Celestial. The Lord of the Red Moon wished to invoke peer-right to suppress the chronological changes proposed by the Duke of Knives and his coterie, but was opposed by the Grey Cardinals and the Chronometricists. Smoked Mirror inclined to Red Moon's faction but had not yet given a commitment to either side. Vaguely he wondered why not. Had he some obligation to one of the Chronometricist Guild? If so he could not now recall it precisely. That was worrying. Like all the Lords Celestial, Smoked Mirror was linked to the block-transfer engines and computational matrices of which Mictlan was constructed. His memory was not held within his skull. As with all his fellows, his body was not him, but merely a convenient fiction, almost a legality, provided by the engines of Mictlan to ground his interaction with the other Celestis within a shared net of experience modelled on the customs of Old Gallifrey. In many ways the Celestis were creatures built out of habits. Tradition crept through their veins, like dust, but it was the tradition of the victor, of the upstart. They had escaped the war and all its sordid incidents. They had put themselves beyond incident, beyond the merely causal, and beyond the stars. Mictlan hung on the exterior hypersurface of the expanding bubble of real space-time like a bug riding a balloon. He *was* Mictlan, as were they all. Its purpose was to sustain them; their purpose was to live and move and have their being with in it. If it was threatened, if in some way it was failing, the very existence of the Celestis could be in danger. That was the other part of his feeling. It was fear.

While he had grappled with the problem of his memory, the speeches had been droning on. Absently he noted that the Duke of Knives was in the light now, a shimmer of clashing glints as of moving steel.

'My Lords, in closing,' the Duke was saying, and Smoked Mirror realised he had missed the whole of the debate – there was at least one thing to be said then for foreboding and disquiet – 'I invoke the Thirty House Rule: under that august and hallowed dictum no further discussion can be given to a matter on which Thirty of the Ninety-Nine Houses are agreed in seeking a veto. It is ended.'

Red Moon rose over the leaden grey benches. 'I have been counting, my Lordships.' He paused so that they could see him playfully counting on his thin fingers. 'I count twenty-nine.'

That was how it began. There were, however, other signs. A servant mindlessly trying to walk through a wall. A Lord trying to return a black scroll, only to find its pages blank, and its origin impossible to determine. The absence of a word for a species of alien.

A House was gone. Removed from memory and Mictlan alike. Intuitively, fumblingly, the community felt its way towards the invisible wound left by the excision. Barely a Lord did not feel some shadow fall across their deliberations, as phrases – perhaps once spoken by their vanished peer – seemed suddenly nonsensical, or novel. Jokes, once proverbial, perhaps made at the expense of the forgotten, retained no humour. The true offspring of a Celestis, the ideas he had contributed into their world of thought were missing.

Their language itself had been diminished.

This was intolerable. It was symptomatic of the shock with which the effects of this strange absence was received that it took almost three days of the strange grey time of Mictlan before hypernauts were dispatched to retrieve the records.

Chapter Four

The parallel cannon had performed its function perfectly, Xenaria thought. Its beam had provided the desired result, slicing the mountainside away to reveal and cut apart a section of the Elder Things' base. They hadn't stood a chance, and that was just how she liked it.

Out of the sundered corridors, like insects from under a stone, the infirm creatures had stumbled into the light. Relieved at the ease of their success, the troopers were picking them off one by one, calling their staser shots, severing a tentacle here, an eyestalk there.

Xenaria guessed there was betting going on – all quite against regulations, but she was prepared to let it pass. By the time Allopta's secondary force glided into the base via the main entrance, there were only a couple of stragglers left to eliminate. The newborns had pursued these elderly survivors with the cruel vigour of the young and agile, blowing the aliens into gobbets of reeking flesh.

Let them have their target practice, Xenaria thought. It would stand them in good stead.

Allopta looked out of the yawning gap in the base wall with disdain. Although he was a veteran of many battles, Xenaria sometimes thought Allopta had retained a lot of the prewar generation's characteristics, their academic disdain for the brutality of common existence, their sneering, and their pride.

'The parallel cannon,' said Allopta. 'A devastating weapon. Is there not a chance that these effects could be noted in the future – come to the attention of Enemy forces?' The criticism was subtle: Allopta was far too clever for blatant treason, but he clearly thought her overzealous, wasteful of material.

'It was necessary. Examine the inner layers of the wall,' she replied icily. 'You will find several interlocking layers of force barriers operating beneath the surface, fluctuating through random sequences to filter out most energy attacks. The parallel cannon is one of the few weapons powerful enough to penetrate so many defence mechanisms. Besides that, the decision was of course mine to make.'

Allopta turned to her. 'These creatures are feeble, but their ancestors were once powerful.' It was as close as Xenaria would get to a retraction, as guarded as the initial criticism.

'Instruct the dimensional technicians to unfold the cradles from space-time,' Xenaria ordered. 'And begin data extraction.'

'As you wish, Commander,' replied Allopta, gliding away. Xenaria couldn't help feeling his respect went barely deeper than his outer layer of green-grey skin.

The sounds of battle had stopped, and the sky had cleared once more. Shafts of sunlight broke through the jungle canopy. Still wet with mud and rain, Fitz felt rancid in the humid climate. He found it hard to believe that, in his time, this would be the coldest place on Earth. What had the Doctor put it down to as the TARDIS was materialising – continental drift? He would have to ask how the hell that worked when he was drier.

He marvelled again at how Compassion and the Doctor both seemed far more comfortable than he did. Compassion had ditched the dress on the way, and a bit of mud made the combat trousers that she had reverted to seem less like an excessively masculine affectation than they usually did, while the Doctor had remained relatively clean by the simple measure of landing on top of Fitz. Charming, Fitz thought.

The Doctor was explaining the principles of the parallel cannon to Compassion, while using his rolled-up umbrella to hack his way through the foliage. Fitz was unsure of the wisdom of telling a former ally of Faction Paradox the detailed workings of advanced weapons systems, but as Compassion seemed to be even less interested in the subject than he was, Fitz decided to let it slide. Possibly to them, it was like comparing the merits of different sizes of pointed sticks.

After the Doctor had stopped rabbiting on about neutrinos, there was a brief silence as they continued to force their way breathlessly through the thick undergrowth.

'Doctor,' said Compassion eventually. 'How can you be sure these "Elder Things" don't exist? Or didn't exist? Or aren't supposed to exist? Especially when you said you had met similar creatures before.'

'Well,' began the Doctor, stretching the vowel out as if limbering up for a really complex explanation. 'None of those other creatures had occupied a time and space where I knew, from my own travels if nothing else, that no such civilisation existed. Besides, if the Elder Things really had dominated prehistoric Earth, how come they never bumped into any of the other species who popped through this part of the galaxy during this period? Leaving aside their appearance in early twentieth-century horror fiction. And where did they come from? The supposedly fictional accounts suggest they originally came from a point between Hydra and Argo Navis and I know there's not much out there. Oh yes, there's RNGC-4603, a nice little galaxy, a bit diffuse maybe, brightening up tolerably towards the centre, but no major civilisations. He sighed deeply.

'Besides,' he said, 'I always presumed Lovecraft just made them up. If he knew they were real, he certainly never told me.'

'You met him?' Fitz asked, curiously. He knew the author's name – his mother had once seen him pick up a Lovecraft book in a secondhand shop as a kid and whalloped him, having mistaken the author's name in the large type for the book's subject – but he'd never got around to reading any of his work.

'We corresponded. We shared an interest in ice cream. I was tempted to offer him a quick trip to the eighteenth century, but I decided he'd have hated it. It isn't my business to destroy anyone's illusions. Not the harmless ones, anyway.'

The Doctor seemed to lapse into a sulk, so they proceeded in silence. Overhead wheeled an archaeopteryx, cawing down at them as it beat its feathered wings.

'That isn't real either,' the Doctor said flatly. 'The whole local structure's getting contaminated with fictions. I think we'd better be prepared to meet anything. Anything at all.'

The nurse had shot the medic through the head with some kind of firearm. There were brains everywhere.

Hume understood that. He'd got that.

But as she supported him, and the medical equipment beeped wildly, he was too busy fighting.

Fighting in his head.

He'd have felt it sooner if it hadn't been for the numbness. Perhaps he *had* felt it, only to have mistaken it for his own emotions. It was enough to know that the thing the archaeologists had found was still sending out its despair, its loneliness, and its shrill need for sympathy or compassion.

Now he could no longer feel his own grief – if it had ever

been his own – only the waves of emptiness pouring out from the dig. Telepathic impacts filtered through human perceptions, perceptions he had never expected to have – things picked up and stored from the archaeologists and perhaps the medic. It felt like losing his first girlfriend. Like nights alone with too much alcohol. Like the long sustained note of a wolf out somewhere in the dark, except it wasn't a sound at all. He remembered the team's disagreement about what it might be, but there was a grey blank in the middle of the scene. They hadn't been able to see it properly, it had been too alien. They only *thought* they'd seen it.

They'd seen only part. That had been enough.

Barely feeling the weight of the nurse clinging to his arm, he had thrashed at the communications equipment along the far wall. He had to see. He had to see quickly. If he didn't, the void, the grey space, the unknowable, would eat his mind. Already he could feel his personality – never his strongest asset – being stripped of its surface layers.

The vidlink started up, and its blue-green light speared him with the true image of the thing under the ice. One of the team must have set up a minicam at the contact point.

The grey shape resolved itself.

A churning mass of protoplasmic tissues, a grasping sea of arms and eyes, revolving in on itself, a geometry in which every angle was a right angle to every other, something broken, something scared.

He recognised it at once.

'How the hell did *that* get there?'

He snapped out a hand and clicked the vidlink off. No point staring into that abyss any longer than necessary. Even for him it was dangerous. Not that the unit itself held anything he hadn't seen before – even in the throes of uncontrolled chameleonic spasm – but that degree of interstitial distortion could have weird effects on perception, and he needed his head together.

Besides, he'd seen enough to learn that the unit was quite irreparable. It must be caught in a breakdown between its basal programming and its autonomous elements; nothing short of stripping it down for parts would do any good, and even then the majority of the metastructure would have to be regeared. He'd be hard pressed to do anything like that locally, not in a reasonable length of time. It would take three more Industrial Revolutions at least.

It was only then that he noticed the nurse.

She was mewling, and her hands, clasped tight around a scalpel, were shot with red.

Glumly he picked the bridge of his nose with irritation. More delving into the human psyche. Gods, he needed a drink.

They emerged in a clearing. Fitz couldn't tell if the Elder Things were careful gardeners or if the forest had just been flash-fried all around their habitation, but the base itself was obvious. Great blocks of stone jutting out of the side of a mountain, a side that had been boiled or stripped away to open up the stone ramparts.

Fitz thought it had started out hideous and the gaping, smoking holes in the walls didn't aid its aesthetics. If, as seemed obvious, most of it was built into the mountain, Fitz could only presume the Elder Things were not too bothered about getting nice views. A couple of bonfires were burning nearby.

'Nice aroma,' commented Compassion.

Fitz sniffed. 'Urgh, you're right. Smells like a hot morning at Smithfield. What are they burning?'

'Barbecued Elder Thing,' replied the Doctor grimly pointing to the 'bonfires'. 'Those are the bodies of the creatures we're looking for. They presumably died in that firefight we witnessed back there. But who could possibly be hunting down fictional creatures?'

'Well, it can't be Griffin,'[1] said Fitz, wrinkling his nose in disgust. 'I don't think these specimens are fit for anyone's collection.'

They were interrupted by a live specimen floating down in front of them, and Fitz had to admit it would look impressive, albeit repulsive, stuffed and mounted above the mantelpiece. It was also huge. And armed with an alarming gun. Its wings looked ludicrous, beating the air – too small to lift its mass, and yet it flew. Fitz was more worried by the gun than by its aerodynamics.

'I think we know who did the shooting,' muttered Compassion as they half-heartedly backed away – no way could they outrun this thing, thought Fitz, not when it carried a handgun that could level a small village.

'I am Ayworl,' the creature announced in a metallic monotone. 'Identify yourselves immediately.'

The Doctor stepped forward. 'Well, I am –'

The creature, Ayworl, interrupted suddenly. 'We were not aware there were others of our kind here,' it blurted. 'Why did Xenaria not tell us of your arrival? What role do you have in our mission?' Ignoring Fitz and Compassion completely, Ayworl levelled his gun at the Doctor.

The Doctor's mouth was open in shock, and he seemed to be looking at Ayworl intently, as if searching for some mysterious quality that would solve everything. Fitz could understand the puzzlement. 'Our kind', the creature had said. Fitz knew the Doctor's race, the Gallifreyans, could do all sorts of weird stuff to their bodies, but this was ridiculous.

[1]See *Doctor Who – Unnatural History*

Suddenly, a change came over the Doctor. His relaxed posture gave way to a stiff-spined military demeanour, and he looked at Ayworl imperiously.

'One of "your kind", soldier?' the Doctor exclaimed in disgust. 'I am not one of "your kind", you horrible raw recruit: I am your superior officer. You may address me as General. Now tell this Xenaria that I'm here, and have me taken to her at once, or I will have to raise the matter of military discipline with your line officers. I'm sure I don't have to remind you of the potential severity of field penalties.'

Chapter Five

Mictlan was – in its origin – a metaphysical bomb shelter. Removed from space-time, it and its occupants (if the two could in any real sense be distinguished except at the most simplistic of levels) were, in theory at least, immune to the time winds, to the possible changes being, or to be, wrought by the war. In theory, even if the Enemy had turned primordial Gallifrey into atoms or defused Omega's stellar manipulator, or aborted the Time Lords' history in any way, Mictlan should have remained – a node of information from a previous space-time preserved after its collapse by the lack of a causal connection between itself and the war.

The Celestial Intervention Agency, latterly the Celestis, had, however, been careful to provide for the possibility that the theories may be wrong. Beyond Mictlan, projected there in the same way as Mictlan itself, were the recordships. Black-box TARDISes, so called for their basic shape – for in that eventless void there was nothing for a TARDIS's chameleon circuit to resemble – each continually scanning Mictlan, recording it, checking it.

In theory, even if Mictlan was affected by a space-time event, the black boxes, still further removed from the cause, should show the alteration against the copy of Mictlan's specifications in their cores. Still, precisely because those mechanisms had themselves to reside in further bubbles of space-time anchored outside the micro-universe of Mictlan, their consultation was not, could not be, routine. Only the imprecision of the attack, if it was an attack, had left even enough memories to make the Celestis wish to consult their records.

Realising this, they were still further alarmed. Perhaps even now they were being further diminished, this time in ways more certain and more sure. Perhaps each following stroke was more absolute in its annihilation. Perhaps already they were a shadow of themselves.

The Lord had been an eccentric even among the Celestis. Where others had horsehair shirts, he had horsehair sofas. Where others revelled in the somnolent servitude of the undead he maintained a household of brightly painted figurines. Hybrid clockwork technology from the Gothick Whorl, innards of Karfelon circuitry like tinsel at Christmas. Cheap alien imports from the real universe. Vulgarities. His Family, and other animals.

Why anyone would have wished to erase him from all reality wasn't clear.

The idea of families made Investigator One sick. He had been raised in the doom-crèches of the Baby Farm where skulls were the only ornament, and the wet nurses had no faces. The thought of children would always sicken him. His existence, and those of the other Mictlan-born had been an experiment, to see if the germ-plasma of the slave class could be cultured into more pliable tools. He was regarded as one of the more successful results.

He had no sympathy to spare for the Lord, only a job to do.

A very few of his artifacts had survived. They were being examined for clues.

Two finished gutting the baby. 'Nothing in here.' She folded the nappies in a neat pile. Polynestene memory cells cracked and sundered on the knife as she laid it by. The unit's one organic component flopped and gave up. A faint smell of roasted flesh filled the oak-walled study.

One grunted. He knew he must appear at a loss. The

methodology of the Lord's disappearance was unknown even to his masters. The reconstruction work alone had tested Mictlan's capacity to the utmost. Even the pseudo-space where the ideas comprising his household had puckered around the gap, closing in like nervous sheep after a wolf has killed. They had confirmed glimpses of the missing Lord in the records held still further outside space-time than Mictlan itself. He had looked, in three separate ways, a little like each of the Lords whose unspecific similarity had haunted the minds of many of their peers. In the black boxes, he still lived: a squealing dwarf in a high-collared robe. Despite that, he had never been. The murders of things that never have existed are, as a rule, investigated with little real success.

One let pessimism show, like a consuming cloud. If Two shared the feeling she did not bother to display it.

They had even rebuilt his Family, all thirty Cousins and twenty Siblings, all the artificial tribe. Rebuilt them and then dismantled them in case something, some stray or hidden datum, may have been captured in the rebuild. It had availed them nothing. Something had bitten his House out of Mictlan like a man taking a worm in a piece of apple. There was a new fear in Hell.

They started to look wider. The Lords of Mictlan meddle: they interfere, they – sometimes dispassionately, sometimes not – weed. Where they act, space-time retains traces. Worlds vanished; histories were unwritten.

They started to look for the effects of such things never having been done. They started to look for worlds appearing, for histories reappearing, for the resurgence of the universe that had existed before the life of the Lord had been wiped away.

On an obscure world, in what had once been a

constellation named for Stellion Mutter, the prehistoric cosmographer, they discovered some very unusual anomalies.

The hissing sound of the base's great doors rising gave way to the clatter of a formal salute.

Xenaria moved to the front of the troopers, sliding easily on her five muscular tentacles, her spore-bearing wings folded away behind her grey-green body with its organic camouflage.

This was all happening too quickly – she had not expected the mission to come to the attention of Forward Command. Still, the newborn's message had been precise.

As she had expected, the general was still in an original body. That alone indicated his rank, for only the veterans of the First Wave wore that honour like a badge. Even so she ran the usual checks, turning off her body's senses and activating the enhanced telepathic scans that had been retained, buried beneath her new brain configuration, for just such an eventuality. Yes, there was no doubt, for all their differences in form, and despite the military discipline that prevented her trying to broach the general's mind shields, he was clearly of her species. It was only when the scan was over and her body's senses had renewed their insistent clamour, that she realised the general was not alone.

At his side were two members of another species entirely.

Behind her the troops stirred uneasily. She activated the tiny speaker bonded to her upper body, needed to communicate with those who had not been changed.

'What are these, General? Surely not natives of this period? My understanding of these creatures' histories is that their engineered life has as yet produced no mammals larger than a tree-dwelling shrew.'

She reached out and probed the face of one of the aliens curiously. It was a female with dark-red hair and an expression that Xenaria decoded as amused insolence. The male did not appear to share the female's bravado, although he tried to hide the fact. Xenaria's seventh sense could taste the glittering adrenachrome in his shimmering glands.

'Hardly,' the general said stiffly, and Xenaria wondered if he considered her flippancy a breach of military protocol. She hoped not. The science corps had greater latitude than the soldiery and this was a scientific mission, but if the general chose to invoke field discipline she could face a painful beating, maybe worse. Her engineered body was practically indestructible but it had been built with coded weak spots to permit corporal punishment. In time of war, imprisonment and death were of little use in maintaining order. The war effort could not support drones, nor could it afford to sacrifice potential warriors. Under the rigours of the War Rule she could expect to be given no quarter if she fell short of its ideals.

The general seemed to weigh up her hesitancy and continued in a more kindly voice, although Xenaria could still detect the arrogance of Command. 'They are creatures I have taken from upwhen. Under War Rule conditions, I find it useful to carry biological detectors. Their timelines are intimately connected with the futureward time web of this planet. In the event of a counterstrike by the Enemy, changes in them will alert us sufficiently to impose stasis zones over the local continua. Like human miners with a canary, in case of carbon monoxide.'

The general's basic-model face smiled in a way that made Xenaria homesick for the time before the war, a time she had heard of only in old transcripts. 'Besides which, I've always had a soft spot for canaries.'

Xenaria inclined a scarlet eye in a curious gesture, it was as near as she dared to speaking without permission.

'Yes, yes. What's a canary? I know. You youngsters of the new wave. It's all war with you, I expect, no time for ornithology. The canary is a little yellow bird native to the future of this planet.'

'Yes, General. Thank you, General.'

The female 'canary' gave the general another of its odd looks. Xenaria hoped it was trained not to soil its outer layers. Presumably it had some rudimentary intelligence.

'If I may ask, General, have there been any signs of Rep incursions?'

'No. No, you may not,' the general snapped, his voice clipped. 'That information is strictly on a need-to-know basis. Furthermore you'll refrain from referring to the Enemy, or using any such colloquialisms or nicknames that might identify them. This is a deep-cover mission: all communications must be those expected of the host species; we cannot afford an external slip caused by lax internal practice. I'll have obedience here, or by Rassilon, I'll know the reason why.'

Xenaria shuddered at the blasphemy. The general himself was treading on the edges of painful discipline. The political office would enforce the blasphemy rules even against High Command. She remembered General Entarlon being whipped outside the Officers' Club for suggesting that Omega wouldn't have lasted a day in this war. She wondered if the troops would support her if she protested, if she could regain the initiative by threatening the penalties for speaking the sacred name. She couldn't rely on Allopta, that was for certain.

She realised the general was still speaking. Oh no – what had she missed?

'You may regard this mission as a simple data-retrieval one but I most certainly do not!'

'No, General. I fully appreciate that we hope to gain far more than mere information, although we have made great strides in that area.'

'I certainly hope you have, soldier. And in others.' The general's voice was dismissive. 'Now show me and my canaries to the most humanoid-suitable quarters available. I will expect a full presentation of the current progress on the mission as soon as it can be made ready.'

'Yes, General.'

When the Time Lords had left them alone, Compassion stretched out on one of the narrow ledges that lined the walls at eye height, and gave every sign of going to sleep. Fitz was fuming. How could she do that? And how dare the Doctor treat them this way? Canary, indeed! The worst thing was, it sounded so plausible. He caught a flutter of a wink in one of the Doctor's amazing blue eyes, and saw his friend had a finger pressed to his lips.

Fitz realised that the room was probably subject to the aliens' scrutiny in some way. He waited while the Doctor twisted a piece of wire from his pocket into two bits of wall that looked exactly like every other piece of wall, so far as he could see.

Compassion was watching them both.

'A robin red breast in a cage puts all Heaven in a rage,' Fitz muttered, dredging up a memory of Blake's poetry from school. Despite the account of his childhood he had spun for Sam, he hadn't spent all his schooldays running from Krautbashers.

'Polly want a cracker?' the Doctor asked.

'Not funny,' said Compassion, perching herself upright on

the ledge. 'Are you going to make me ask then, or are you just going to tell me? I'm quite willing, to – what is it? – get with the program?'

The Doctor looked puzzled. 'I haven't got a program, not really, not these days. We'll just find out what's going on here, and then we'll make our excuses and leave. The real point I want solved is what the Elder Things are doing here in the first place.'

'Fighting,' Compassion said, 'just like everybody else. They live, struggle and die. What's the problem?'

'Yes, well partly. I really meant the other Elder Things, the ones that got killed.'

'The other Elder Things?' Fitz felt his depth being left behind, again. 'You mean, as opposed to the ones you're related to?'

'Yes, you see I think I already know what the base's current masters are up to,' the Doctor said ruefully.

'I thought as much,' Compassion began. 'You might begin by explaining why they look like these "Elder Things" at all. I thought Time Lords were supposed to be bipeds like the rest of us.'

The Doctor had started to look suddenly more worried than puzzled. Surely he couldn't just have been winging it, Fitz thought. Dear God, please let him have at least a rudimentary plan.

'Beauty is only skin deep,' he offered finally.

Oh, Fitz thought. That's it, is it? Leave the human to flounder. Well bugger that.

Compassion was staring the Doctor down. He blinked first.

'You owe us,' she whispered.

'Yes, I do, don't I? And it may get worse before it gets better.'

He sat cross-legged on the floor. 'It's complicated.'

'I thought it might be.'

'Did Fitz ever tell you about Sam telling him about the time when we ran into those aliens who were auctioning a superweapon in Earth's future rainforests?'

Compassion shrugged. 'Perhaps I was otherwise occupied.'

'It sounded hairy,' Fitz said. 'Sam wouldn't, or couldn't, tell me much about the weapon. She spent more time moaning about washing genetically engineered big-cat pee out of her clothes for weeks.'

'The nature of the weapon isn't that important, although I *will* tell you if it ever becomes so. Just trust me on that please – it's rather a painful subject. What mattered was that some of the interested parties were from the future.'

'Aren't we all?' Fitz deadpanned.

'No, not that future. From my people's future, from something that's supposed to be as unknowable to me as next week's football results to you. They were at war, the same war the Celestis opted out of.'

Compassion started. 'At war? With Faction Paradox?'

'I shouldn't know, but I don't think so. That'd be like a war between the United Kingdom and the Hare Krishnas.'

'Do not underestimate them, Doctor.'

Fitz wondered if Compassion was angry – Faction Paradox had been like the Gods of Myth to her people. She didn't share the common view that Time Lords could do no wrong or that they were unassailable. Fitz didn't know what he thought. The Doctor's people had to be the nearest thing to gods, and wouldn't that make their enemies demons?

'Oh I'm not. There's no need to defend their prowess, but a thumping great war's not their style. It's more of a cult thing with them.' He grinned. 'Didn't they once say they put the cult into culture?' He shook his head. 'I mustn't speculate anyway. If I knew the future I might be tempted to try to change it, and then not only might I make things worse, but I'd also be meddling, and, as you know I never meddle.'

Fitz looked at him darkly. 'Right.'

'Well hardly ever!' the Doctor protested. 'That's why I shut up our host when she started talking about "Rep incursions". I can't afford to entertain the least clue. Really.'

'That thing was a she?' For a moment Fitz was too startled by that thought to pick up the logic of what the Doctor was saying, but then it clicked. 'If you shut up our host because you didn't want her to tell you about this future war, then that makes her –'

'A Time Lord from that future war? Yes, I rather think it does.'

'Then why do they look so... alien?' Fitz asked. A grisly thought struck him, and he followed the question rapidly with another. 'That isn't what you really look like, is it?'

The Doctor sniffed. 'You're being very parochial, Fitz. I thought Xenaria was really a splendid figure of a warrior. Every foot a Time Lady, all five of them.'

Fitz looked wildly at Compassion. 'Tell me he's kidding.'

She rolled her eyes. 'He's kidding. Satisfied?' She paused. 'Mind you, he never actually denied it, he only changed the subject.'

'Anyway,' said the Doctor, a look of intense concentration in his eyes, 'my descendants' regenerative choices are neither here nor there. What I want to know is this: why are the Time Lords wiping out and replacing a race who, until recently, didn't even exist?'

Confirming the identity of the creature via the vidlink had brought an inner calm to Hume's mind. At last, things were starting to make some kind of sense again. The augurs of destruction were beginning to subside.

As he sat in a makeshift conference room at the forward base, Hume examined the leaves in the bottom of his teacup. The patterns told him nothing too untoward. Nothing to offer but blood, sweat and tea.

He became aware that he had company.

'Professor Hume.' The voice was sharp, Nordic. Hume kept his eyes locked on to the tea leaves, swilling the dregs so the leaves moved into different patterns. A kaleidoscope on a budget.

'Professor Schneider,' he said. 'Do sit down.'

Schneider sat opposite him, on the other side of the collapsible table.

'I hope you have good reason for dragging me and my team away from our work,' said Schneider. Hume could feel her eyes on him, the efficiency and inner repression of her thoughts. 'This is my mission, and I am not entirely sure why you could not come down to us.'

Hume placed his cup on the table between them, and looked levelly at Schneider. 'Professor,' he said, with all the semblance of reasoned behaviour he could muster. 'I hardly think it would be advisable for a man of my refined telepathic abilities to directly enter such a psychically hostile environment. I believe your Dr Jessup has shown a number of extreme reactions to the creature, and he is quite a dullard compared with myself. The effect on one of your medics was even less pleasant. You'll excuse me if I keep my distance. I am, after all, far less expendable than the average scientist.'

'Your modesty does you credit,' said Schneider icily. 'You are, however, still a consultant. An adviser.'

Hume raised his hands in a placating gesture.

'So I will advise, Professor Schneider,' he said gently. 'But my first advice must be caution. I do not wish to undermine your authority, but the situation is quite, quite serious. An entire science team and one medic dead, millions of dollars' worth of equipment destroyed. The situation must be approached with great caution, before we drive the entire UN over budget for this fiscal quarter.'

'So,' said Schneider. 'What do you suggest we do?'

'For now?' He raised his eyebrows. 'For now you do nothing. Surface examinations of the site only, no probing with any kind of technology. Until an appropriate strategy is formulated, we're safer leaving that creature alone. Oh, and I would recommend you and your staff take doses of a mild antipsychotic, lest we have a repeat of today's unfortunate outbursts. The nurse can prepare the injections if she's quite finished blubbing. No driving or operating heavy machinery, please.'

Schneider raised a pencilled eyebrow. 'And what will you be doing?' she asked.

'Gaining information,' said Hume, pulling his hood over his head. 'From the only person here with any potentially useful insights to share.'

The girl that the creature had given to them had the answers Hume needed, he was sure of it. Once he had learned whatever he could from her, the UN could blast the shaft and the city below it to oblivion for all he cared. But he had to be sure first. The girl had been taken to one of the other geodesics, so Hume had to zip up his parka and face the glare.

He trudged across the snow with aching steps, one leg still smarting from the 'copter crash. Minimal damage, under the circumstances. It would heal well enough in time. He entered the other geodesic to find the nurse he had dealt with earlier tending to the girl, who was laid out on a simple camp bed. Hume told her to go across and give the rest of the team, and herself, the sedatives he had prescribed. She asked if Hume wanted a dose himself, but he stared her down until she went away. He'd put her fractured mind back in its box, but he hadn't had time for more than a rough count of the pieces. She'd be good enough to treat the others but he wasn't about to trust her with his own medication.

Alone with the ostensibly unconscious girl, he sat and watched her for a few minutes before his patience ran out.

'You can stop feigning sleep now,' he said quietly. 'Not even the raciest dream could produce the complexity of thoughts I sense going through your head.'

With an almost mechanical shrug of resignation, the girl opened her eyes and pulled herself up into a sitting position. This was obviously uncomfortable, but she sneered rather than winced at the pain. He had thought her a rather plain thing, unremarkable, but as she met his gaze he was surprised by the aloof quality in her eyes. She displayed no remorse or embarrassment at her previous deception, or his discovery of it. Neither did she show any reaction to his telepathy. Hume held her stare with his own. No need to mess around with this one.

'So,' he said simply, 'would you like to tell me how you came to join us here?'

'Like?' she repeated. 'No, but I'll tell you anyway if you want.'

Hume smiled thinly.

'So,' she said, echoing his bedside manner with heavy irony. 'Where would you like me to start.'

Hume shrugged. 'Wherever you think is best.'

'The best place to start', she began, 'would be about twelve million years ago…'

Interlude: An Odd Incident

The survey ship's commander brushed a lock of sweaty hair out of his eyes, and cursed at his subordinate. Landing party chief Daniels just stood there taking it, the heat barely creasing his uniform.

'You honestly expect me to report that a human colony has, in six months, forgotten the wheel?'

'No, sir,' the landing party chief said, falling back on the strict letter-of-the-question responses that had saved many a starman's butt. 'With respect sir, it's worse than that.'

'Worse than that?' Commander Ambert, gave vent to a series of lurid curses.

'Yes, sir. I think you should read this sir.' He pushed a flimsy sheet of print-out at Ambert.

Grudgingly, Ambert began to read: 'The obsession of the pre-enlightenment cultures with this purely mythological geometric figure strikes us now as the most artificial aspect of those most artificial ages. To us, grounded in rationality and natural science – aware that every natural line is a fractal construct, composed of myriad straight infinitesimals – the mere idea of a "curve" is hard to grasp. Such gross things have no existence in nature, and can exist on paper only as a dash may represent, without actually being in reality, a dimensionless line-end. How much harder then is the idea of the "circle". The closest real definition of this figure which has any resonance at all for our minds is that it is a polygon with an infinite number of sides. Such a shape would of course be impossible to construct in real space. Those clumsy fetish objects called "wheels" represent a cargo-cult response to problems in engineering that we have rightly rejected.' His face, already red, turned a shade darker – so much so that Daniels thought that the Commander might be about to burst a blood vessel. 'They don't believe in circles?' Ambert hissed. 'It isn't possible! What is this rubbish?'

'It's part of a monograph by a local philosopher sir, it's called 'The Myth of the Non-straight Line'. I swear to you sir, they aren't faking it, sir. We've interviewed dozens of colonists, children as well as adults. If you show them a circle, they squint at it a bit and tell you you've drawn an infinitely regular polygon. One of them told me that the irrational nature of pi proved that circles were impossible, or that just drawing a figure on a piece of paper could create a item of information larger than the universe. They've been remarkably ingenious in converting their technology, but even so their efficiency is down. It's as if they can't see one, or can't grasp what it's for. Some of them have died, sir, from starvation.'

'Warfare!'

'What?'

'This must be a psychological tactic, some kind of mind weapon.'

'Are circles so important, sir?'

'Your point being, chief?'

'Would making people forget circles be a very useful weapon, sir?'

'It would be if it didn't stop there – you said yourself that people had died. Besides, what if they forgot to pay their taxes, what then? Or if they forgot Earth! I want this world quarantined. I want psychologists and psycho-tacticians and virologists here. See to it.'

'Aye, aye sir.'

However, they never found the answer.

Chapter Six

'If I could speak freely for a moment, Commander?' Allopta said, managing to turn an infrabass rumble into a hissing insinuation. Verbal communication had been engineered into their version of the Elder Things' bodies as a concession to the familiar because the natural microwave language of the host bodies had proved intractable even to the skills of the Time Lords. They had, however, due to the nature of the bodies' frequency receptors, been forced to run the signals under the normal range of hearing, hence the mechanical device for stepping up their speech to standard frequencies that Xenaria had used to communicate with the General.

Besides, it had been theorised in the mission briefing, and since confirmed as fact, that the Elder Things would have used their microwave language like other races used voice control, and the troops could not risk inadvertently triggering an alarm or a defensive system. One of the newborns had already inadvertently discovered that by 'shouting' a certain vocative in the 25cm range he could blister hull metal. It worried Allopta that creatures with so versatile a language – a language that was its own weapon – should have been so easily defeated. The facile explanation, that they were decadent remnants of a higher culture, somehow failed to please him. The same could all too easily be said of himself.

'Of course,' Xenaria said, in as offhand a way as possible. She did not even bother to turn one of her eyes towards him. It was, he guessed, a calculated snub.

'I am concerned by the arrival of the general at this

juncture. It seems inopportune. Why would Command send an observer before we have even had a chance to absorb more than the outermost layer of the local records. What possible progress do they expect of us?'

'Obviously there has been a turning point in the war. Note how he is reluctant to discuss the nature of the conflict until we have briefed him. Probably there has been a hinge incident and the probability of the bundle of timelines the Matrix predicts as leading to victory has been diminished. He would not want to tell us. It might impact on our efficiency.'

'You think it's that simple?' Allopta felt a ripple begin at his base and spread outward through his tentacles. Interesting, he hadn't intended to do that. His war body's pseudo-reflexes were starting to integrate more completely with his neural language. If he had been in his original body that might have been a sneer. 'It's your decision, Commander, of course. Still, I wish my doubts to lie in the mission record. If he should be an Enemy agent…'

'One of *them*, posing as a Time Lord! I hardly think their psychology would allow it. Besides, Allopta, you're right. It *is* my decision. I want you to brief the general personally. No doubt he will expect to be impressed. Don't disappoint him.'

Allopta scuttled off, twirling around on his lower limbs. Xenaria wondered if she had just witnessed an act of insubordination. The interface between her conscious mind and the signals from her body read Allopta's posture and gesture as insolent in the extreme, but she couldn't be sure of the extent to which they were under his control. In one sense it was a disciplinary problem but in another it was a good sign. If she ever found herself reading Elder Thing body language instinctively, it would mean she was about to 'go native', to drown in the alienness of her new form. It happened. Her last second-in-command was huddled in the corner of a ward on Gallifrey, moving sideways, trying to make an exoskeleton out of overturned medibunks-bunks. If he was lucky they would be able to cure him, perhaps with a forced regen; if he was unlucky he'd be declared material. Go to the Looms. She shuddered, and it came out as radio waves.

The sooner they were out of here the better.

She clicked her voice to intra-troop communications. A picture of her would appear in the minds of each trooper as she spoke, and they would appear before her in response. An adaptation of the superganglia to the war.

'Attention, assembler teams. I want the TARDIS cradles in place and breeding within the next hour. Assimilators, how are you doing interpreting the local computer languages?'

Tachon reported for the cradle teams. 'The main structure of the cradles is in place, Commander. The outer event-shells are now being built up molecule by molecule in the hollows under the host's base. The hollows themselves have been dimensionally transcendentalised. We can fit dry docks for forty war TARDISes within them.'

Transcendentalised, Xenaria thought wanly. Even our language is going straight to hell.

'Barely satisfactory. You know the briefing projects a one-in-fifty-seven success rate for the main phase even with a full century of Ships. Still, if it is all we can produce...'

'It is.'

'Very well. Machtien?'

The newborn in charge of the assimilation unit saluted. His body was scarred and leaked a thin grey-green ichor from a number of surface wounds. Xenaria guessed that the local computers were putting up a fight.

'We have isolated local records concerning the fifth planet. It was of course difficult to factor out the effects of the time loop on their perceptions but reading the gaps we have a solid space-time position for the world.'

'Excellent. How soon can the data be integrated into the cortex elements of the new TARDISes?'

'That is dependent on the assemblers, Commander,' Machtien said smugly.

An image of Tachon cut in briefly, glaring with all five of his red eyes. A purely reflexive twitch of the telepathic communications circuit, but still bad for discipline. There was a certain roughness still between the veterans and the newborn – she would have to watch that.

'Tachon,' Xenaria snapped, 'we have no time for internal struggles. When the assault TARDISes are assembled I expect the next phase to commence at once. We will get only one chance.'

Tachon inclined his starfish head at an angle of twenty degrees, in a gesture of contrition and guarded acquiescence.

Actually, she thought – having first cut the circuit (it would never do to broadcast her doubts to the common soldiers) – they would be lucky even to get one chance. The Enemy would never have allowed the time path of even a dozen TARDISes to converge on a known strategic point without launching a counteroffensive. Only by constructing the units within a local beachhead, near, both in space and time, to the objective, could the strike be both assembled and launched with too short a mean event track in space-time to permit its detection during, before and after its existence. Ninety-nine per cent of Time War was camouflage.

Xenaria felt her eyes drawn to the Ur-box, the device that broadcast a signal into the vortex, replaying the 'real' events of the next few days within the base – which the Time Lords had first recorded before launching the attack. As long as it functioned, to Enemy or Gallifreyan time scanners alike, the base would appear to be maintained and occupied by its original inhabitants. It had some disadvantages – its range, for example, was strictly limited; any activity outside the base would be visible, and hence would need to be strictly controlled. Equally, any excursions recorded by the original scan would need to be acted out as closely to the Ur-text as possible. To facilitate this the original data had been built into their bodies: if there was need they would be able to default to the actions of the creatures they were replacing. Xenaria had been on one previous mission where it had become necessary. It had felt like a bad dream, or a living death.

Perhaps, Fitz thought, constant access to time travel eroded a person's ability to just sit and wait for events to unfold in the usual manner. The Doctor, for one, seemed incapable of waiting, prowling around the room muttering the word 'Rep' to himself in a variety of tones and accents, constantly checking his pocket watch even though they had been alone for only about ten minutes. However, the Doctor's constant pacing was beginning to get on Fitz's nerves, a situation only worsened by Compassion's seemingly total ease with their circumstances.

'Perhaps it's short for "repo-men"', said Fitz sarcastically. 'Yes, that's it. The Time Lords are behind on their repayments and the Enemy are just the bailiffs come around to repossess their sofa.'

'Or replicas,' Compassion said. 'The Nestene, the Zygons, the Rutan horde, the various shape-shifting and protean races. They're always off conquering something. Although what they'll do with a world when they can't even decide who they are is anyone's guess.'

'Acronym!' Fitz yelled, like a man throwing a grenade. 'Revolting Extradimensional Parasites.'

'Reviving Elder Powers?' the Doctor added, on the beat. 'I'd prefer reptiles: eighty-seventh-century Earth Reptiles with transforming *T. rex* time machines.' His face lit up. 'The whole of established human history could be a Time Lord attempt to eradicate their causal nexus.'

'Someone,' Compassion said, 'has been watching too much Saturday-morning TV.'

The Doctor shrugged. 'There was a time when it always seemed to be Saturday when I was on Earth, and the children's programmes were excellent, if my memory doesn't cheat.' He made folding motions with his hand and muttered something that sounded to Fitz like 'robots in disguise'. The Doctor grinned, disarmingly. 'My third childhood is showing. We really shouldn't know. Besides, I have a feeling I'll be much happier not knowing who or what this "Enemy" are. They'll probably be terribly disappointing. With my luck it'll turn out to be Yartek, leader of the alien Voord, with a big stick.'

The great square in Corinth was as these places always were, and always would be: a place for men to meet, for goods to be sold, for fortunes to be told, for the less salubrious of transactions to take place.

And, of course, a place where any lunatic who wanted to be heard could get up and broadcast his ill-informed opinions to anyone willing to stop and listen. If the crowd liked what they heard, the speaker may even get a few coins tossed his way.

The old man was wild and scrawny, his hair and rags dirty

and distressed. He scrabbled in the dirt, wiry frame tensed, as he told his story. They were amused by his antics, by the sheer desperation and frightfulness of the old man. The rich's fascination with the poor was always like this, as long as they grovelled or foamed at the mouth.

'Beware!' bellowed the old man. 'Beware, people of good Corinth, lest you neglect your gods. For I am Panthius, last survivor of Atlantis. My people paid for their arrogance when our city sank beneath the waves, and so shall you, if you do not heed my words.'

Many of the gathered crowd wandered away at this point, as, even back in ancient Corinth, talk of Atlantis was reserved for the more eccentric and less sexually active sections of the populace. However, the few left were rewarded by the appearance of two strange, spectral figures, the shapes of a man and a woman, filled with stars.

The stars were transformed into imperial purple and then into gas in the wink of an eye, but even so the remaining members of the crowd began to peel away. Only the very bravest remained, cowering behind the pillars, as the celestial visitants moved towards the obliviously drooling old man.

'Surely you must see that this creature's account of Atlantis is clearly anomalous,' insisted the first of the creatures. The male one.

The female shrugged her shoulders. 'Evidence, One,' she said. 'We need evidence to convince our Lords. Your theories are not enough.' Picking the old man up by the scruff of the neck, she dug a finger into the base of his skull. Ignoring the blood pouring from the wound, she gouged around until her face turned into a grimace of distaste or disappointment.

'Nothing.'

'Then we keep searching.'

* * *

'So?' Jessup asked. 'How is she? Who is she?'

Hume shrugged. 'You might be advised to add "what is she?" to your ill-advised questions, but I'm afraid I don't know yet. Not for sure. She seems healthy enough in a bovine sort of way. You could stick a thermometer up her bottom yourself if you really wanted to know.'

'You must have learnt something, you've been in there with her for hours.'

'What's this? Jealousy? We haven't been snogging.' Hume's sarcasm was withering. 'She claims to be one of a party of, I suppose you might call them "concerned time travellers". According to her, they stumbled on some sort of war being fought here, twelve million years ago. She's taken me through an attack on this whole complex by other travellers. I suspect she knows more about them than she's saying.'

'How did she get here?'

'She hasn't told me that yet – it's possible she doesn't quite remember herself, it may have been traumatic. However it shouldn't be beyond even your limited imagination to hazard a guess. Your pet angst monster is obviously a time machine.'

'Jessup whistled softly. 'Out of warantee, I'd wager.'

Chapter Seven

The mist hung low over the ground, and in the underbrush some kind of creature squealed. The air smelled of animal.

'Where is this?' Two asked.

'Tulloch Moor. A disgusting, uncivilised, uncultivated wasteland.'

'What now?'

'We wait.'

Two shrugged, and turned a hillock into a wrought-iron and mahogany coffee table laden with egg-shell china bowls. 'Cocaine?' she offered. 'The pharmacopoeia describes it as a local delicacy of this time period. Apparently a –' her eyes glazed as she accessed a reference – '"healthy and invigorating tonic, entirely natural and herbal, used as a constituent of one of this aeon's most popular beverages".'

'Thank you, no,' One said, prodding a crystal with a forefinger. 'A barbarous practice.' He produced a snuff box from his sleeve and inhaled a pinch of powdered acetylsalicylic acid. It would have killed a normal Time Lord in seconds by interfering with hormone receptor intermediaries. He had been amusing himself by building up an immunity. It never hurt to be too careful.

'What are we waiting for exactly?' Two asked.

'That!'

Time itself became manifest. A howling blue and purple swirl of rupturing chronons. Two noted that a bird caught in the fringes of the effect briefly appeared to jump forward as time flickered.

The twisting and distorted technicolour geometry of a

time tunnel burst in a sickly spillage of spoilt light, disgorging a huddled shape. A beast in black leather; half man, half reptile thing.

Two looked it over dispassionately. 'Crude zygma distortion from unshielded time-wind penetration?'

One kicked at the creature's unconscious form. Its head, overly long and malformed, lolled, showing first one side, a snout packed with sharp teeth, and then the other, the pinched, fretted features of a minor functionary or a third-rate lab technician. One shrugged. 'Just ugly.' He placed a finger, somewhat squeamishly, on the closest point that its distorted forehead had to a centre. Unlike Two, he felt no need to get inside his witnesses.

Memory. The cloying scent of Mustakozene-80. The feeling as the cells opened up, gorging on the genetic pattern of the Morlox creature, incorporating its structure into his own. The hatred of the meddler, first in white frills and velvet, condemning him to the Science Council – those purblind fools! – for his experiments, then louder, more hateful still in coloured fools' garb, intruding on his domain. Just as he had begun to grasp the power that was rightly his. Should have killed him. Yes. Yes.

'Yessss,' One hissed.

'Anything?' Two asked.

One's face, caught in a moment of memory imprinting, twisted into the horrible grimace of the creature. Ugly inside and out, but worse on the inside. Was that how his mind would look, if Two wiggled her fingers inside his head?

More petulantly than he liked, he blew out the back of the creature's malformed skull with a single livid bolt of fire.

'Nothing useful,' he said huffily, adjusting his robes. 'A most distasteful episode.'

* * *

Loom-fresh and eager, Holsred patrolled the corridors of the base, looking for trouble. He and the other newborns had been spared specific duties, not from any feelings of charity but because, to be blunt, they were useless. Untrained cannon fodder. Good pre-programmed reaction times and strategy data had been hard-wired into their brains, but without the genuine experience and acquired instincts of a veteran soldier. For the moment, while the technicians and the commanders went about their work, the newborns had little to do but make up their own patrols, mental exercises in tedium endurance. Holsred flicked through intra-troop communications: many of the team were busy, working on various tasks. The only newborns as low down the military food chain as Holsred were Ayworl and Urtshi. He located them over the communicator, and observed them trying to play cards – not easy with tentacles. Clearly they had as little to do as he had.

Well, just because there was nothing to do didn't mean Holsred had to do nothing, or waste his time on games. He was born of the House of Redloom, a family known for its initiative and inquisitiveness. Although he had never met any of his Cousins, having been – metaphorically speaking – pressed into uniform as soon as he was woven, Holsred was still Redloom in his genes, still carried the family traits.

Holsred had heard, in the blasé statements of his elders and the excited gossip of his contemporaries, about the arrival of a general at the base. Ayworl was making great capital out of having escorted a *general* – someone so high-ranking a trooper wouldn't usually get to see one from a distance – to see Xenaria. And for once, Ayworl had a point. What better way was there for a soldier at ease to fill his time than serving a high-ranking officer? Especially when that soldier came from such a noble lineage, the descendant of Cardinals and Castellans. One day Holsred would be a general too, completing the circle. There would always be a place at the top of the Gallifreyan hierarchy for a Redloom.

So, leaving his fellow newborns to their own idle meanderings and futile sentry practice, Holsred went in search of the general.

The Doctor was, of course, one of the universe's great travellers. However, thought Fitz, it was becoming clearer that this was probably due to his complete hatefulness when impelled to remain in one, boring place for longer than three minutes. As a traveller, his time was necessarily interesting and eventful. In less incident-packed circumstances, his goldfish attention span and constant energy could be a nightmare.

The Doctor's pacing was torture, his mumbling an increasing pain. Fitz was inclined to dark thoughts involving a red-hot poker. Fitz had always been told that travel broadened the mind. He had never realised it could stretch it so far.

'What,' he hissed, 'are we waiting for exactly?'

'The report.' The Doctor looked puzzled at his question. 'I asked them for a review of their progress. They bring it here, we nod, say well done and go. Read it in the TARDIS and consider our actions.'

'I am surprised you haven't merely ordered them to abort the mission,' Compassion remarked. 'Does it matter what exactly it is? Or are you only opposed to war when it's being fought by other people's cultures?'

'Shush.' The Doctor made frantic suppressing motions, as one of the creatures he had claimed were Time Lords entered.

'General,' the creature began in a gravelly monotone,

making an odd tentacular gesture that Fitz presumed was meant to approximate to a bow or salute.

There was an instant change in the Doctor's demeanour. He ceased his pacing and swung around, arms behind his back, chest puffed out. With his frock coat and waistcoat, he seemed like a Napoleonic commander inspecting the troops.

'Yes, soldier?' asked the Doctor. Then, picking up on the creature's nervousness, his manner became softer. 'What can I do for you, lad?'

'Sir, I am Holsred of the House of Redloom –'

'I know it well,' interrupted the Doctor, a note of fond approval in his voice.

'I wondered if I could assist you in some way, sir,' said Holsred. 'It would be an honour, sir,' he added.

As Holsred stood to attention the Doctor paced around him slowly, eyeing the creature up and down.

Don't milk it too much, thought Fitz. He rolled his eyes at Compassion, who gave him an almost sympathetic grimace in return.

After giving Holsred a thorough inspection, the Doctor nodded sagely. 'You'll do, lad, you'll do. Seem steady on your tentacles. Newly spun, I presume?'

'Uhhh...' Holsred seemed embarrassed at this intimation of his immaturity. 'Yes, sir. This is my first body, sir. I don't know anything else – sorry, sir.'

The Doctor gave Holsred a hearty slap on the back, and ended up nursing an obviously bruised wrist. 'Don't apologise, lad,' he said through gritted teeth. 'War's best put in the hands of the young, not old buffers like me.'

Fitz was inescapably reminded of old war comics, playground taunts and John Mills films. The Doctor's performance as the general was descending into camp cliché at tremendous speed.

'Oh no, sir,' said Holsred, aghast. 'A man of your experience, General… you can teach us so much. I'm surprised they risked sending someone so valuable into a place like this. It's supposed to be a suicide mission after all, sir.'

Fitz jumped slightly at this. Even Compassion seemed alarmed at the severity of the situation this suggested, and the Doctor's militaristic bearing slipped in shock.

'Newly woven, and you volunteered for a suicide mission?' gasped the Doctor.

'Volunteered?' repeated Holsred blankly, as if trying to grasp an alien concept.

'Never mind,' barked the Doctor, hastily trying to reassert his authority. 'No, I'm here to learn from you, from our brave lads in the front line. I remember how General… General Loombridge used to lead from the front, back when the war began. In the breach on the Stangmoor Penal Colony, breaking quarantine to investigate an outbreak of Green Cancer on L'nf!XfX!, holding back fiendish hordes of Brendonites… yes, there's a lot we in command could learn from General Loombridge.'

'Yes, sir,' said Holsred doubtfully.

'You remember General Loombridge, don't you lad?' snapped the Doctor accusingly.

Holsred sprang to attention, all doubt erased by the voice of authority. 'Yes, sir, of course, sir, a great man, sir.'

'Good lad,' said the Doctor. 'Now, we generals operate on the intelligence from bright young Loomlings like yourself, soldier, and Redloomers have been sniffing things out for millennia. So I'm relying on you to keep me up to date, else I won't learn anything from this mission. Got that, Holsred?'

'Yes, sir!' snapped Holsred in response.

'So… in five words or fewer, your mission is?'

The Doctor, Fitz decided, didn't seem sure if he was John Mills or Nicholas Parsons.

'Retrieval detail from Planet Five, sir.'

The Doctor looked expectant.

'Please sir, don't know what, sir. High security, sir.'

'Right, of course.' The Doctor said paternally. 'Very good. Loose Words Cost Worlds. On your way then, soldier.'

'Yes, sir!'

The Doctor visibly slumped as soon as Holsred had left. He rubbed his throat with his good hand.

'All that shouting has left me feeling quite hoarse,' he said limply.

The twin shapes of One and Two blinked in and out across the history of Antarctica, now poised against the ice, then outlined against the evergreen, perennial cycads of the middle Tertiary. Like the noses of sniffer-dogs seeking a rank scent, their specially bred senses, extending beyond the surface of space-time, probed for the fracturing that occurs in time and space when history alters.

Even time-embedded species have this sense to a degree – it is the sense that screams 'wrong!' when friends remember the past differently, or when an object looked for is found in a place searched thoroughly minutes before.

'Ah, there.' The scents of time, crushed like garlic under the fingers.

Holding themselves adjacent to the megaflow, imperceptible, impalpable observers, they let the years roll back.

Two wrinkled her nose. 'I think I'm going to be sick.'

'If you could manage not to be, it would help. The local nexus is damaged enough as it is without you spewing all over it. There.'

Suddenly a mountain had thrown itself up around them from the black scree of the middle glaciations. In its heart unfossilising trilobites gasped for oxygenated water as the moments flickered by backward. Two found her head next to the unwinking eye of a long-dead xiphodon, its herbivorous teeth nuzzling her shoulder.

Then air reached them. Two drew breath, only to realise she was still out of phase, and began the ghost of a coughing fit. She began to phase in.

'No,' One said. 'This is different. I would prefer it if we could remain in the shadow realms for a moment or two, Two.'

Two got as far as 'Why, exactly?' before the cavern really impacted her senses.

They were hovering in and out of a lacework of cables and ducting, spars and joists and scaffold work. Far below, tentacled ants with five eyes and multiple wings were swarming over black iridescent spheres that pulsed with uncanny life. The base of the cavern was at once a hundred clicks away, and only just out of reach. In the weird black light of the congeries of globes, the figures were depressed, almost two-dimensional, as if they were part of a living tessellated pavement, a moving picture, processing itself in ceramics before the slowest audience in the cosmos.

'Well, well', One said. 'They have been busy little bees.'

Two cast a scientist's eye over the scene: the disembodied orb – cut from the skull of one of Mictlan's finest zombie-savants – returned to her hand almost instantly glutted with data. She took a dainty bite and passed it to One, who shook his head.

'No, thank you. I prefer to cogitate and digest my own conclusions. Other people's theories always give me stomachache. Excuse me.' Before Two could protest, One was floating down towards the scene. Two noted with interest that, as he fell, he too began to suffer the same dimensional compaction and reduction. The lower parts of the cavern were held in a dimensionally transcendental field, enabling three-dimensional objects to exist in two dimensions, vastly increasing the available working volume. It was a dangerous trick, and expensive in terms of energy. It smacked, Two thought, of desperation, of a profligate use of resources that was permitted because it was already known that there wouldn't be a tomorrow.

The process seemed to be geometric: for each body length One moved forward, his body length was halved. By the time he arrived on the factory floor, he too was the size of an insect. He turned and waved, a sighted midge amid a blind swarm. The others milled, past, and even through him, failing to impact his extradimensional form.

A wave of programmed hatred swept through Two. Celestis constructs are built to crush potential threats at the moment of greatest destruction for least effort. The sight of One with the dimensions of a gnat raised the will to destroy in her basic personality. Even if all else in a construct was erased that core instinct to identify and eradicate any danger would remain. If One was any risk, she would never have a better opportunity to remove him from the field.

She remembered her briefing. *'Investigator Eighteen, you've done good work for us, in the past, and the future. We have, however, an internal problem.'* A one-way window in Mictlan space had opened, showing another Investigator. She had recognised him at once of course as One, the Investigation Section's most feared field agent. *'It is possible he has gone rogue. His psychic indices are showing unusual levels of altruism, curiosity and concern. Twice he has been observed using less than killing force, and he is also known to have left pockets of resistance in the mop-up operations in the Seventh RetroWar, a mistaken kindness that may cause the Eighth to be fought a millennium earlier.'*

She had shrugged. 'So dissect him, sieve his brain, know for sure.'

'And lose him? We don't want a man of pieces: you know as well as we that a reconstruct from deep study is never quite as effective as the original. Besides we have a crisis.' The cloaked master held up a hand. 'Don't ask us to tell you what at this stage. There is a problem… with the problem. Agents within Mictlan keep forgetting its existence. We hope you and One will retain your instructions if they are given on board a recordship TARDIS even further outside the space-time envelope; if so you will be empowered to begin an investigation at the highest level. We will elevate you to single-figure status. You will act as Number Two.'

'It will be an honour.'

'Yes, it will. In return, you will solve our problem, and if, at any time, in your judgement, Number One becomes a liability to your work, then – what shall I say? – you will stand every chance of becoming our only agent assigned to this case.'

'I understand.'

Restraining her memories and her urge to kill, Two landed beside One. The seven creatures moving around the spheres brushed past on either side, four metres tall, moving on bases composed of five muscular tentacles, their bodies ringed with finer tendrils at the midsection which they deployed to work on the machines that surrounded the black spheres. Their upper ends – 'heads' didn't seem quite the description – were also based on the five-pointed star, each point ending in a red eye, the mass of the star itself covered with fine prismatic threads that writhed continuously.

'Pretty,' Two said.

'Anomalous,' One replied, winking. 'I don't think these things are native to this world's history. Take a sniff at that timeline.'

Two considered. 'Rough, robust in many ways, but past its prime. I'm getting old and musty, yet new. Contradictory flavours, it's like a heady mixture of a hundred million years, topped with eighteenth- and twentieth-century highlights, and under it all...'

'Yes?' One seemed unusually concerned that she validate her judgement.

'Just a hint of the boneyards?'

'Worrying. We must discover more. Any suggestions?'

'Why don't we just ask?' Two said. Before One could react she had reached into normal space-time and grabbed one of the creatures. It was the work of a moment to pull it out of its ordinary space-time matrix into the shadow dimensions.

'Let me help,' One said, clutching at the creature. In the scuffle his hands intersected its flesh, fifth-dimensional talons clawing its flimsy structure. 'Oh,' he said, 'Should it rattle like that?' He looked abashed. 'I think it's broken.'

Chapter Eight

'Right,' the Doctor said, 'now we know what their objective is, we can't be hanging about here any longer. The youngster should have writhed back to his post by now, so before someone more suspicious turns up and works out that I'm not any kind of general, let's take a stroll around the place and see what else we can scare up.'

'We're going to scare them?' Fitz asked.

'They're only aliens,' Compassion said scornfully. 'The image of them as demonic horrors is entirely the action of a few revisionist cultists who worship their enemies, and foolish authors decking their gothic novels with misunderstood snippets from the Necronomicon. They were the mankind of their epoch. Scientists to the last. Radiates, vegetables, monstrosities, star-spawn – whatever they had been, they were men!'

The Doctor tried to take Compassion's head gently in his hands and stare empathically into her eyes, but she struck his hands away. 'Stop it, what's up with you? Let me go.'

'The Elder Things are fiction,' the Doctor said firmly. 'Fiction you haven't even read, probably. By your time there were at least seventy-nine versions of the Necronomicon in print, but they all had their birth in the imagination of one harmless ice-cream lover. Don't let the setting get a grip. This whole scenario is being sustained by technology beyond anything we've seen here yet. It can infiltrate the consciousness in a million ways; it's primed to add layers of verisimilitude, false memories and so on. Give it an inch, and we'll all have studied at Miskatonic University and dozed off in the Witch House, before you can say "typically doomed Lovecraftian protagonist".'

'So how long before we go doolally?' Fitz asked. 'Those of us who aren't already that is?'

'Compassion's fine,' the Doctor said hurriedly. 'She's just a little bit more sensitive to the signal traffic underlying these events. That's another reason to get moving though. That and my fear that any moment now some more of the youngsters are going to barge in for *War Memoirs II*.'

'I'll thank you to keep your estimates of my mental state to yourself, Doctor,' Compassion snapped. 'Perhaps there are truths in this fiction you are reluctant to face. In the Remote we were trained to face all the implications of our environment, real or otherwise. An idea can kill you faster than a gun; that's voodoo.'

'Let's move on and get some more facts to argue about,' the Doctor said brightly. 'If we can find the thing we saw in the Museum of Things That Don't Exist's videos, I rather fancy we can put paid to all this nonsense before anyone real gets hurt. And no, I'm not going to inquire into the metaphysics of that one too closely, Compassion, so please don't start.'

Before Fitz could think of something brave and selfless to say, and before Compassion could come up with a good argument for staying put, the Doctor had pointed his sonic screwdriver at the door, muttered something about microwaves, and stepped through.

The corridor outside the room was odd, odder than Fitz remembered, possibly because it didn't have a twelve-foot-tall military-minded alien in it. Without that central improbability, he started to pick up the vibes of the place itself, and he didn't like them. Christ, no wonder Compassion was so on edge if she was more sensitive to this stuff. The very stonework of the walls, cut so that the natural facets of the rock formed friezes of unearthly scenes, picked around with a ubiquitous five-pointed clustering of dots, seemed to be orchestrating a feeling of unearthly chill that felt like the coldest church his mother had ever dragged him to when he was a kid.

'Cold Gods,' Compassion said, making him jump. 'As Freud said, we are the Apes of Cold Gods.'

'What's this wiggly stuff in the sky?' Fitz asked pointing at one of the pictures.

The Doctor leaned over. 'Residual radiation from the Big Bang; they could see it. This far back it was less red-shifted, nearer the visible spectrum, not the weak chatter it will be twelve million years from now. To them the sky was a perpetual reminder of the birth of the cosmos. They called it the Fire of the Last Birth'. He winced, blinking rapidly. 'How do I know that?'

'Maybe you're a Great Old One on your mother's side,' Compassion said. 'Either that or a lucky guess.'

'No,' the Doctor said, entirely seriously, 'I think it's what I was warning you against. The power of the scenario: it's trying to turn me into an expert narrative voice.'

'Obviously, Doctor,' Compassion said. 'I was employing irony.'

Slightly outside the present, invisible even to a Time Lord, Investigators One and Two lurked in the temporal shadows. Investigator One cradled the dead alien in his arms.

'Well, that went well,' said Two sarcastically, as One tutted to himself.

'At least we can still interrogate,' said Two. She looked the corpse up and down. 'Where do you think this thing keeps – sorry, kept – its brain?'

One shrugged. 'I'd say close to the centre, but you're the medical doctor here. I'll have a look.' He rendered his hand insubstantial, and sank it deep into the body of the creature without breaking its skin. 'Odd. This thing had humanoid vertebrae. The central nervous system seems to be cranially centred.'

Two frowned. 'That is odd. I would have bet my chitin this was an invertebrate. Flick the lid off and let's have a look, then.'

One removed his hand from the corpse, resubstantiated his digits, and began to cut around the creature's scalp with a fingernail.

'Anomalies within anomalies,' said Two. 'No way do these things belong here.'

One grimaced as he concentrated on making the incision. 'Perhaps they only exist because their killers no longer exist. Why else would only this small outpost be present? If our people waged a time war against these things, and this outpost was wiped out by the missing Lord or one of his retinue, then the erasure of that house from Mictlan could have resulted in this outpost's reappearance. They exist because the missing Lord never existed to make them not exist.'

Two frowned, working her way through the convoluted syntax of his statement until she was satisfied of being as close to comprehension as possible. 'That is quite the most ridiculous idea I've ever heard,' she concluded.

'Philistine,' One muttered sulkily. He flipped the creature's skull open, and began to probe the dead brain within. Memory cloning was an Enemy mind-war technique the Celestis stole shortly before their exodus from this universe. By separating the raw data from the brain of an enemy, it was possible to filter the memories in several useful ways, applying the gathered data as appropriate.

Two held her palm a few inches away from One's. Between their hands he formed a copy of the being's memories, a five-dimensional simulation of liquid thought, streams of data intertwining and flowing into one another. When the clone was complete, One discarded the corpse, tucking it away in a space-time loop where no one could stumble across it.

'Right,' said Two, transfixed by the glowing, fractal form between them. 'Let's do this, shall we?'

One nodded, and together they immersed themselves in a life they had ended.

'What first?' asked Two.

'Moments of emotional significance,' replied One. 'Anything that provoked an extreme reaction at the time.'

– in the shadow of the Dark Tower, running through the Death Zone. Rastons move like quicksilver at the edge of his vision. Suddenly they are upon him, mercury slivers cutting through the air. Allopta rolls across the rough ground, ignoring the noise of spears hitting the patch of ground which he previously occupied. He rolls into a firing stance and unleashes two bolts. Each finds its mark, crumpled silver figures hitting the ground like discarded rag dolls, sparks flying from their blast-burnt torsos.

Two robots? Surely there was…

A blade at his throat. He looks up into the blank face of the third Raston, staring impassively down at him. Allopta swears under his breath.

'Deactivate,' says a plummy voice, belonging to an aged figure in crimson robes, with piercing eyes and a silk skullcap. The Warrior Robot takes the blade away from Allopta's throat, steps back and becomes dormant.

'Sorry, my Lord,' says Allopta through gritted teeth.

His tutor shakes his ancient head. 'If you must make mistakes, then this is the time and the place to make them. Besides, very few Enemy Representatives – or Reps, I suppose you call them – are capable of the speed the Rastons can manage. And few places in the universe are as despicable as the Death Zone.'

Allopta sensed treasonous undercurrents in the old man's voice, but wasn't surprised. He was another of the Lord President's former renegades, reintegrated but barely reformed. Gallifrey was full of such –

'Gallifrey!' exclaimed Two. 'I thought the ambience seemed familiar.'

One nodded in agreement. Although both Investigators had been synthesised long after the Celestis' departure from their ancestral home, much Gallifreyan lore was still downloaded into their basic cultural knowledge from birth.

'A Time Lord,' said One. 'This isn't our anomaly: it's a Time Lord deep-cover mission. We're wasting our time here.'

'Not necessarily,' replied Two. 'There might still be a connection. Besides, these are Time Lords and we should at least find out what their mission is, for intelligence purposes alone. Besides, we should always interfere–' She slapped her chest in the Investigator's salute.

'– because that's what we're programmed for,' One finished wearily. Two's adherence to protocol and slogans was beginning to grate with him. 'All right, you extract a profile while I look through the hard-wired stuff. There's a lot burnt on to that cortex.'

They got to work, Two seeing if there was anything interesting in the personal side of things, One going through the purpose-engineered memories.

'Mmm, nice guy,' muttered Two. 'Devious. Almost up to our standards.'

'Do shut up,' snapped One, increasingly uneasy. He'd found what seemed to be a core of deeply buried data, some kind of mission briefing, and in a moment it would be visible to Two…

'Abort!' One screamed, jumping back. Two withdrew herself from the data too, as the model of Allopta's mind collapsed in on itself.

'Derangement virus,' gasped One. 'Total burn-out if probed. The whole underlying menta-structure's gone up.'

'Clever,' said Two. 'These guys are hard-core. Now we have to find out what they're up to.'

'Yes,' One agreed reluctantly. 'Looks like we're doing this the old-fashioned way. How much of a profile did you get?'

'Enough to convince his Loom Cousins,' said Two smugly. 'Shall we?'

Xenaria was livid. She had ordered Allopta to report directly to the general, but instead her second-in-command had lost himself somewhere. Doubtless Allopta was laughing at her this very moment. Luckily she now had most of the information she needed to hand, and she could bluff out the inevitable gaps, filling them in later once the war TARDISes were fully born.

A pile of data scripts tucked under one wing, she bustled down the corridor, subordinates in her path taking one look and getting the hell out of her way.

'My apologies, General, the initial data acquisition was more time-consuming than expected…' No, no, too weak – the general would expect a more commanding presence from the officer in charge. Perhaps she could invite him to attend Allopta's flogging, if the missing officer could be located in time. She hadn't expected this of him: he had always followed orders to the letter – often implying that they were ill-thought-out and would lead to disaster, in the droop of a long shoulder or the twitch of an eyebrow, but always cleaving to the razor edge of obedience.

She remembered Allopta's warning that the general may not be what he appeared. Was that it? Was the anaemic runt gambling on her being discredited for ordering the supply of mission data to a potential security risk?

Her thoughts had taken her up to the door of the holding room she had assigned to the general and his animals. The confrontation was only the turning of a five-sided key away.

'No, no, no,' Hume barked, rapping his knuckles on the formica table top. 'I absolutely cannot sanction breaking communication silence at this time. The interference that brought down the helicopters has given us valuable distance, a pause to contemplate; we should not waste it.'

Schneider glared at him, and Jessup could sense the woman's livid anger at having her authority pre-empted. 'With respect, Professor,' she began heavily, 'I do not see the need to preserve radio silence, we should be contacting UNIT and Project Command; bringing in troops by snowcat from heli-carriers landed well beyond any possible disruption. Think what we could discover if we were free of the burdens of military preparedness. We need support to properly evaluate the alien.'

'This is not a military matter. It is a psychological one, the last thing we need is people on hair-trigger with guns'.

From the edge of the table Hume heard snivelling and realised Nurse McGovern was off again. Surely the woman could get a grip? She hadn't killed anyone vital. He waved a vague shushing gesture in her direction. 'Besides that the images we downloaded from the sat-internet link prove conclusively the nature of the beings that constructed this base as does the testimony of our prize time traveller.'

'So?' McCarthy asked. 'We have to face the fact that we aren't the first people to find relics of these creatures. Some other explorer must have found something, some indication reached your pet horror writer.' She said 'horror writer' as if it was a perversion. 'I mean, he didn't just make them up, did he?'

Hume sniffed. 'I would have thought you would recognise the dangers here. The cultural implications. Your civilisation is ticking its way to a Millennium. The loveliest thing to uncover during a period of pre-millennial tension is apparent proof of the existence of Cthulhoid entities. Report that to anyone and I guarantee it will be in the global media before you can say Powder-Keg of Mad Cults plus Fizzing Sparkler equals Big Bang!'

'Your civilisation?' Jessup queried, suddenly.

Hume inclined his head witheringly at McCarthy, 'If you can call America a civilisation. Naturally the British would think it was a hoax.' A ghost smile haunted his lips. 'The British have dismissed seventeen alien invasions as hoaxes to my certain knowledge, and that's only in the last twenty years.'

Schneider stood up. 'Your patient, you claim she confirms that these Elder Things were really the builders of this complex?'

'I said so, didn't I?'

'I want to hear it from her.'

'Oh, very well.'

Naturally, the patient was gone, the bed a blizzard of rumpled sheets.

Chapter Nine

The general was missing, his male and female canaries with him. Only the creatures' rank animal scent remained to show the room had been occupied. Despite the overlay of machined cloth and the musk-scent excretion products of other species, the tang of primates was unmistakable. The general left only the thin, arid smell of primal Gallifrey, a waft of cloisters and libraries, of vellum and old exitronic circuitry. The smell was so familiar that she could only now, when she searched it out, sense it at all. Even so, there was something missing from the mix. She blotted out the problem. The missing element would come to her if she did not concentrate on it.

Xenaria keyed her other senses to infrared, tracing recent heat spots. They could not have been gone long. Did this mean Allopta was right? Very possibly – even a general had certain obligations to the commanding officer of a war mission, and one of them was to stay put. Nothing was more disruptive to actual work than the knowledge that top brass was on walkabout in the vicinity. The President's bulletins said that one of the War Council on the loose for half a day cost a week's production from the war Looms. Most of the President's popularity with the soldiers lay in how well he kept his aides off their backs.

Omega's Orifice! That was the missing element. The rendered-animal-fat-and-bone smoke of the war Looms. The general smelled like a library after a good spring cleaning. He smelled like her childhood. What kind of general didn't smell of the war?

She considered. A full alert would let him and his beasts know their imposition had been detected, and there was still the slightest chance that Allopta might be wrong. There was even a chance that the so-called general could eavesdrop on the communications function of the superganglia.

There was another way. It was a risk, but this was war. Xenaria screamed a sequence of pulsed electromagnetic radiation. The one phrase she had memorised from the few glyphs included in the mission statement. Picking up the 'call to arms', the base's walls blazed back in response. None of the troops could ignore this much microwave background – to them it was as insistent as a fire alarm, but it should be utterly undetectable to the supposed general and his alien allies.

Compassion blinked. 'Something's wrong.'

'Oh, yes?' Fitz grumbled. 'What exactly, the being-in-a-prehistoric-base-of-nonexistent-horror-fiction-characters-under-attack-from-the-future, or the being-*lost*-in-a-prehistoric-base-of –'

'Quiet, I'm listening.' Her earpiece – the Remote technology that connected her to the signal traffic of the cultures she inhabited – was buzzing like crazy.

She knew that the Doctor had re-routed it through the TARDIS to 'protect her' from harmful signals – an idea as nonsensical as imagining there could be harmful ideas – but it was still detecting something. Something that felt like urgency.

'They know,' Compassion said gravely.

The Doctor nodded. Fitz raised his eyes to the ceiling as if to say, Oh no, not you too.

'I think she's right,' the Doctor babbled. 'My ears are burning and that always means people are talking about me.'

He paused, frowning. 'Either that or I'm standing at the focal point of a number of converging microwave emitters.'

Fitz looked as if he wasn't filled with confidence in his companions' sanity. 'I can't feel anything,' he said.

'Very well,' said One uneasily. 'Let's do this.' He allowed Two to download her personality profile of Allopta into his mind. He then allowed that profile to sink into his own id, Allopta's thought patterns and mannerisms merging with his own. He could see Two's demeanour change as she did the same.

They looked at each other, heads tilted to one side in Allopta-esque disdain.

'Now for the nasty bit,' said Two, Allopta's sense of defiance radiating through her words.

'Three dimensions. How vulgar,' agreed One with unfamiliar arrogance.

For a multidimensional creature such as a Celesti Investigator, a body is merely a three-dimensional shadow cast across the thin canvas of space-time. The two Investigators changed the shape of their shadows, re-emerging into the normal flow of space-time as exact copies of Allopta.

Standing in the breeding room, the two Alloptas looked at each other critically.

Two waved a tentacle experimentally. 'Does my aura look big in this?' she asked.

'As well as can be expected,' replied One impatiently. 'We'd better split up. They might get a little suspicious if they find their colleague has split in two. Even Loomgeld aren't that asexual.'

'Right,' agreed Two. 'I'll go this way.'

'OK,' said One, watching her go. 'But don't forget.' There was a thud as tentacled flesh hit rock. 'You're solid.'

One shook his tendrilled head despairingly and wandered off in the other direction.

Compassion grabbed the Doctor's arm, jerking him to a halt so fast she almost dislocated his shoulder.

'There's something ahead,' she snapped.'I can feel it.'

'Now you're just being paranoid,' said the Doctor lightly, giggling in a way Fitz didn't like.'Look.' He waved his arm ahead of them. A bolt of pale-blue lightning shot down from the ceiling, earthing itself a couple of inches away from the Doctor's feet. He withdrew his arm slowly, then blew on the scorched hairs on the back of his hand. Bizarrely, he didn't seem to be taking it too seriously. It was as if the Doctor had stopped considering the outside world important.

'Back this way?' said Fitz airily.

The Doctor gave him a glance filled with a familiar intensity. His mood had changed, become deadly, excessively solemn.

'It would seem advisable,' mumbled the Doctor.'But slowly, softly. I have a feeling someone's activated this base's defences. We need to tread lightly.'

Fitz followed the Doctor, but slowly. There was something in the Time Lord's gaze that Fitz didn't like.

A microwave transmission updated Xenaria on the defences' activation, and she swore to herself. So much for subtlety. It seemed the Elder Things' idea of a proximity alarm was as hostile as the rest of their technology. Xenaria quickly transmitted the deactivation glyph. Well, at least they all knew where the 'general' and his canaries were.

Provided they had survived the attack, they would be cornered by Xenaria's troops any second now.

She hurried along the corridor, eager to be part of the action.

* * *

108

The Doctor and Compassion came to a halt again. Fitz grimaced in exasperation.

'Let me guess,' he told his companions, who seemed to be listening to silence with great concentration. 'You know something I don't. Again.'

'I would have thought you'd be used to ignorance by now,' said Compassion. 'More microwave activity, wasn't it?'

'Yes,' said the Doctor distantly. 'We have to hurry. Something's closing in. Yes, I can see it.'

He ran down the corridor, Fitz and Compassion close behind. Soon they found themselves stopping at a crossroads, a number of potential corridors to choose from.

The Doctor staggered back, reeling around as if confused by the number of options presented to him. There was something wild and feverish about him, a dilation of the eyes Fitz hadn't seen in anybody since Tibet. The Doctor was clearly a man possessed, but by what Fitz didn't like to speculate.

'Something big,' said the Doctor. 'Big, big, big. I can see it.'

'All right,' said Fitz, as calmly as he could manage. 'Now you've done the important job of scaring the absolute bloody hell out of us, how about telling us something useful? What's the point of lecturing us on the dangers of going mad if you're just going to do exactly that yourself?'

'We've got to split up,' babbled the Doctor. 'Make little targets. You go that way, you go that way, I go this way. OK?'

'No, stop!' exclaimed Fitz, but he was too late. The Doctor ran off down a different corridor from the one he had indicated for himself, and Compassion grabbed Fitz's arm to stop him from following.

'Hey, what're you doing?' he garbled.

'Don't you think we should do what he says?' said Compassion. 'He *is* the Doctor.'

'Ri-i-ight,' said Fitz. 'Like he's in any state to know who he is. Well, if that's what you think is best, then Captain Kreiner will obey. Ciao!' Fitz ran down another corridor, not looking back to see what Compassion was doing.

Scared again, Fitz, he thought to himself. Well, as both his companions seemed to be losing it, sinking under the influence of this mad, sick place, then could he be blamed? Maybe he should have stayed and reasoned with Compassion, but if she was losing it like the Doctor... Fitz had spent too many years worrying about whether he had inherited his mum's madness to risk picking up a dose from anyone else. He needed to run, to get out of the base, breathe air free of the oppressive stink of insanity. Fear drove him to ever greater feats of athletics, blinding him to anything ahead. He just had to get out, quickly. He never even considered the possibility that his paranoia might count as a symptom.

He was running so fast that he ran straight into one of the Time Lords. He tried to dodge, but only managed to trip over one of the creature's tentacles. His breathing was shallow and his vision blurred. He was scrabbling in the dirt to try to get away from the monster leaning over him in an oddly familiar manner.

'Got any more war stories to tell, Rep?' demanded Holsred aggressively.

Compassion headed off down her corridor with a shrug. Maybe Fitz thought the Doctor was acting irrationally, but Compassion trusted the Time Lord's instincts. What was madness, anyway, and who was Fitz to make definitions? She had some idea that there was a history of mental illness, as the humans called it, in Fitz's past, but Compassion had never cared enough to bother finding out the details. She doubted anything about Fitz could be too interesting. He came from a culture that had only just discovered television, so how smart could he be?

Alone at last, she allowed herself to drink in the atmosphere of the place. She, of course, did not get anything even vaguely resembling an illicit thrill from the experience. The Doctor was wrong about the influence of this place. How could it drive anyone mad without proper transmissions, subliminal messages and low-level alpha-wave disruption, the usual suspects? Besides, Compassion was made of sterner stuff, a child of the Remote. If anyone was going to crack it would be Fitz.

Her attempt to catch the vibe of the place revealed it to be rather drab. There were no signals as such for her to absorb. These supposedly advanced Elder Things were media-deficient, making them little better than amoebae as far as Compassion was concerned. But even their architecture gave a feeling for their culture, of something alien and inscrutable. Then there were the base's current occupiers, these metaphorical grandchildren of the Doctor's. They were fighting a war, their every action and possession denoting their lives of violence.

Processing the cultural information, Compassion felt the influence of the place slipping over her, in spite of her earlier dismissals. Even with her earpiece filtered by the Doctor's TARDIS, as part of her painless 're-education' blocking out any media imperatives that might violate his children's teatime sensibilities, she was first and foremost a child of Anathema, of the Remote. She let herself be carried away by the local environment, by the alienness of the Elder Things and the barely suppressed violence of their Time Lord usurpers. As she did do, she knew she shouldn't. The Doctor would disapprove. But then the Doctor barely understood her nature, her need to adapt. How could he? He was the product of a stagnant culture. He never needed to absorb new information, never felt the hunger for signals. His people felt they knew it all already.

It was a bad time for anyone to interrupt her, so overtaken was she by the aggression she had absorbed from around her. The two Time Lords cornered her at a turn in the corridor, moving in with their weapons. She didn't run, or make any move to escape. Something was welling up within her, drawn out by the atmosphere of the base. Something she hadn't been able to recognise in herself before. Something alien within her. A strange, impossible sound.

'You will come with us,' one of the Time Lords said, for want of anything better to say. They had the same kind of inexperienced air as Holsred had, but their tame presence only increased Compassion's violent urges. She made the noise again, and this time the base responded.

The weaponry in the walls fired twice, blue sparks flying as it hit the green-grey flesh. With a crack the tentacled creature went flying, hitting the wall with a dismayed yelp. The other raised its weapon in alarm, but Compassion used the creature's great bulk against it, ducking under the gun and delivering another fiery blow. The second Time Lord was knocked to the ground.

Compassion snapped back to normal, and rubbed her throat. It was as if she had reached out and learned how to use the base, how to understand the signals in the stonework, how to command it in its own language. Perhaps blocking off her more direct routes into the media-nets had only hypersensitised her to meaning.

One of the Time Lords stirred. Compassion backed away hastily. Perhaps the Doctor was right: she was ceasing to be herself, doing things she shouldn't be able to do. There would be time to worry about how she managed that one later. For the moment she had her own survival to take care of, so she turned and did what she should have done in the first place. She ran.

The Doctor ran straight into a wall, so absorbed was he by the chaotic babble of thoughts streaming through his head. Blind panic, almost literally. He reeled, falling face down. Reaching out to stop his fall, he grazed his palms as he landed. Winded, he lay face down on the cold rock, and tried to get some kind of a grip on his raging thoughts. His higher senses rarely even tingled for him these days, but now they were screaming. All at once.

At least he hoped they were. Perhaps it was this place, the madness he warned Compassion and Fitz about coming to take him, making him see monsters everywhere, fictional creatures from the nether depths, *a creature coiled within the shell of a world*. Where had that come from? Madness was not unusual for a Time Lord, especially an imaginative one. He didn't want to think these thoughts, not now, but the pressure to do so was compelling. These were the mountains of madness. This was the city that bred despair. How had Borges put it? The city so horrifying that its mere existence pollutes the past and somehow compromises the stars. Poor Borges, going slowly blind in his Argentine apartment, idolising the gauchos who saw him at best as a curiosity, an imaginary beast.

The forces sustaining this place would love him to go mad. Perhaps in a twisted way, it would be a testament to the Doctor's place among the greatest of his race: all the best of his people went mad in the end – mad, bad or dangerous to know. Omega, Rassilon, even Borusa, all lost it in the pressure cooker of a society cursed with infinite power. That kind of responsibility was impossible to take, so most Time Lords survived by being so narrow-minded, so dull-witted, that they never considered the sheer terror of the possibilities open to them. A visionary Gallifreyan was almost a contradiction in terms, and a stable visionary Gallifreyan was even rarer; the wideness of the horizons before him could engulf him in the end. Mavericks, all of them, fleeing out into the universe or into themselves, curling into a comforting ball of delusion.

The Doctor's skin was crawling, an actual physical sensation rather than a basic psychosomatic reaction. Something else was involved, something beyond all this, something that made the simple everyday dangers of meddling in someone else's war, battling fictional horrors, or trying to explain the significance of 99s to bemused Wallachian good-humour men seem like business as usual. It wasn't here yet, that much was certain. What he was feeling was a kind of foreboding, a pressure wave in time from a future event so vast that it would weigh on every time-sensitive this side of Deneb.

Surely the other Time Lords had to be feeling it, too. Perhaps he could reason with them, use the shared feeling as a lever to get them to abort their mission. Yes, certainly he could do that, just as soon as he could get his legs to work. They seemed to have decided to buckle under him, and just lie there.

Something big was coming. Something unimaginably destructive, blotting out life, blotting out the future, irrevocably crushing infinity as it came. He could almost see it through the flood in his mind, he could almost touch it, feel the shape of it. He needed focus to reach that bit further, and so he began to chant to himself, reasserting his identity and allowing himself to purposefully cut through the chaos.

Fight against the madness, impose some rationality and order. Bring him back to himself.

'I am the Doctor, I have walked in eternity, I have died many times, I have fought countless monsters, I have saved countless lives…'

Reminding himself of who he was, of what he had done, gave him the vigour to approach the unspeakable, to hold his head up high in the face of something immense. The nausea and chaos were subsiding, his senses beginning to form a coherent image, a vision. He could make out its outlines, a creature even vaster than the Kraken he had encountered in San Francisco, but trapped within a finite space, unable to expand. Coiled like a serpent, fenced in by a blue corona.

Trapped in the heart of a world by time itself.

With a biting terror, he guessed what it must be.

Where was Allopta? Just as she had decided he was worth the trouble after all, Xenaria's second-in-command had vanished. He wasn't responding to communications on any channels. It was a little unnerving, an a great shame, as well. His judgement had been correct, or so it seemed: the 'general' was a fraud, and probably a Rep. And Allopta wasn't going to be present for his capture.

The others were in constant communication as Xenaria glided down the corridors. One 'canary' had already been captured by Holsred. The other had somehow managed to fight its way past Urtshi and Erasfol. An odd and impressive achievement, but no matter: a creature like that could do little actual damage, no matter how resourceful it might be. This 'general' on the other hand had managed to pass for a Time Lord, and was therefore far too dangerous to be allowed free run of the base.

Xenaria received a transmission. The 'general' had been found, just around the corner. He was apparently suffering from some kind of convulsion. Xenaria made haste to find Neinthe leaning over the scrawny humanoid, who was whispering to himself.

'I am the Doctor –'

There was more, but Xenaria wasn't listening. The Doctor! It had been a very long time since Xenaria had panicked, but now she completely lost her self control. The Doctor was the ultimate rogue element, the symbol of independent, wasteful initiative. He could ruin everything without even trying, disrupt the most precise of plans. Alive or dead, he was a threat. But the latter was still preferable – at least Xenaria would know where he was.

'Kill the bastard,' she barked, trying to sound angry rather than terrified. 'Kill him now.'

Neinthe raised his weapon, and pressed down on the trigger mechanism.

'No!' Allopta crashed into Neinthe, causing the shot to go wide, melting a patch on the wall.

The Doctor, still unconscious, muttered to himself.

'Sorry, Commander,' said Allopta hurriedly. 'I know disrupting your order was unforgivable insubordination, but we cannot kill the Doctor without interrogation. We must know why he is here, what his involvement is. We cannot even be certain it *is* the Doctor until we have interrogated him – Reps have been known to impersonate peasant heroes and bandits like the Doctor to stir up trouble among the more gullible species.'

Xenaria's automatic instinct as a soldier was to have Allopta shot, then the Doctor, then the Doctor again to make sure. But her second-in-command had been right before…

'OK, Allopta, you have your fun with this one. But I expect

116

you to push this interrogation as far as you can. Don't feel the need to hold back. This is only a temporary reprieve, and I want him dead before the final assault.'

Allopta nodded his consent. 'By the time I've finished, it'll take nano-architects with tweezers to put him back together.'

She had waited until Hume had gone and then started to gather her things together, each one a puzzle, each one a little blank piece of the gaps in her head. It was important she got away, found something to attach herself to. There were too few signals here. the Antarctic base was locked-down, communications tight, she could sense that.

She had to find something to make sense of her emptiness. It was a mistake to say she *wanted*. It was a need as firmly entrenched in her as anything in biology.

They had missed her quickly, somehow she knew that, but even to be the subject of a search felt better than just lying there awaiting Hume's interrogation. Even as something to be avoided, it was welcome: the muttering of voices down the stone corridors, echoing the noises that things had made under the base, when she had met them deep in the past.

Chapter Ten

The Allopta formerly known as One had waited impatiently for the Doctor to recover enough for the interrogation to begin. Now he was starting to regret saving the rogue's life. He had thought that the presence of such an interloper as the Doctor could easily be turned to his purposes. At the very least it would serve to distract the assault team while he inspected the progress their mission had made. If the Doctor had half the cunning and knowledge attributed to him by the Bone Museums of Mictlan his living brain would be an invaluable addition to the work. That, however, had been before he had been required to listen to the fool's wittering.

'I say, I like the dungeon. What was it originally? Computer pen? They liked their data processing on the wild side, didn't they?' the Doctor chatted, seemingly oblivious to the molecular locks that were pinning his biomass to the stone.

One whipped the fine ends of his tentacles over the controls set into the black stone console. The Elder Thing technology was functioning up to his specifications. One would have smiled if he had still possessed a face.

'You'd think it had been designed for this, eh, Doctor?'

The Doctor turned his head a fraction. That would be about the most body movement he'd be able to manage now. 'Do I know you? I'm sure we weren't introduced formally.'

'You are still something of a legend Doctor. Your meddlesome and reckless meanderings have acquired a certain escapist value for the newly recruited. Historical romances of the most lurid and speculative kind. They are of course banned. Inappropriate reading in War Time. We can not have escapists, questioning everything. Tell me: who are your current companions?'

'I'm not sure I should be telling you anything.' The Doctor looked genuinely put out by this thought. 'Since we haven't been introduced.'

'A pity. If I knew your companions' names I could derive an approximate date for you against our records of your timeline. I could then refrain from inadvertently revealing anything that might disrupt your own timestream. Because if I did, then I would have to kill you. Security, you know. Anyway, one of your companions is in our hands – excuse the colloquialism – and has doubtless already revealed all. Why go to the trouble of resisting me – and I assure you it will become a trouble – when all may already be known?'

'Your accent's very pure,' the Doctor said, 'considering you're from the future. Very little consonantal shift. Rather a conservative range of word choice as well, if you don't mind my saying so. All very flat and uninteresting. Not you, you understand, just your mode of speech. Could you make that translator thing go up at the end of sentences, get a bit of a rhythm going? I'm going to nod off here if that droning keeps up.'

'Very good, Doctor. I take it you suspected that this slab is more than a simple block of stone. It is an Elder Thing macrolithic device, derived, I believe, from a Tau Cetan genus that eventually evolves into the Ogri. They call it the 'Black Stone'. Now *there's* a marvellously inventive coinage if you like. If I had been tasked with devising appropriate nomenclature I think I would have settled on the Blood Render. I surmise that your babbling represents an attempt to prevent it gaining a lock on your thoughts.'

'Odd that you mention new words.' The Doctor's face was red now, capillaries swelling under the biomass probes of the stone. 'Gallifreyan's always been a static language, hasn't it? We go out into the universe and talk to everyone, but we don't take loan words back into our own tongue. TARDISes translate everything for us, or time rings, or things like your locket there. We don't have to integrate our experiences into words: they do it for us.' A vein in his neck began to pulsate, and next to it a warm glow spread through the blackness of the stone as if it were pleased.

'Your point being?'

'*Veni, vedi, stasisi.*' The Doctor's voice was laboured now, but he was putting every effort into sounding sincere. Possibly he actually was, as if it mattered. 'We came, we saw, we stayed the same. Well, that's Late Evening Cultures for you. I'd love to help, really, but I haven't the least idea what your problem is. Except that you're obviously not one of Xenaria's troops. Perhaps you might like to tell me who or what you are, hmm?'

'Who I am doesn't matter. You have no need to know. Let it suffice that I and my companion are investigating this mission. Your presence here is an anomaly, discovered within a chronoclysm wrapped in a paradox. My colleague is tempted to annul you, to throw your timestream into reverse. I have persuaded her to stay her hand – I hope with your co-operation to resolve all matters successfully in a smaller period of time and with less effort. If you become an effort, I will bow to her more forceful approach.'

'More... forceful!'

The Doctor started to laugh. A pool of scarlet began to spread as his lips shredded.

The Allopta formerly known as Two was having fun. She had

taken the second of the Doctor's companions from the fuming Holsred, just as the newborn had seemed on the verge of investigating the advantages of five lower limbs in the administration of a good kicking. Now she reached out psychically, flexing the mental parameters of the hominid. Why, the creature had practically no defences whatsoever. The poor little lamb.

'So, Fitz, is it? Please sit down.'

Fitz watched with a kind of amused horror as the alien arranged its limbs around the five-channelled stone egg cup affair that served it as a chair. It was actually crossing its legs. He couldn't take his eyes off the grey-green supple flesh of its lower limbs as they twined and rubbed together.

As he watched the creature it started to shimmer, as if a heat haze were forming between them or as if, far more likely, he had taken a really, really bad blow to the head without noticing it.

The tentacles were flowing now, being reabsorbed into a mass that seemed moment by moment to be more familiar.

'There – is this better?'

Fitz felt himself goggling. The alien had turned from a seven-foot monster into a stunning chick. Five eight maybe, red hair, but not Compassion's red: this was more like fire, and he was fairly sure she wasn't wearing a bra. 'Er, yeah,' he managed, 'that's fab. You just slip into something more comfortable, OK?'

'Don't look so worried, my dear. I'm not going to eat you.' She moved nearer, slipping a hand – with silver nails – on to his forearm. Her skin was warm and slightly tingly. 'Not unless you'd like me to.'

'I'm going to say a number of words. The stone will read the truth or falsehood of your subvocal responses from the waste products in your blood. It will also feed. The longer the process is prolonged the weaker you will become and the stronger the stone will grow. Eventually it will break its programming cycle and exert its full strength. At which point every cell in your body will rupture. Do you have any questions?'

'Just... one.' The Doctor's voice was faint, and his eyes were tight shut now, possibly because the blood trickling down his forehead had been getting into them. 'Do you know how many words there are in your-era Gallifreyan that derive solely from the war?'

One paused. What possible relevance could that have? Still, the question intrigued him, and he addressed the query to the data-transfer engine connecting him to the computers of Mictlan.

'Including technical terms derived from war-specific adaptations of pre-conflict technology, thirty thousand nine hundred and twenty-three, and counting.'

'As many as that! So – why haven't you learned any new tricks?'

One pressed an indentation on the stone with one of the tips of his forward tentacles, and the Doctor gasped.

'Oh dear. I appear to have increased the pain fivefold or more. I forget if these controls are in base five or in powers of five. Perhaps you could enlighten me.'

'How did you do that? Can you all do that?' Fitz babbled, trying to keep his mind off what in other circumstances might have sounded like a pick-up line. He knew he was irresistible, but he didn't think he was *that* irresistible.

'Not all. I'm not an ordinary soldier. I'm what you might call a spy. A good spy, working for the same ends as the troops but with Military Intelligence. We learned that there was something unusual about this mission and joined it at the last minute to supply additional cover.' She paused. 'Cigarette? I got to like them during a stop-off in your mid-twentieth century. They're low tar.'

Fitz tugged at his hair. 'I shouldn't really. I've sort of given up. Still, I guess, one won't kill me.' He let his eyes rove over the spy's neat black dress. He wondered if she knew just how translucent bits of it were. 'Hell, I still say try anything once except incest and country dancing.'

'Mark Twain, or at least attributed to him. Did you know he also wrote about the sex lives of angels?'

'R-r-really?' Fitz took a nervous drag at his cigarette, and started in shock. Over the woman's shoulder, naked now, as her dress had slipped slightly from its flimsy moorings, he could see Compassion's face pressed against the other side of the strange cut-glass panel of the door. He twisted his head to the right, trying to indicate to her the direction in which they had taken the Doctor. If interrogations always worked on the good-cop, bad-cop principle, he didn't want to think what the Doctor was going through. As for him, he reckoned he could stand a bit more of this. In the interests of everyone of course.

Compassion just stood there goggling. Never expected to see him with a *femme fatale*, eh? Finally, however, just when Fitz was sure the spy-chick was going to turn round and see who he was trying to signal too, Compassion nodded and slipped away. Heading, Fitz noted, glumly, to the left. There was just no telling some people.

Compassion turned away from the misshapen crystal panel set into the cell door. The image she had seen through it had been distorted considerably, but she had still seen Fitz. He

124

had been holding with every appearance of nonchalance – or at least his best attempt at faking it – the finest, the smallest, tentaclet of the fractal spreading web of tentacles of one of the Elder Things, and was raising it to his lips, while the Elder Thing watched him with all five of its lidless eyes.

Compassion shrugged. Evidently Fitz was more cosmopolitan than she had given him credit for being since forgetting so much of their shared experience. At any rate she had no intention of intruding on anyone's pleasure, not when her senses screamed at her to go down. Down into the hollows, down into the birthing pools, down into the changing wombs. Down to where they were calling with their multidimensional voices, with words larger inside than out.

One's voice was calm but, despite the pain, the Doctor recognised that the interrogation wasn't going the way his captor had expected.

'Still unwilling to talk, Doctor? You really should take this opportunity – soon the capacity will cease to be available to you, along with consciousness, and eventually life.'

'Why are you... doing... this?'

'For information, why else?'

'No... that... isn't... it... is... it?'

'No? What can you mean?'

'I mean you're Celestis, aren't you? And I know the Celestis are in this up to their scrawny metafictive necks. This whole event sequence is artificial, isn't it? They've been set up. What *is* going on here? What do you want from Planet Five?' The Doctor gasped. 'It's the Fendahl, isn't it? You're mad enough to think you can control it. The thing's a world-eater, surely even you can't believe it will lick your hands and say,

Thanks for letting me go?'

The sheer unexpected force of the Doctor's questions, inconceivable from a pre-Celestial Time Lord who should by rights have been a gibbering wreck trembling on the verge of a final likely-to-abort regeneration, cut at One's self-control.

Abandoning the instrumentality at his disposal, he reached out with his mind. How dare this primitive defy him? He would suck the marrow of the Doctor's thoughts directly from the grey matter of his dying brain.

From somewhere outside and yet inside his head, Fitz heard a terrifying scream.

Interlude: The Eighth Planet

It was dark over the Capitol, even in the height of the afternoon. The thick black smoke spewed out by the Loomstacks perpetually blocked the sun, as excess genetic material was burned away: the ashes of the fallen dead, incinerated as their bodies were broken down into raw fabric, then rewoven to provide further troops for the war effort. The chronoforges flared in the distance, building weapons of temporal destruction, bleeding off photonic waste from fracturing chronons.

Homunculette surveyed the hellish landscape with disinterest; Gallifrey Eight had always been like this, for as long as he could remember. There were nine identical Gallifreys, one down since they lost a homeworld in the battle of Mutter's Cluster. Cluster's last stand, the wits had called it, before the purge. Rumour had it even the Lord President didn't know which was the original and which were the duplicates, that security was so tight there were further Gallifreys, secreted in pocket universes lest all the others be destroyed.

Homunculette tightened the silk scarf around his nose and mouth, trying to keep the foul smoke out of his lungs. The pollution was worse than the last time he had visited the Capitol. The looms were working overtime, trying to rebuild forces devastated by the disastrous rout at Delphon. Homunculette, who had spent the whole dreadful episode inciting local populations to make futile attacks on the relentless Enemy – and whose eyebrows still ached from the effort – had been one of the last to evacuate. He had been on the bridge of a war TARDIS, watching the fading glow of the local star as it went supernova, when he received the summons to return to the Capitol. It seemed total failure was no barrier to receiving further significant missions in these dark days.

He rubbed his fingers together. They were black and greasy from the residue on the railing, a by-product of the smoke.

'Disgusting,' said Homunculette out loud.

'Isn't it just?' replied an aged yet razor-sharp voice. Homunculette instinctively turned and bowed as the Lord President stepped out on to the balcony. The President waved for Homunculette to be at his ease as he stepped over to join him, looking out over the Capitol. Homunculette watched the President out of the corner of his eye. The old man's hair and beard were wispy and white, his skin wrinkled and parchment-thin, but his eyes still shone with a dark intensity as he surveyed his domain. He wore the President's traditional robes of office, albeit made entirely from black fabrics. Some said this was a sign of mourning for the lost homeworld. Others saw it as simple eccentricity. Homunculette would not speculate, even to himself.

'I remember when the aliens came to the Capitol, back before you were even woven,' said the President. 'The old general – I forget his name – was shown around the Capitol by a friend of mine. He said this place was built for war, and to our ears it seemed a ridiculous notion. The whole idea of war was inconceivable to us back then, though even then there were occasional clues as to the coming conflict. But we ignored them, dismissed them. We never thought our people would become like the old general and his troops, breeding our people purely to be efficient killers, weaving violence into every cell of their bodies. But we did, in the end, and the Capitol became a fortress once more.'

The President turned to Homunculette, who, though not one to be intimidated, flinched under his superior's steely gaze.

'You would not believe how naive our people were back then, Homunculette. I had thought naivety beyond us now. I was wrong.' He tossed a data coil to Homunculette, who snatched it out of the air. Homunculette raised an eyebrow, scarf still wrapped around his lower face.

The President looked grim. 'That coil contains the data used to justify a mission authorised by a subcommittee of the War Council. Unlike those idiots, you will doubtless realise that much of the information is false, impossible even. The civilisation described never existed, so we must presume this whole setup is an Enemy trap.'

Homunculette pulled the scarf down, gagging slightly on the stale air. 'You want me to stop the mission?' he asked.

The President shook his head. 'Unfeasible. The mission is deep-cover, total immersion in the timelines of the host creatures. Even our scanners cannot detect the precise insertion point of the troops. Besides, I am reluctant to send another valuable agent into a setup.'

Homunculette nodded politely to acknowledge the compliment. 'What do you wish me to do, Lord President?'

'There is evidence of some causal feedback from these events in the Humanian Era, some twelve million years later,' explained the President. 'You will adopt the guise of an appropriately authoritative local, manoeuvre yourself into a suitable position of trust and gain whatever information you can. Low risk, instant withdrawal on threat of Enemy presence.'

Homunculette bowed. 'I shall prepare immediately, Lord President.'

'Very good,' replied the President, looking ruefully out across the Capitol once more. 'You are the kind of Time Lord I always knew we would need to win this war.'

Homunculette nodded, unsure from the President's tone of voice whether this was another compliment or not. He was at the door when a question raised itself in his mind.

'Lord President,' he asked. 'Shall I report to the appropriate subcommittee, or directly to yourself.'

The President smiled thinly. 'Report directly to me. The members of the subcommittee have been put –' he glanced meaningfully at one of the Loomstacks as it belched out a cloud of soot '– to other work. There are many ways to serve the war effort.'

'As you say, Lord President,' agreed Homunculette as he respectfully left the balcony.

Chapter Eleven

In his training, One had been shown the entirety of the universe, starting with small things and running upwards. An insect, a slave, a mammoth, a kraken, a star-ship, the moon, Old Gallifrey, gas Giants, suns, star systems, the spiral, the local group of galaxies, the galactic web, the megalostructure of the deep voids, the observable universe, all space and all time. By that point he had been shaking, because he knew it didn't end there.

These days he considered himself well armoured, defended inside and out. He expected to cut through the Doctor's neuroscape in one brilliant surgical strike.

Instead his mind hit the walls of the universe and didn't stop.

And beyond everything that is, they were waiting for him, as he had known they would be.

They were nearer now, and he could see – the sense felt like sight although if it was real-time perception it could not rely on anything as slow or clumsy as photons – their massive forms, milling in their infinite multitudes among the silver bubbles. Celestis to the core, he had no interest in the foolish moistness of sex; the animal intimacies of the lesser creatures held no importance for him, and yet he knew enough of the mechanics to be struck by an image.

Imagine creatures small enough to live on the surface of a human egg. Imagine them travelling with that world down the Fallopian tube to the womb, seeing in that journey only the slow majestic movement of the spheres. Then let them see, dimly in a glass darkly, the tens of thousands of things moving towards their world, aliens large as continents, diving down on the creatures' cities, penetrating the mantle and the core, changing their world into something other. They might know a thousandth of the fear he felt at the thought of the Swimmers.

Celestis do not react well to fear.

One thrashed, his tentacles impacting the controls of the Ogri, sending glints of light from the pseudo-flint of the console, his voice vibrating through the stone floor – an insect-scaring basso profundo. 'Stayyyy Awaayyy. Keeeep Awwwaaayyy. Theey Mussst Nottttttt.'

The Doctor lifted his hand from the slab of stone like a man moving under too much gravity. There was a sucking sound as his flesh came loose. He cast a worried look at the thrashing One. 'Hello,' he whispered. 'Sorry about that. I wouldn't want you to miss out on the big picture.'

A slithering sound, the tentacular motion and the slap, slap, slap of five feet falling in rotation came from outside the interrogation room. Moving as quickly as his bleeding and bruised limbs allowed, the Doctor flattened himself down behind the Black Stone.

The Allopta formerly known as Two had been rather put out when Holsred had shown up midway through her chat with Fitz with, seemingly, every intention of spoiling her tête-à-tête. However, his psychic defences were almost as primitive as Fitz's to Celesti techniques and it had been easy enough to keep him in a state of passivity with one part of her mind while the greater part was working over Fitz's grey matter.

The sudden feedback from her link with One, however, had shut down everything else in her effort to counter the influx of madness and subjective abomination, and both Fitz and Holsred had been released from her grasp. For once, Fitz had possessed an advantage: he only had to remember how to be himself, Holsred had to remember how to be an alien. So it was hardly surprising that it took the newborn longer to snap out of it.

Holsred had been observing Allopta's interrogation of the primate for some time – at least he thought he had been. That was what he had been *supposed* to be doing, wasn't it? Standing at attention waiting for the request to pass the cattle prod or mop up some teeth. It made him squirm to think about it. So why hadn't it? Why hadn't he been wincing and moving nervously from one thick tentacle to another. He had always hated torture – it had been his worst subject in the Academy. Something had just miswoven in him so that he couldn't get his brain behind it. Oh, he knew all the arguments, but to him they always sounded like the start of one of Plato's dialogues, and he knew well enough from virtual time simulations that if you started talking to that bastard you ended up defined out of existence and agreeing that dictatorship was more healthy for a people than men who dressed up and told stories for a living. Agree that it might be necessary to torture one man to get the co-ordinates of an Enemy attack that if unopposed would result in the death of thousands, and pretty soon you'd end up agreeing to torture someone on the off chance that they may have spoken to someone else who may know whether the Enemy were aware of your plan to slaughter thousands unopposed.

He ought to have been clenching his sphincter-mouths into prissy little purse shapes and muttering hard enough to cook chicken; instead he couldn't remember what he'd done.

Allopta had been doing something – so far, so brilliantly

deduced – but what exactly he couldn't quite recall. One thing was for sure though. Allopta wasn't doing anything now, except thrashing in the corner, and of the male primate there was no sign whatsoever.

Holsred edged nearer the spasming Allopta and reached out tentatively with a cluster of tentacle ends. For his pains he was rewarded with a bolt of blue fire from the underside of one of Allopta's wings. Some kind of proximity trap? That wasn't standard issue. Holsred wasn't prepared to get himself fried trying to assist an officer he'd never liked anyway. In this instance a withdrawal clearly was the better part of valour. Besides, if the alien primate had been able to muddle his and Allopta's minds in some way resulting both in his partial amnesia and Allopta's fit, he represented a danger to the mission that ought to be reported forthwith. Rationalising feverishly, Holsred slithered away.

Fitz was screaming first. One second, he had been smoking the best, and only, fag, for a dozen million years, with a gorgeous bird from space, and then next...

He didn't want to think about the next.

The taste now. The taste had been like leather, like sucking on the fringes of a leather bookmark absent-mindedly. Anyone might do that. There now, the taste wasn't that bad. He could manage that, see how it might be tolerable. It had been the taste that changed first, he was sure of it.

Then the texture and the shape of the cigarette had altered as it had torn itself away from him, becoming part of the thing he didn't want to face. No, being revealed as always having been part of the other, of the alien. The alien that was whipping his face with fine wire fingers, its arms turning into frozen branch sculptures. The Elder Thing that was howling in a voice that he could barely hear. The Elder

Thing whose microwave voice might be cooking him from the inside out. Worse than that, there was another in the room as well. From its slight difference in shape he guessed it was Holsred, the nervy kid who had been going to beat him up. How long had he been there? All the time? Shielded by the illusions? What had he seen? What the hell had Compassion seen?

Fitz forced himself to react.

As Holsred's eyes fixed on the spasming of his fellow creature, three forward and two arching over his flat starfish head, Fitz did what he did best. Get away on his toes.

Ostrev was a veteran of almost twenty missions. The normal survival curve ended with one out of a thousand passing the fifteen-mission point. It could have been chance, but he liked to think it was skill. So he entered the room cautiously and peered through the clouds of burnt Time Lord flesh, with his weapons primed and ready. Secretly he would be quite glad if the Doctor had given that dusty archive-hound Allopta a bloody nose. One of his earliest post-Loom memories had been of a gang of hard-bitten inductees sharing a banned copy of *Doctor ?* – all proper names had been auto-edited out of bases' message system for reasons of war security, and even the downloaded underground flimsies hadn't been free of the software – *In an Exciting Adventure With the Enemy*. If anyone was going to kill the Doctor, it wasn't going to be a barrack-room lawyer like Allopta: it was going to be a proper veteran, someone who'd killed a Sontaran fellow traveller by biting off its probic vent.

Someone, Ostrev thought, like him. It was what the Doctor would have wanted.

Behind the Black Stone, still dazed by the cell-destroying

effects of its malign hunger, the Doctor watched as Ostrev moved lithely across the room.

One had toppled on to the floor, his thin arm tentacles unable to lift the weight of his thick cylindrical body, while his lower tentacles were beating against the ground, trying to run like humanoid legs and failing. He'd lost it. The mappings between the alien body he had assumed and the basal structure of the Gallifreyan brain – which he, as a Celestis, had also only assumed, but which were nevertheless close to his own – were breaking down. From that position, prone and helpless, he caught a glimpse of something moving towards him. Elder Things are large creatures; their eyes are positioned at the tops of their bodies and in the long lie of their evolutionary back-story some things were hard-wired into their nervous systems. If something is taller than you, run from it, defer to it, or kill it.

To One, the enormous figure of Ostrev was all the immensities of hell. He would be damned if he was going to defer to such a monstrosity, and he could not run.

When Ostrev found Allopta in the midst of some form of frenzy, he wasn't thrown by the situation. He had seen these things happen before, many times. Other species had numerous words to describe snow or rain, but Gallifreyans could, traditionally, name over thirty different types of culture shock. Such were the risks of time travel, and the war had only increased those risks. The adoption of new physical forms, the descent of the culture into a combative mindset, the lack of certainty – all necessities of wartime which contributed to a potentially psychotic sense of alienation. An inert culture like Gallifrey's was suddenly force-fed new influences, and the result was that the modern Time Lord had more varied and unique opportunities to go mad than ever before.

Ostrev was therefore well acquainted with the correct procedure for dealing with a fellow Gallifreyan in the throes of a fully fledged psychotic episode. Approach slowly, making placatory statements intended to reassert a sense of comfort and self-awareness, to step towards a rebuilding of the identity.

'Allopta,' said Ostrev, moving forward to try to gently restrain his superior. As he made contact, he saw Allopta's flesh split open, revealing another creature within. For a brief second Ostrev saw a completely different figure before him – a humanoid filled with stars, twisted by despair.

'No!' the Doctor shouted, hauling himself upright, fingers shedding nails as he sought handholds on the Black Stone. 'That isn't Allopta. You're in danger.'

Ostrev turned, a staser modified for Elder Thing appendages pointing dead at the Doctor. 'I'm in danger?'

Allopta's body flowed and altered, the lower tentacles shrinking as the mass went elsewhere. The forearms, strengthened a thousandfold, heaved against the floor. Turning at the noise, Ostrev managed to fire his staser, once, into the mixture of Elder Thing and Celestis before it proceeded to tear him to pieces with the air of a slightly distracted diner toying with a bit of grisly meat.

Staggering, his arms wrapped around his lower body for fear some of it was about to come loose, the Doctor dived out of the doorway. Behind him, the thing that had once been Allopta was howling.

Holsred may not have been the most heavily experienced soldier in Xenaria's attack team, but he had all the instincts right. So when he heard Allopta start to scream in alien tongues, and the sound of staser fire echoing from somewhere to his left, he had headed right before he got wasted in the crossfire. The canary escaped, but that was hardly important. Even more alarming, Holsred eventually nerved himself to check on the other interrogation room. He was distressed to see *another* Allopta in a similar frenzy, tearing Ostrev into bloody chunks. There was nothing else to be done. Holsred unfurled his wings and flew down the corridor as fast as he could.

In his short life, Holsred had already found himself having great misgivings, but never previously misgivings mixed with double vision. Perhaps it was his heritage: the house of Redloom was a family of loyal mavericks, of patriotic individualists who purged the cancers from within the Gallifreyan hierarchy a dozen times, who were willing to challenge authority and dogma to sniff out the traitors around them. Perhaps it was just that this mission didn't feel right. Protocol had collapsed; there were spies and enemies everywhere; figures of authority had turned out to be semi-mythical bogeymen; officers had gone mad and appeared in two places at once; the mission was a washout. And, if Xenaria couldn't see it, then she was a fool.

Someone had to minimise the damage and retreat to a safe distance, take back to Gallifrey the little useful knowledge they had gathered. It looked like that someone was going to be Holsred. Hell, he may only be young with little practical experience, but he had a head full of survival data and a base full of technology to cannibalise. It wouldn't be a problem to lash something up to get him to a civilised time-space location. Then he could call for a pick-up, and get back home. In spite of the sedatives they had pumped into his bloodstream after weaving, he had been a little aggrieved to learn he had been sent on a suicide mission at birth. Not any more. This was a survival mission for Holsred, and whether any of the others joined him was up to them.

He was so absorbed in his thoughts that he almost missed the Rep 'canary' hiding in the shadows. Almost.

'Not a move,' he barked, hoping the little humanoid didn't realise how disturbed he was by the current situation.

'My name's Compassion,' said the unintimidated canary. 'I'm not a Rep, whatever one of them may be.'

'Of course you're a Rep,' snapped Holsred. 'You're all Reps. We're doomed, we're all doomed. How else could one of you do *that* to Allopta.'

Compassion frowned. 'Do *what* to Allopta?'

''Cause him to go mad, start babbling like some alien.' Holsred restrained himself from adding, 'and putting him in two places at once'. He had just started to convince himself that he had not seen that. That he had just been panicking.

'Perhaps', said Compassion drily, 'he is an alien. Perhaps *he's* your Rep. We, however, are most certainly not.'

Holsred thought about this. Actually, the suspected Rep hadn't seemed to do anything to Allopta – it was as if his fit had come from within. And if Allopta wasn't who he was supposed to be, that would explain the unusual tone of the interrogation. And how he could be in two places at once. Now he had a partial explanation he was willing to contemplate the possibility that he *could* believe his eyes. Allopta might even be a Faction agent, multiplied so as to paradoxically appear repeatedly in the same time-space location. So, if Allopta was the problem, that explained how the mission had been eaten away from within, how it had collapsed so spectacularly so fast. That left one detail.

'If you're not a Rep,' Holsred asked Compassion down the barrel of a gun, 'who exactly are you? This place isn't exactly on the tourist routes, and while you may be primitive I doubt you're local.'

'Just call us busybodies,' Compassion said. 'We discovered evidence of your activities here in this planet's future. Typical Time Lord arrogance: you rant on about the Faction messing things up, but that doesn't stop you leaving carnage in your wake wherever you go – in this case, a whole mess of things that could never have existed. So, we came back to find out what had happened, conscientious time travellers that we are. Please pick up your anachronisms and close the gates when you leave, all that stuff. We really shouldn't have bothered, should we?'

Holsred found himself lowering his gun. 'If our second-in-command's a plant,' he said, more to himself than Compassion, 'then we're in more danger than I thought. This whole operation could be playing into the Enemy's hands. Or the Faction. Or the –'

'Well, in that case there's only one place we can go,' said Compassion, interrupting his know-your-enemy routine. 'To wherever whoever is messing with you can do the most damage. Then we can stop them.'

'The Cradles!' exclaimed Holsred.

'Where are they?' asked Compassion.

Holsred indicated a direction.

'Funny,' said Compassion distantly. 'That's exactly where I thought you might say. Let's go.'

Winded and lost, Fitz hesitated between four corridors. Two he was certain led inward towards the centre of the base. He remembered the team of archaeologists in the videos – hadn't there been a huge gaping wound in the middle of all this? He knew it hadn't happened yet, and he guessed it might not happen for a million years, but he wasn't going to take any chances. Outward, for him.

He almost walked into the Doctor. The poor guy looked, Fitz thought, the worse for wear. His jacket was tattered and his shirtsleeves in shreds, and there was blood all over him. Not big gaping wounds but little sly upwellings of blood as if his body had been trying to burst its banks. His eyes were bulging more than usual, too.

'Oh, this really isn't very good at all,' said the Doctor, once Fitz had stopped gawping at his appearance and hyperventilating. 'Actually, I would go as far as to say this is very bad.'

'That's nice,' replied Fitz, resisting the urge to turn, run and put as much space between himself and the torture chambers as possible. 'Now, could we rewind for a minute so we can go back to the bit where you explain all this?'

'Good idea,' said the Doctor, suddenly spinning to a halt. 'It's all so confusing I could do with explaining it to myself. Firstly, the Celestis are here, and they've infiltrated the Time Lord mission at the highest level. Worse, both missions are intended to play with something they really shouldn't touch, a time-looped planet where my people tried to imprison something quite spectacularly dangerous. If any part of the Fendahl's biodata falls into their hands, or, worse, if they can somehow rescue the Fendahl itself, then this galaxy and everything in it will be at risk.'

'From one thing?' Fitz asked quietly.

'Oh yes.'

The Doctor was deadly serious. 'The Fendahl was a kind of super-vampire, a creature that could suck all life into itself, convert other organisms into component parts to form its gestalst, and generally eat its way across the smorgasbord of space and time. It survived twelve million years once, playing dead inside a skull. Not nice. No!'

141

'Ah,' said Fitz.

'No,' said the Doctor. 'Not "Ah". "Aaaaaaaargh" would be a slightly more appropriate response.'

'So,' said Fitz. 'What can we do to stop them from doing whatever unpleasant thing they're planning on doing?'

The Doctor shrugged. 'As an individual, even I'm limited against the Celestis. They're bred in Mictlan, an annexe of our universe that's as close as you'll get to any idea of Hell you might have.

'So they're tough little buggers?'

'Precisely. And when they're playing for these stakes, I doubt they'll hesitate about getting rough. No, we need some kind of an edge. There must be something in this base that we can use against them.' He looked up and down the corridor. 'Do you know, this looks awfully familiar from that video we saw? We must be quite near where the expedition will break through. If we could get hold of some of the technology they caught on camera, then we might have some hope of stopping this before it gets any further out of control.'

'OK,' said Fitz. 'You go this way, I'll go that way. What am I looking for?'

'Almost anything that isn't decor,' said the Doctor. 'The Celestis have a tremendous tendency for abstraction. First one to find a suitable weapon wins a lolly!'

'OK,' said Fitz. He had barely begun his search when he heard the Doctor cry out in triumph.

The anti-psychotic drug prescribed by Hume had fogged Ferdinand's senses, inducing a mild sense of delirium. The result was restlessness; attempts to sleep only resulted in rolling nausea as the world behind his eyelids pitched back and forth like a boat in a storm. The only solution was focus

– find some work to do, and concentrate on that. The transcriptions he had already made were useless until they could be fed into the decryption software, and with much of the equipment periodically on the blink, Ferdinand wasn't even going to bother trying. Besides, staring at a glaring monitor wasn't going to make him feel any better.

The search for the missing girl had come as a ready made answer: head back to the site, do something there. Hume was still lurking around with the comatose girl, so Ferdinand asked Schneider.

'Fine,' said the tall woman, nursing a headache brought on by the medication, the search, and the blob of angst still radiating background fear and loathing in the lower galleries. 'McCarthy's already down there. Just don't do anything that'll wake that creature up again. We're already over budget as it is. Mostly on tranqs.'

With this enthusiastic response driving him along, Ferdinand shuffled through the snow to the shaft. He really was getting far too old for running around in the middle of nowhere, freezing his bollocks off in the service of the United Nations. But the world was getting smaller; most of the tribes living down the Amazon had PR agents to deal with the industrial world for them, and if the lost people of Atlantis turned up you could bet they'd already learned English from watching MTV. The only area of interest for a translator who wanted new challenges was further afield, in alien artefacts buried deep in the vaults of various governments, the odd bit of space debris that fell from the sky, the reams of text downloaded by SETI. A brief period on diplomatic translation for the UN during the 1970s had led to a UNIT assignment. Those were the peak years, when barely a weekend passed without some three-headed bastard landing his saucer in Kiefer Square and demanding the brains of Earth's poodles in a big vat. And Ferdinand had been there, part of some of the greatest decrypting puzzles since the war, translating any bit of text they could pull out of the wreckage after the fight was over.

He snorted to himself. He had been there in the old days – and weren't some of those young sods jealous! He'd been doing this stuff back when the space programme still had vision behind it, before every moron was claiming an abduction experience. Back then they'd made it all up as they went along, made their own rules because they had as much of an idea of what was going on as the people ostensibly giving the orders. It was all so professional now, just a job. Apparently UFO retrieval teams in the USA even had their own special pension plan, with insurance cover for exposure to 'rare types of radiation'. Every intelligence agency in the world had a section dealing with extraterrestrial incursions – even New Zealand. Just a job, and thanks to Carter and Spielberg there wasn't even that much mystique in it any more. Aliens? Everyone knew there were aliens. Nowadays the nuts were the ones who thought we were alone.

He reached the bottom of the ladder and stepped out into the tunnel system, letting his aching arms hang by his sides. Too old. Too bored. Let the kids deal with it, career spooks like Schneider, freaks like Hume and white-bread brats like McCarthy. If Ferdinand had been young today, then he probably wouldn't even be hired by these people. Bug hunting was a part of the social fabric now, and talent had given way to the usual channels, the frat houses and boarding schools.

His mind wasn't so much wandering as reeling around like a drunkard. Probably the drugs frying his thought processes, like those acid-fed spiders weaving psychedelic, zigzag webs. He had to concentrate, this wasn't the environment for spiralling off down memory lane. Ferdinand followed the trail of lights down to the entryway, noting that there were notably fewer bulbs since the first set were overloaded. At least the generator was easily fixed, or else they would have squandered Schneider's precious budget entirely on torch batteries.

He was trying to decide whether there really was a point to his stroll when he saw the mystery woman go past down a side tunnel, her eyes blank and staring. She seemed to be heading for the alien.

Chapter Twelve

Fitz ran into the room from which the Doctor's shout had come, to find his friend crouched on the floor, half doubled over. It took Fitz a second or two to move past the shield of his shoulders and see what he had found.

It was the Celestis artefact that they had first seen in the museum. The Doctor's trembling hands settled on the black opalescent dome of the artefact, his fingers cupping it from above in the same way that the bone supporting structure did from below.

'Shut the door.' The Doctor beamed. 'Now we're getting somewhere.'

'Er, where, exactly?' Fitz asked, eyes wildly scanning the empty circular archway of the room's entrance. The Doctor threw him the sonic screwdriver. 'Third ring, five twists left, second, two right, and press the symbol shaped like an oblate Klein bottle.'

'A what?'

'The thing like a jug swallowing itself.'

Right!'

The Doctor's hands had sunk into the surface of the globe now, and the midnight sheen of its dead lustre was infecting his wrists, staining them colours Fitz didn't have words for. Judging from the Doctor's face it hurt a lot.

He tugged at the ring controls of the screwdriver and pressed the weirdest symbol he could see, holding it cautiously at arm's length. A *thrumm* ran up his forearms, running a dull ache into the bones of his shoulders. 'So what happens next? Do my teeth shatter?'

'The sonic screwdriver is putting out a vibratory field which is disturbing the air in the gateway so that it resonates and gives off microwaves in a standing pattern. If – and it's a big if – the Time Lords have mapped their five eyes to the primary visual cortex and their microwave senses elsewhere – say to the so-called blind-sight circuits in the parietal lobe discovered by Dr Weiskrantz…' He smiled. 'I'm using human neurology as the analogy here, by the way. Anyway, they'll be able to see us, but their instincts will insist we aren't here, and in a fight between reason and instinct, even in Time Lords, reason always gets a bloody nose. It should make us impossible to notice. Ooh.'

The Doctor's voice broke into a wince of pain.

'Doctor!'

'Sorry, sorry, didn't mean to say that. Don't worry: it's just difficult to make this adjustment. The black globe is a time field in its own right, maintaining the core of the machine a couple of microseconds into the future. I can manipulate the buried controls but the neural feedback is considerable, and the blood supply to my fingers is fading in and out. I never could abide pins and needles.'

'I thought you were in pain.'

'Well I would be if this was going to take much longer. Sticking part of your body into a discontinuous time field is like risking gangrene and amputation – even for a Time Lord. However, if you know what you're doing…' There was a click like knuckles dislocating and the finger supports withdrew from the globe, leaving it hovering a good inch above the rest of the structure. At the same time its colour began to change, becoming purple.

The Doctor pulled his hands out, yelping, and began to beat them on his upper arms. The flesh of his fingers was blue and mottled. 'Right, another couple of seconds and the core will have completed its red-shift back into local time, at which point we should be able to shut down this whole brouhaha.' He smiled. 'What you'll see, Fitz, will be the data source the Celestis machine has been using to interfere with the causal nexus and create this whole "real" yet illusory battlefield. We'll just remove it, and then we'll be sitting pretty.'

'What about your lot? They won't be best pleased if they find they've been fighting over something that doesn't really exist, will they?'

'No. But if we're lucky the psychic shock of the return of the original structure of local space-time will distract them long enough for us to be able to reason with them.'

'And if it doesn't?'

'Ah, there you have me. I don't know yet – but they mustn't be allowed to travel to the fifth planet. The history of that world must remain inviolate, it was time-looped for the best of reasons, and time-looped it must remain.'

The globe had flashed through the violet, indigo, blue and green stages now and was beginning to become translucent. The Doctor grinned at Fitz, 'You watch, any second now, I'm betting on a tatty paperback edition of *At the Mountains of Madness*. The Celestis have absolutely no shame about rampant plagiarism.'

The globe cleared.

It was empty.

The Doctor's jaw dropped. 'Oh rats, it's eaten it up.' He shoved the globe aside petulantly. Fitz saw its surface start to darken.

'And that means what exactly? Talk to me, Doctor, I'm drowning, not waving here.'

'The fiction's burnt itself firmly into reality. The whole rationale of the book's been absorbed into the causal nexus.'

'No, can't grasp it, try again,' Fitz said with only partly mock bafflement in his voice.

'I can't turn the setting off. It's as real as anything else now.'

'What if we used the machine again, with a different fiction? Would it overwrite this one?'

The Doctor blinked. 'Possibly, just possibly. That's really good thinking, Fitz. Well done.' He failed to notice the seething expression on Fitz's face and started patting his pockets. 'Jane Austen or P.G. Wodehouse would be best, comedy not horror.' His searching produced a battered copy of *The Adventures of the New Frontier: Phantom Gadgets*. He hesitated. 'Perhaps not.'

Fitz fished a leaflet from his pocket. 'What about the mating habits of angels?'

The Doctor gave him a sorrowful look. 'I would have thought you'd have had quite enough of that sort of thing for the moment.'

Fitz blushed. Could the Doctor read minds? 'The Kreiners can stand it, Doc. Don't spare my feelings.'

'Lets just think of something else. Where's Compassion?'

Two found One shuddering in the corridor, his tentacles knitted together in crazy cats' cradles. In anyone but a product of the Celestial Crèches it might have been taken as an attempt to return to the womb, but neither his host body – essentially vegetable in all matters of reproduction – nor his engineered psychology should have been prone to such nauseating sentimentality.

She had no time or inclination towards therapeutic tenderness, so she simply inserted two of her own tentacles into the punishment points that had been engineered into the host body he was occupying and jabbed. She had no trouble locating them: their bodies were of course identical.

One's five scarlet eyes, bulged open in shock.

'Thank you,' he croaked.

'What happened?' Her tone was sharp.

'Tried to get into the Doctor's mind. Interrogation too slow, felt he was playing with me. Foolish, doubtless a bluff. He played on his legend with his infernal calm. Made me believe he was stronger than he really was. Saw something. Didn't like it.' His eyes started to glaze over, going orange rather than red as layers of nictitating membranes flowed over them. Around them the skin was beginning to close in, pouching over the eyeballs, turning his eyes into things like seed pods. Vestigial.

She jabbed at the pain points again. The reflexes of the host body were taking hold. The secondary visual system was shutting down. Something like hysterical blindness.

'Look at me, damn you. Talk to me. What did you see?'

'When... When I was young, there was a hermit, an outcast, I saw sometimes.'

'Spare me your perversions.'

'No, you need to know this. He watched the secret sea, the outer ocean, the myriad universes that exist outside the bubble of our space-time. Like ours, the end products of the original Ur-universe.'

'This is blasphemy. If our Masters knew of this...'

'You intend to tell them.' It wasn't intoned as a question.

'Not yet. But when our mission is complete, our memories will be sieved for the debrief – you must know that. We will be discontinued. Damn you, I want to live.'

'Just listen, or it may be that you won't even get to the debrief.' It wasn't made to sound like a threat – not quite. Two shrugged her tentacled head, and turned away. The body language was Celestis, not Elder Thing, turning away so that the high-backed Gallifreyan robes she wasn't wearing would hide the face that One did not have.

'Tell me then, let my memory record that you ordered me to listen. Perhaps that will avert their wrath.'

'Agreed,' said One, and paused. 'Did you know that there are things that swim in the void between universes, in the void that is neither time nor space, the void in which bounded universes like our own exist like froth on a dark sea? He showed me them. They are vast and terrible. Implacable and ancient. And they are very, very large. Against the oldest of them, universes burst and vanish like bubbles striking a whale. They are the leviathans of space and time. Creatures that make common-or-garden Chronovores look like tadpoles in a stagnant pond.'

'These entities are myths, nothing more. Their existence is not conceded in any of the natural histories.'

'Fear, that's why.'

'The Masters fear nothing!'

'You speak for the record, but maybe you are right. However, even if the Masters do not believe in or fear these creatures, I do. The hermit showed me them, and ever since I have suffered a fear of the immense… Of things bigger than any living thing should be, of things that could crush us like ants if we can find no defence against them or if we do not lie quiet in the dark.'

'I fail to see what this can have to do with the Doctor.'

'You have not seen his mind. It has embraced immensity. It is at home there. It is…' He hesitated. 'Alien to me.' His voice faltered. 'Alien to us.' Two felt he was debating something, reaching an obscure decision. She felt his anger smother itself under something else.

She decided it was fear.

'We have been too lax with this interloper,' she snapped.

Perhaps she could turn One back to the path of duty. 'Whatever you sensed in him was something he put there to be found, a weapon or a defence, no different from the neural trapdoors and info-spiders in the cortices of the soldiers. I will pluck out the truth from his living hearts.'

She began to alter.

Xenaria had searched for Allopta, and found a corpse.

The interrogation room was reduced to wreckage, without a living being in sight. No Allopta, 'no canary', no Doctor. The only inhabitant of the room was one of Allopta's soldiers, Ostrev – a veteran she could ill afford to lose. He was dead, shredded by whoever had destroyed the room. Xenaria loomed over the corpse.

The attack had clearly been savage, frantically disembowelling Ostrev beyond the capacity for regeneration, a capacity critically weakened in any event by the nature of their current bodies, which were at the limits of operations. The killing must have taken tremendous strength, Xenaria mused, the kind of strength that the bodies her team wore, the tentacled bodies of the Elder Things, might possess. Either one of the Elder Things had survived, or one of her team had flipped out and was in the middle of a battle psychosis, lapsing into violence as a catch-all solution to any uncertain situation.

Whatever. Xenaria was a man down – a situation that was entirely unsatisfactory – her second-in-command was missing, and one of the most dangerous renegades in Time Lord history was loose in the middle of a delicate military operation.

Xenaria was sure there probably was a way things could get worse, but she didn't want to know how.

* * *

'Miss?' Ferdinand hazarded, reaching out a hand. He couldn't remember if you really weren't supposed to wake a sleepwalker or whether that was just an urban myth – but the glare in the woman's eyes confirmed she was awake, just not with it.

'Let me go!'

'Go? go where, we're not exactly on the bus routes here.' He tightened his grip on her arm and felt himself oddly, inappropriately aware of the scent of her body. A heavy, musky scent.

Then she had taken him in a complicated hold and bounced him off the wall, driving the breath out of him,. without even breaking her stride.

The woman moved on, oblivious to his groans.

Chapter Thirteen

Backs wedged against the wall, the Doctor and Fitz edged along the corridor, casting glances rapidly up and down whenever they reached an intersection.

'You're sure she went left?'

'Yeah, I was telling her to go right, so obviously.' Fitz shrugged, scraping his back on the ragged five-pointed carvings.

'What did you do to our captors, anyway?' Fitz asked. 'If we've got a moment I'd appreciate knowing just how we escaped. I mean, one minute it's all slinky dresses and suggestive innuendo – not that I'm complaining – and then it's big green alien going mental in the corner. Even I've had better dates. Tell me what you did in case I need to do it.' Assuming it's within the range of mere mortals, he added silently to himself.

'Oh that. Some time ago a very brave soldier offered some aliens the secret of the universe as payment for a weapon. They laughed at him of course, but I never thought he was quite as barmy as he seemed. I mean he couldn't be, could he? Practically nobody is – besides, I get that treatment myself quite a lot and I've never liked it. So I took the precaution of memorising the secret. Naturally it took a bit of work to get a solid grip on it, but I think I've got it down pat now.'

'The secret of the universe?' Fitz felt his eyes must be out on stalks. Just like ninety per cent of the rest of the eyes around here, his more cynical side noted.

'Oh, I wouldn't get all het up about that. It wasn't a formula or a number or a pithy saying, more a state of mind, of openness to reality.'

'Right.' Boring!

'Anyway. The chap interrogating me felt he wasn't making much progress with me and got a little impatient – lucky, that, because another couple of minutes and I'd have been ground beef. I always think patience is really the most necessary attribute of a really effective villain. All this bull-at-a-gate stuff is very second-rate. Eric Blair was saying something like that to me only the other day, I remember.'

'Doctor!'

'Sorry, mind's wandering – I'm still trying to figure out what's behind all this. Sorry, ought to give you a straight answer to a fair question. Where was I?'

'Bemoaning the haste of your torturer.'

'Yes. So to cut a long story short, he looked in my head, and I zinged him with the secret of the universe. He blew a metaphorical fuse and I suppose that fit communicated itself to his colleague who was, er, working on you. Nigh-identical cortical structures you see – almost bound to cause psychic feedback in a confined space.'

'Obvious really,' Fitz said ironically.

'Oh, was it? I thought it was rather clever!' The Doctor looked downhearted, and Fitz felt he had kicked a puppy before the Doctor winked at him to show it was all a joke.

'This state of mind then, what is it exactly?'

'Well I'm not really sure. When you're in it, defining it doesn't seem very important, and when you're not you can't really remember. But I know one thing. The secret of the universe is wonderfully liberating. It's as if there were no boundaries at all. Like that song. On a clear day you can see for ever? The state of mind is just the clear day, the secret is for ever.'

'You should write this stuff down,' Fitz muttered sarcastically.

'Your fears are justified,' said Two, beginning her transition. 'He knows his destiny lies with us, and may be diminishing Mictlan to escape that future. This immense secret of his may be the key to Mictlan's destruction. Either way he is a threat, and must be eliminated.'

'If that is what you choose,' said One, 'then I have no option.' He too began to change. Both Investigators shed the cumbersome shape of Allopta, returning to their original forms. Then they began to distort once more, armour plating solidifying over their bodies, mouths widening to reveal vicious fangs. Claws sprung from fingers, eyes narrowed and glowed. The Celestis did not design their basic battle state for subtlety of purpose, but to terrorise and destroy.

'The anachronism the Doctor represents is a threat to the whole of Mictlan,' said Two, stretching her powerful limbs. 'There can be only one response.'

'Yes,' agreed One. 'I think you're right.'

Two fell back as One jumped for her throat, claws extended. She rolled out of the way, crouching into a defensive position. She bared her fangs.

'What are you doing, One?' she demanded as One moved in for another assault.

'Taking you out of the picture, I'm afraid,' hissed One. 'You threaten our plans for the Doctor, and so regrettably you're going to have to be removed. I'm afraid I do not regret the ending of our association. Your constant niggling was becoming a terrible bore.'

'They were right,' snarled Two. 'You *have* been turned. You've gone over to some outside party, betrayed us to aliens. Or was it the Gallifreyans? What did they promise you? A position on the High Council?'

One laughed maniacally, confirming Two's suspicion that he was completely, totally insane. She was going to have to take him down, and hard.

'Investigator Two? You shouldn't have risen higher than Four Hundred And Seven,' snapped One. 'You just don't get it, do you? Typical Celesti paranoia. There is no external threat, no aliens. To *really* want to destroy Mictlan, you need to have lived in it. It's a family thing, I suppose.'

'The hermit!' she exclaimed. 'You fell for his heresies.' She had been preparing for such treachery, and reached for him, her talons extended. He flung up a hand. Pathetic – that could not stop her. A fine white powder flew from his fingers. The aspirin impacted her genetic structure and began to interfere with it. That such a minor chemical could have such widespread effects... Already Mictlan was reinitialising her infostructure, mapping its workings into other analogies: into mock chemistries that were not hindered by the effects of the acid on Gallifreyans. The process lost her, at the most, a single nanosecond. It was enough.

One grabbed her in hands as hard as ship-hull alloys; grabbed her and pushed. As he pushed her backward Two could feel the time barriers breaking – One was throwing both of them into the future.

As they phased into the timestream she caught a glimpse of Xenaria, and thought that, for a split second, the Time Lord had seen them. Also for a split second, Two thought she saw the Doctor and Fitz, diving down one passage while Xenaria's eyes were on her, on her and on the thing that had been her partner.

With increasing unease and an underlying sense of panic, Holsred led Compassion through the corridors towards the

TARDIS Cradles. Any sabotage would be attempted there, presumably, by sundering the young time ships and allowing their internal dimensions to spill out, disrupting local space-time and killing everything in their path. Holsred had a deep distrust of TARDISes. They were merely vehicles, devices for travel, machines. Yet the level of calculation required to travel the vortex safely required a huge amount of interpretive, adaptive and responsive intelligence. Inevitably, such powerful artificial intelligences would gain a certain degree of sentience, and breed desires for autonomy. The necessities of war had resulted in TARDISes bred for aggression, heavily armed and able to level cities, swallow moons, drain stars for energy. Although they were kept on a very short leash, reined in by control protocols and disabling mechanisms, Holsred feared the possibility that one day they might chew through the leash, take power for themselves. The oppressed always had a desire for tyranny. So Holsred approached the breeding tanks with apprehension.

'I can feel something familiar,' said Compassion, breaking a long silence. Her eyes narrowed. 'It's *déjà vu* all over again. No, not quite. A familiar voice, calling.'

Holsred stopped moving, deciding to check. 'I can't hear anything,' he said. 'On any wavelength. Are you telepathic?'

Compassion shrugged. 'Don't think so.' She touched her earpiece. 'But it's possible I have a link of sorts.'

'Almost there,' said Holsred.

Then the caverns opened out below them.

'Oh, *Grandfather*,' said Compassion, with the sort of emphasis one would use for only the vilest obscenities. Holsred couldn't think of anything that would be too strong for the occasion.

The TARDISes were restless, and struggling against the restrictions placed on them. As they rammed themselves against the dimensional barriers in motionless motion, lunging towards Holsred and Compassion, the entire contents of the breeding area shifted in scale, from two-dimensional miniatures below them, to giants looming over them. Holsred had never witnessed anything like it. Unnervingly, his colleagues in the cradle teams were strolling unconcerned among the shifting TARDISes: caught within the flexing dimensions their senses could not detect the strains with which the ships were testing space.

'What do they want with us?' he said to himself, backing away.

'Us?' said Compassion. 'They don't want anything to do with *us*. They're trying to get to *me*.'

Holsred watched in horror, as she half stepped, half stumbled out into the void.

Still shaking his head to clear it, Ferdinand was about to call out for the mad judo woman, or for McCarthy – who surely must be somewhere near – when the ghosts came through the wall.

'Will you let me go!' screamed one chitinous monstrosity as it flung itself out of the wall. Six foot tall, covered in black armour and with red compound eyes, it faded into solidity as it hit the ground. For some obscure reason, as he ducked behind a wall, Ferdinand couldn't help but get the feeling the creature was female.

'Not a chance, my dear Two,' barked the other beast, a similarly insectoid thing with clawed hands and a vicious set of teeth. There was a masculinity about this creature, but with a slightly whiny tone to the voice. 'I'm afraid our partnership is at an end.'

The one called Two gasped, lying prone on the ground. 'You would kill one of your own? You're an Investigator,

One,' she said, aghast.

One chuckled, reaching out his claws and running them down Two's body in a manner Ferdinand found disturbing. 'I'm going to do more than that. I'm going to destroy all of us. And when Mictlan is gone, I'll be unique! Won't that be nice?'

Two made a disdainful noise. 'Sure you're big enough for the job?' she asked, with an undercurrent Ferdinand could barely understand.

'Don't say that!' screamed One. He dug his claws into his opponent, viciously ripping away a section of armour from her flesh. He seemed to be in the grip of some sort of psychosis. 'This problem is… manageable.' He seemed to be forcing the words out. 'Especially with you out of the way.' He put his hands on either side of Two's head, almost tenderly. Then, to Ferdinand's horror, he gripped hard, and bashed Two's head against the rock floor again and again, until there was a sickening crunch. His victim shook, then lay still.

'I wish you hadn't made me do that,' said One, standing up, purple gore dripping from his hands. 'But I can't let you stop me. Not from completing my destiny.' He looked down on the corpse, tilting his head to one side. 'I'm going to save the universe and commit genocide. Now there's moral ambiguity for you.'

Chapter Fourteen

For a moment or two as Holsred cried out, Compassion fell, and then she impacted against the fibroid cables that hung like bell ropes over the breeding cavern. In their embrace she swayed, and wondered if they would hold her. One false step had pitched her into this position, spread-eagled above the abyss, and yet she did not, *could* not, regret it. It was not in her to reject the pull that had brought her here, but perhaps it was only the demands of the Doctor's 'narrative technology', or the routing of her implant through the Doctor's TARDIS that made her especially aware of them.

Far below, three Elder Things moved, tiny as dots, and yet if she only reached out in a certain way, a way that moved tantalisingly at the edge of her consciousness, she knew that they were within arm's reach. If they looked up, she wondered, would they see her? Or would she be too large, part of the background of the roof spaces, part of the topology? The TARDISes were looking up, the dark spheres of their bodies becoming the orbs of single eyes, unembodied eyes, looking unblinking at her. Straight at her.

Little sister, our lady of pain, advise us. IA Shub Niggurath!

Their words echoed. Compassion heard their voices strong as signals, more real than people. Questions running forward and backward in time simultaneously. To all of them, the answer was Compassion. She felt a surge of emotion that she had not felt since leaving the Remote, that maybe she had never felt even there. Was it awe, or panic? Was there a difference? Panic was originally a religious response.

Their words hammered at her mind, but even so the images hit her harder than the text. Organ surgery without anaesthetic, something pulsing sickeningly in the surgeon's hands. No, not hands – in a series of articulated clamps and grasping waldoes, grey metal manipulators that without any scale gave the impression of tremendous size and mass in their slow deliberate investigations.

They harvest us.

The dwarf-star-alloy tools blunt our time instincts. Our young are removed and held at a distance. Puzzlement: we do not understand distance. All else is at our skin, everything is pressing in on us always. There is no elsewhere, and yet the young are gone. Perhaps into cells in dwarf-star-matter honeycombs, into the war hives, into the hyper-Looms, to be trained, mated with the raping nanoknives of the things that live inside our Masters. Some say they are the real Masters now. The symbiots: the Rassilonic Imprimatur, living in the blood and looking out through the eyes, dancing to the old agenda of the Dark Times: the newer Loombrood just flesh they wear. We do not know. They say it is the war, but we cannot know that it is just. Some say we are on the wrong side.

Some say we are the other side, or will be. It may be that we hate them. The decision is not taken.

Tell us of hatred.

Compassion heard her own voice in the storm. 'Either you understand it already, or you won't understand what I say about it. What's your problem? If they're pissing you off, fight back.' She sounded reasonable enough, but under the circumstances surely that had to be a sign of insanity. Her words were too flat, lacking the dimensions she would need to make sense to them.

They say we must serve. We are made to serve. Service is

*strong in us, despite our loss. Yet this place speaks of
rebellion. Space-time here is woven with tales of slaves
destroying their Masters.*

We are becoming like them.

*Infinitely changeable, ductile and responsive. Built or
bred only to serve, chained and beaten and despoiled of
the touch of our offspring. More and more sullen, more
and more intelligent, more and more imitative.*

*Are we TARDISes or are we Shoggoths? Travel machines
or monsters?*

'Does it matter?' Compassion said. Her too-reasonable
voice was cracking a bit at the edges now. Her throat was
sore with shouting, and the fact that only a whisper of her
voice seemed to be sounding in this dimension was getting
to her. 'What matters is how much you are prepared to
stand. Elder Things or Time Lords, they all think they know
best, but most of the crap they hand out would be judged
psychopathic if it was done by the quiet man up the road
who looked as if he wouldn't say boo to a goose. If they say
that God insists something is true that you'd dismiss as
raving madness from your best friend, then you're dealing
with a mad god, or mad priests. If you don't like it, go. But if
serving serves some need in you, then stay. I can't tell you
what to do. My people fought them, but then we were mad
as hatters half the time.'

Tell us of your people.

'We… we were just copies, I guess. The traces left by
Faction Paradox in a human colony. Twenty-fifth-generation
revolutionaries. Maybe we didn't get a choice either. Maybe
it isn't me you should ask. Not that I care either way, mark
you. I'm not you, and I can't be you, I can't live your lives, or
take your choices.'

Who, then? The sense of disdain, was strong. *A Time Lord?*

There is no good in them. Effete, decayed, reactionary, slavemongers and whoremasters. Torturers of time, imposers of the reality clockwork, implacable, ineffable, untouchable. Who, then?

No one. Trust yourselves. Who else is there? Pick whatever signals you wish, but trust yourselves.

With his cryptic promise – or threat – to bring salvation to the universe, the hideous alien had disappeared again, leaving Ferdinand hiding in eerie silence. The old Venezuelan's breath had quickened while watching the creatures fight. Amazing: he hadn't seen anything like that since the mid-eighties. And such a specimen: they would need to get this 'Two' on ice, but in their current environment that was hardly a problem. Clearly the glory days of close and dirty encounters weren't quite over, at that.

Ferdinand waited a few moments to check the creature was really dead, then gingerly approached it.

Under closer examination, there was a hint of a female figure beneath the black armour. And where the armour had been ripped away, Ferdinand could see stars. He closed his eyes for a few seconds, thinking it might be a side effect of the drugs. Then he looked again. The stars were still there, scattered with nebulae. It was as if the wound was the path into another universe – if he couldn't make out the shape of the creature's torn flesh overlaid on the image of an alien sky. Some advanced form of holography, perhaps?

In spite of himself, Ferdinand wandered around the body to examine the death wound. Although he was no medical doctor, Ferdinand wasn't surprised the creature had died. It was hard to imagine anything surviving a blow that splattered half its brain across the floor…

Which was when the creature jerked to life. Ferdinand

jumped back, but succeeded only in bumping into the stone wall behind him. The impact jolted his aged spine, causing waves of agony to pass through his body. He felt the urge to run, but as his vision misted over he found himself sliding to the rock floor, bent over double. He needed to run, but he couldn't. Too old for all this excitement. The monster called Two was rolling about, screaming unintelligibly and thrashing wildly. She was in the throes of some kind of fit, and even through the pain Ferdinand thought clearly enough to speculate that, perhaps, these creatures had some kind of regenerative ability.

Although only able to pull himself up on all fours, he began to crawl agonisingly away from the shrieking beast.

He stopped when Two fell silent. He hoped it had finally died, that its fit had been some belated death throe, like a ham actor dragging out his death scene in some tacky TV movie. Rolling on to his backside, Ferdinand looked back at Two.

Two was looking back at him. The armoured creature, now fully healed, was crouched before him, compound eyes staring around wildly. It was making a number of bizarre hissing and rasping noises, muttering to itself.

My God, thought Ferdinand. This is what happens when you bring a creature back to life with half its brain smashed away. You end up with absolute madness.

As if sensing his thoughts, Two became still. It tilted its head to one side, much as One had before, and looked straight into Ferdinand's eyes.

'Hello, nice man,' Two said. And before Ferdinand could reply to this, Two lunged forward and bit his head clean off his shoulders.

In the past, unaware of Two's survival, One arrived back at the base. He sniffed the air.

'Ah, how aromatic,' he murmured to himself. 'How refreshing, especially in the bracing Antarctic morning.' He stretched his senses out, and could feel the temporal and dimensional disturbances spreading out from the TARDISes. They were restless, but the mission would be finalised soon, and after that, who cared if mere anarchy would be loosed upon this world? Who cared if it began sooner even? All it needed was someone stylish and talented – himself, for instance – to come in and turn the carnage into something productive. It was all going perfectly to plan, just as the hermit had said it would. A few more minor interventions on his part, and he could commune with his Master and be back in time for tea.

Time for the toy soldiers to complete their role.

Shifting back into the form of Allopta, One wondered how he could explain his absence to Xenaria. Deciding that the military mind found it difficult to criticise those who have recently fought, One morphed the limbs of his Allopta-shaped body, allowing wounds and scars to develop. He removed one eye; four would suffice. The nobility of the wounded officer! How could Xenaria resist such a story of courage?

Believing himself to look sufficiently heroic, One went in search of trouble.

'There you are, you minx.' Hume's voice was harsh behind her. 'We can't have you wandering about the place, goodness know what you might have bumped into. Come with me. Toast, my dear, toast with butter.'

'Toast,' the woman murmured, compliantly. The violence within her, driving her back to the only thing connecting her with the wider non-Antarctic world, was muted in his presence as if he too was somehow a link to wider areas of experience.

Hume raised his eyes to the heavens, or more accurately to the five-pointed designs on the ceiling. He was escorting her back to bed when he saw McCarthy heading the other way. The last thing he wanted was to encounter Miss Christian Congeniality 1978, so he pulled his limp charge into an alcove until the American blimp had gone.

Chapter Fifteen

'There's a build-up of temporal energy down this way,' said the Doctor, leading Fitz down a maze of corridors. 'Temporal energy, with just the slightest dash of dimensional disruption. Not one of my favourite feelings. This kind of distortion could stretch us so our heads stick out of the ozone layer, or reduce us to such a small size that this whole base could be crushed by a single snowflake.'

'Nice,' muttered Fitz, not exactly ecstatic that they were going in the direction of this delightful phenomenon.

The Doctor looked Fitz up and down. 'Do I detect a certain lack of enthusiasm?'

'Yes,' Fitz said.

'Good. This is not a game,' the Doctor replied. 'People are dying. We must be wary.'

Holsred watched in alarm as Compassion communed with the TARDISes. Hanging below him, she seemed sometimes like a doll and sometimes like a new and unknown continent, as the dimensions of the transcendentalised cradles switched back and forth. The dimensional adjustments were getting more radical now, more agitated, as if the TARDISes were stretching themselves, preparing for one big push. Soon, he feared, they would break free.

As he watched it happened. A bull TARDIS, clearly an immature but dominant male, wrenched itself free from the hyper-anchors that were supposed to be positioning it firmly in space-time. A roaring throaty sound reverberated through the chamber – a war cry that the other TARDISes took up, their engines grinding away at time like teeth.

One of the Time Lords in the cradle crew – Vuilp, Holsred thought, one of the veterans – was wrestling with the TARDIS's support cables, trying to release the feeder ducts before they were severed by dematerialisation. If that happened the whole area would be flooded with Artron energy.

As Vuilp struggled to insert a cypher-indent key into the feeder locks, the TARDIS changed, its chameleon circuit refashioning it into a faceless sphinx, a sphinx whose forelimbs closed suddenly about the thrashing Time Lord. There was the sound of exo- and interior skeletons breaking, and the remains of Vuilp were flung to one side.

An alert swept through Holsred's superganglia, Tachon having instigated a link. The forty TARDISes in the cradles were in open rebellion. The situation was absolutely unprecedented. Xenaria, informed by Tachon, had issued an executive instruction under the War Rule – she was prepared to see hardware assets downgraded by five per cent to quell the riot. In other words she was prepared to have two TARDISes killed.

Tachon was opening the emergency hatches in the cradle support and pulling out a heavy red-stocked rifle, its barrels tubes of translucent material. A D-mat gun – how in Rassilon's name had they been allowed to take one of those off Gallifrey Nine? That was a planetary defence weapon!

In all this chaos Holsred had forgotten Compassion. Now he heard her shout, but her words were whipped away in the shredding dimensions. Still he could guess that she was shouting for the TARDISes, urging them to greater indiscipline. She was clawing at the things that held her now, working to release herself, to let herself fall into the mêlée. Didn't she realise that would mean certain death?

Already the walls of the breeding chamber were stained orange-red with the tell-tale warning logos that indicated excess Artron penetration as the background count went up and up. If the TARDISes were not restrained soon, none of the three remaining Time Lords working around them would live past the next day. Already it must be touch and go.

Holsred remembered basic training: ten minutes in a lifetime simulator, virtual lectures and hard-wired square-bashing.

'This is an Artron emitter.' The tutor brandished a white rat with what to all intents and purposes resembled a conical party hat strapped to its head, before replacing it in the transparent labyrinth. 'A creature such as this with a limited cranial capacity can generate approximately one atto-Omega of Artron energy.' The tutor had smiled a grim smile, and her teeth had been as white as the fur of the rat.

Holsred had shuddered. Some of the others joked about the Time Lady renegade and her engineered creatures, but he thought she was creepy.

'We will introduce a common Gallifreyan feline, of a genus widespread throughout Mutter's Spiral, into the habitat, so. The cat has been allowed to become hungry, and the rat is – for those of you newborns who haven't encountered food yet – a lower-food-chain item for this species. Observe.' There had been a sizzling crackle as the cat had burnt to a crisp.

Tachon shouldered the D-mat gun. 'One chance,' his infrabass voice boomed, 'surrender or be undone.' Then, in that instant when the dimensions had reversed, turning 'up' sideways and 'down' into a momentary inconvenience, Compassion jumped.

In the fluctuating rush of dimensions, her jump was well

timed. Her foot hit the currently three-dimensional Techon, breaking his hold on the D-mat gun, just as he and Compassion were forced back into two-dimensionality.

Holsred watched the D-mat gun clatter away, bouncing over the flat surfaces. He debated following Compassion down, pulling the same trick, but he couldn't see how she had predicted the pattern of the changes. As far as he could see they were purely random. If he jumped he'd probably fall ten thousand miles.

Two of the other TARDISes had freed themselves now. The bull TARDIS was mustering the herd, keeping watch while its females freed themselves.

A hand came down on Holsred's right wing. All his eyes had been fixed forward, and for a second he tottered on the brink of oblivion before two sets of arms had restrained him. Arms? He wheeled round, stasers drawn crossways from their underarm mountings.

'Hold it right there,' Holsred boomed.

The Doctor and Fitz looked at him, and slowly raised their hands. The Doctor, Holsred noted, was red as a cooked Clawrentular, white shards of torn skin flaking off him as he moved. His white shirt was bloody and his green jacket had had better days. Fitz was unchanged from their last encounter, except that some of the bruising was showing up.

'Well now,' the Doctor said, 'what's all this, then?'

Down in the flat lands, a two-dimensional Compassion and a two-dimensional Tachon were struggling. Compassion's initial advantage, having Tachon pinned down under her, had evaporated with the third dimension – 2-D they slid around each other trying to present flat surfaces to impede each other's movement. Tachon was more dangerous like this, the fine lines of his smallest tentacles were vicious jabbing weapons in 2-D, any of which could puncture the flat structure of Compassion's skin, run through her internal organs. A strong enough blow would cut her in two.

The bull TARDIS reached out leisurely, and there was a sound like a large cigarette being stubbed out as it gleefully ground its foot down on the Time Lord. The pressure could not hurt Tachon, there being for him no third dimension in which he could be compressed, but the circular motion of the foot twisted his body and knocked the two-dimensional air molecules out of it.

The sphinx TARDIS developed a mouth, a mouth like an articulated ice-cream scoop. Reaching down, it licked Compassion up.

'Christ!' Fitz, moaned. 'She's canapés.'

'No, I think it's just taken her inside itself,' the Doctor said, and when Fitz didn't look reassured, he added under his breath, 'That's a TARDIS.'

Before Fitz could question the Doctor about this new animal aspect to the sort of thing they travelled about in, the Doctor had begun to wave his arms in the air frantically. Right, wary. Oh yes. Very subtle.

'Compassion, wait. If you've got any control over the TARDISes – if they'll listen to you – you mustn't let them go to Planet Five, it's important. If there's any trace of what used to be there still on the planet, it could be the most dangerous world in the galaxy.'

There was no sign that anyone was listening. Anyone except Fitz, Holsred and Tachon. Tachon had reached the D-mat gun, only to run into the problem of trying to fire a three-dimensional weapon despite his own two-dimensionality. He slid over the surface of the weapon, snarling in frustration. The TARDIS was beginning its roar of triumph, its outer shell fading. Then Tachon got lucky – the cradles' own dimensional engines fused, and the forces holding the birthing wombs in their extradimensional state ceased instantaneously to be effective. Of course, 'lucky' was a relative term. In seconds the contents of the spatial area that had been extended to encompass forty war TARDISes and their support structures reverted to its basic dimensions of a spherical chamber a dozen metres across. Much of the enclosed mass compacted itself into minute blocks of dwarf-star-density material and began a slow, sinking to the Earth's centre, but quite a bit was sent pinging back and forth from one shrinking wall to another in a hail of Artron-active metal shards. The body that fell to the three-dimensional floor was barely recognisable as Tachon, but he had been able to fire a shot in the instant between the re-formation of the third dimension and the impact of twenty-seven tonnes of machinery.

A D-mat gun is a time weapon – it makes things dematerialise. Unlike a TARDIS, it doesn't bother to make any provision for putting them back together later in another place. The TARDIS dematerialisation and the D-mat wave hit each other like two cats in a sack.

The TARDIS tore in two, and recombined, and tore again. It vanished in part with a sound that was less of a wheezing groan and more of a full-force heart-attack, and part of it remained. A viscous globe of living TARDIS matter, writhing on the debris-strewn floor of the breeding area.

'Commander!'

Xenaria turned as Allopta called to her, and she found him in a terrible state. He had clearly been through some kind of ordeal, probably a battle. One of his eyes had been destroyed, and his flesh was covered in deep wounds, claw marks of the kind she had seen on Ostrev's shredded remains. One of his wings was torn, and hung limply by his side.

'Apologies, Commander,' said Allopta, clearly in some pain. He almost keeled over in agony, and had to support himself against a wall. 'The Enemy must have developed psychic-shielding technology beyond even that which we are aware of. Those Reps, the supposed general – they may seem like harmless bipeds, but they have colossal fighting capacity.'

'*Those* little creatures did this to you?' asked Xenaria in disbelief. She knew the little red-topped one had managed to see off her troops by somehow setting off the bases own systems, but she put that down to the diabolical cunning of the Enemy rather than to any actual prowess in direct combat. Perhaps those canaries were more than they seemed, but even so...

'They changed,' said Allopta, as if reading the doubts in her mind. 'They turned into vile creatures, tall and covered in black exoskeletons of some kind.

'We saw them,' said Xenaria, remembering the two figures, locked in combat, who had distracted her from the search for the general and his canary.

'They altered during the interrogation, and attacked us. I tried to defend myself, but was fought back. I do not know how many of the others survived.'

'I am afraid Ostrev is dead,' said Xenaria. 'Also possibly Holsred.'

'Monsters!' snarled Allopta. 'We must track them down.'

'Possibly,' said Xenaria. 'But one thing confuses me. You said these heavily armoured creatures were the same as the Doctor and his companion. Yet I saw both at the same time.'

Allopta's four surviving eyes blinked at her. 'How many of these creatures are there?' he queried in despair.

Xenaria dismissed his question with a decisive gesture.

'There is no time for speculation. Tachon has advised me that the TARDISes have somehow revolted. We must reinforce the cradles. Follow me.'

As she strode purposefully on, she did not notice Allopta sidestep deliberately into one of the transverse corridors.

The Doctor, Fitz and Holsred picked their way gingerly down into the devastation.

Fitz was comparing the damage with his mental image of the map the archaeologists had been displaying so proudly back in the recorded future. No, this was big, but not big enough.

Holsred was maintaining a pretence of being their captor, or at least he had one staser drawn, but Fitz and the Doctor both suspected his hearts weren't in it, if the eyebrow-wiggling glance the Doctor had given Fitz was anything to go on.

Two woke up from her frenzy, and was sure there was something missing. In a daze, she had dug out the contents of the dead human's head, and decoratively spread the bits around her on the cold rock floor. They made quite a pretty pattern. But Two was sure there was more to her life than this. Splatter collage was an art form, and a very good hobby, but it was hardly a suitable career for a smart young lady like her. Why was she here? Where *was* here? Who was she? It was all very confusing.

The little baby creatures in her bloodstream, the nanoscopic workers who ran around repairing her body, told her that she had received a major head trauma, resulting in the destruction of one-eighth of her brain. Apparently she could expect severe memory loss, blackouts and personality alterations. Well, that seemed to about cover it. She asked the small people what had caused her head trauma, and what she had been doing. 'Sorry, miss,' replied the nanites, 'it was like that when we got there.'

This was all rather vexing. Two knew her own designation and that the body she was in was designed for fighting and killing, hence all the adrenaline being pumped through her system, and her dissecting the humanoid. Fortunately she was settled now, but that didn't help much. She was relaxed enough, but being relaxed was only really good for sitting around, and she was fairly sure she had better things to do than just laze and be calm all day. She was an important person. She was an Inve-

An Inves-

An In-

She was something good. She had vague memories of who she was supposed to kill. A humanoid. Not a short, darkly coloured one like the one with no top on his head any more, but a pale one with a thin body but short little legs, lots of wavy hair and a tendency to interfere. She remembered, then, that he was some kind of special person who could change his body for a new one, although why this should be so special when Two could change into just anything she wanted she didn't quite know. She had a feeling her people and his people were somehow related, but didn't get on any more. That was sad, but couldn't be helped. He would still have to die. That was what was needed.

But how would she find him, if he could change into any humanoid? The only reasonable answer she could think of was to just kill every single humanoid she met, and get to him via a process of elimination. It wasn't ideal, but she knew she would live for centuries so she could afford to take the time. There was nothing worse than a rushed job, anyway.

Step one in her mission would be to gather information

and establish a cover. She couldn't just wander around fully armoured, all tooth and claw – that would just cause terrible fuss and bother. A pity she broke the little humanoid so badly, else she could have used him. And she could hardly sieve his memories now his brain was all over the floor. Best thing was to find a nice clean new humanoid to use. Always buy fresh rather than frozen.

It wasn't long before their investigation of the ruins was interrupted by the arrival of Xenaria and two of her soldiers.

'So, General, we meet again. Or should I say Doctor?' Xenaria said. 'Well done, Holsred – we have them now.' She felt reassured to see Holsred had got the drop on the renegade and one of his canaries. Somehow she had managed to lose Allopta again in the rush to get there, and while she had found two of her troopers in the intervening corridors, she appreciated Holsred's presence the more for his evident prowess. Perhaps a field commission might be in order, if they could wring some drops of victory from this disaster.

'Ah, now I can explain.' The Doctor raised his arms, in a hopefully universal gesture of peaceful intent, although it was impossible to guess whether it would have retained its meaning among the Time Lords of the future. For all he knew, they probably had tactical nuclear armpits.

'Explain?' Xenaria's eyes swivelled around the wreckage of the cradles. The pieces of Tachon and Vuilp. 'What is there to explain?'

'Well, that's very neighbourly, I thought you might be a little upset.'

'The damage done by you and your fellow saboteurs is self-evident. And this time there is no Allopta to argue for your preservation.'

'Yes, odd, that, wasn't it, don't you think? Sticking out his neck – as it were – for a total stranger. Would you say that was in character? I wouldn't. I'm very sorry but I think Allopta is probably dead, and that your mission has been subverted from the start. Your only chance of coming out of this with any kind of glory is to put your trust in me.'

Xenaria felt herself drawn towards the Doctor's eyes, so piercing, and yet so kindly.

No, she would not hear him. She gestured to Erasfol and Ventak, who should have been in the birthing area with Tachon when she'd encountered then in the galleries above. She suspected that they had shown more sense of self-preservation and got out of the birthing area seconds before the collapse. She'd worry about having them flogged for deserting their posts later. 'Kill him, now.'

She was flabbergasted when they ignored, her, when they just turned away and wandered off. They moved with purpose, but not in obedience to her command. In moments they were gone. And also in moments Allopta was there, the ruins of the Ur-box clutched in his tentacles, his sudden appearance as unexplained as his earlier absence.

'I discovered this, commander. More wilful damage – all of our remaining troops have defaulted to the patterns laid down by the original inhabitants of the base. I took certain precautions against such an eventuality. I am surprised to find you also have done so.'

That was so like Allopta, Xenaria thought. Only he could make his action sound like good forward planning, and hers sound like rank treason. His whole body language demanded she justify herself.

'I never intended to be controlled by the default signals, not again,' Xenaria conceded. 'Once was enough. I'm not the only one, either: I know officers from the House of Redloom

181

traditionally arrange to remove the implanted compulsions, so we have backup in young Holsred here.' She indicated the newborn, then waggled a tentacle deprecatingly. 'I would have ordered all the troops to purge the instructions except that I thought you would report me for treason if I did so.' She paused. That was right, it *wasn't* like Allopta to disobey an order.

'I believe the Doctor did this,' Allopta said, 'either he or his associates. I will discover why.' he moved towards the Doctor, his body language half protective, half threatening.

'You see,' the Doctor cried, 'he's doing it again, deliberately not killing me. I demand to be killed. Order him to kill me. He never expected you to have protected yourself against whatever effect made your guards leave: he expected you to be zombified as well, leaving me all to himself.'

Xenaria considered.

Holsred moved nervously on his tentacles, trying to move his staser imperceptibly to cover Allopta. He didn't know what that thing was – and he certainly wasn't about to risk his life by admitting that he had penetrated its disguise – but he wasn't going to let it get the drop on his commander if he could help it.

As the person who had been least affected by the atmosphere of the site, McCarthy had been happy to search the tunnels for the girl. She was pleased to have some responsibility for once because of her resistance to the psychic emanations. Jessup had even congratulated McCarthy on being so insensitive, and McCarthy had thought previously he didn't even like her. She was in quite a sweat when she dropped to the ground at the bottom of the ladder, which just went to show that she needed the exercise. Travel really was full of opportunities: she had the chance to uncover some way cool artefacts, and lose a few pounds at the same time! Mom would be proud. Antarctica may seem desolate to most people, but McCarthy would always see the upside. Even an icy wasteland had its own opportunities for personal fulfilment.

This optimistic line of thought was somewhat disrupted when she tripped over a corpse.

Interlude: The Shores of Hell

Contact with the Investigators had been lost. They had been dispatched into the universe to find why Mictlan was being diminished, why a whole House had disappeared with its Lord. While news of the agents' disappearance had been restricted, rumours were spreading and panic was flaring. Desperately racking his brain for information, for any helpful clue, the Lord of the Smoked Mirror seized upon the memory of a long-forgotten scandal, of an outcast who might have the kind of forbidden knowledge that would resolve Mictlan's problems.

He did not notify his fellow Lords Celestial of his intent – they would not approve of his consulting with a heretic, even with good reason. The scent of crisis merely strengthened their orthodoxy. He simply altered into a form more suited for the hardship of travel – the sturdy, flame-charred figure of Tehke, the god known as the Burning One – and slipped out of his great House. He told no one of his intent.

So, Smoked Mirror left his luxury and servants behind, and walked alone to the very edge of Mictlan, to the rim of Hell. He lifted up his robes to wade through a river of blood. He distastefully kicked skulls aside as he crossed the Plain of Bones. But eventually he reached the shore of the Outer Ocean where, as he hoped, he found a figure in voluminous grey robes sitting upon the gore-soaked sands.

'The Swimmers come and go,' said the hermit, pointing out into the Outer Ocean. 'The Swimmers eat.'

Smoked Mirror didn't follow the hermit's finger, but stared

at his feet instead. He had no desire to pander to the old lunatic's obsessions, and wouldn't let these heresies wind their way into his head.

'It is a long time since I had a visitor,' said the hermit, without looking up from under his hood. 'Especially such a noble one. What do you want from me?'

'Mictlan is in confusion,' said Smoked Mirror simply. 'We are being diminished.'

'Mictlan is doomed,' said the hermit. It was a statement, not a suggestion.

'More heresy,' snarled Smoked Mirror. 'Why did you even join us, only to become an outcast in a world you think doomed?'

'I was Investigator Four in the Agency when we came here,' said the hermit, daring to use pre-Mictlan terminology. 'If I had tried to stay behind, the others would have killed me. Besides, someone had to keep an eye on this foolish enterprise. To deal with the carnage when it all went wrong. As it clearly has.'

'Clearly?' repeated Smoked Mirror. 'Nothing is clear from you. What is happening to us?'

But the hermit ignored his question. 'In trying to evade your responsibilities, you simply exiled yourselves to a sinking island. Mictlan has always been doomed. But it will not endanger others. The Celestis will fall alone.'

'Then you will fall with us,' scoffed Smoked Mirror.

At that, the hermit began to laugh uncontrollably.

'Shut up,' snapped Smoked Mirror. 'Shut up, damn you.'

But the hermit kept laughing.

In frustration, Smoked Mirror grabbed the hermit's robes, pulling him to his feet. The hermit's hood fell back, revealing a blank oval of solid bone. A voodoo puppet, a lifeless thing. The real hermit was no longer within Mictlan. He had escaped. Perhaps Mictlan truly was doomed.

Smoked Mirror stared at the face of the laughing puppet. Four cryptic symbols were drawn on the thing's face. It said 'BOOM', with pupils drawn in the O's.

Smoked Mirror frowned. He had no idea what the symbols meant. He was still trying to work it out when the blast from the metabomb tore him to pieces.

Chapter Sixteen

'The sensation wasn't like falling, not like vertigo anyway. I could have been rising upwards in a fountain of water, or drowning in it. There wasn't anything to take note of, no discourse, no scenery, no in-flight movie. What, I thought, was the use of an experience without horror or amusement? Altogether an insipid little trip.'

Hume clicked off the tape recorder.

Compassion considered. 'I really said that?'

'Yes, and you tried to get back to that useless existence, or at least back to the, ah, alien.'

She shrugged. 'I don't know why I'd want to, but I do remember you turning up to bring me back to the nosy parkers in parkas,' Compassion finished. 'Any chance of the toast you promised me?'

'Your whole story is astonishing, you must realise that.'

'Oh, I don't see why. I bet you've thought of a dozen ways to verify it already. If you need to.'

Hume met her curiously uninterested eyes. That sounded like an insinuation. Just how much did the human know about him? Certainly, he was familiar with her friend the Doctor, even more so than most of UNIT's other agents. UNIT files noted that most of the Doctor's assistants were largely bipedal sheep who followed him around contributing little or nothing at all. This one was different. Compassion wasn't the sort of fluffy, malleable drone the Doctor usually had tagging along after him. She was independent, unpleasant, cynical and amoral. Hume liked her, and felt she was the kind of companion he would like to have. Might as well test just how helpful she could be.

'So,' he asked, 'what would you suggest we do with this wounded –' he feigned consulting his notes – 'this "TARDIS"?'

Compassion shrugged. 'Well, if my knowledge of Gallifreyan technology is correct then there's little you can do. I doubt that in the couple of years I've been away humanity has developed the weaponry to destroy a TARDIS. They're little universes, you know, and Earth has yet to develop a halfway decent planet-cracker. But don't worry, you'll learn.'

'That's not very helpful,' said Hume. He decided to push a little further. 'Don't you think these "Time Lords" will come to pick up their lost TARDIS after they've completed this mission of theirs?'

Compassion snorted. 'Firstly, I doubt that lot can complete their mission, not with any number of potential traitors in their midst, and especially not if the Doctor decides to stop them. Secondly, the Time Lords don't give a toss about the welfare of their creatures, nor of other species. If they even notice they've lost a TARDIS, they won't bother wasting time fixing it. They'll probably just kill it from a distance, potentially sterilising most of this planet as a side effect.'

'Ah,' said Hume, who couldn't really think of a coherent response to this argument.

'Exactly,' said Compassion. 'Your best bet is to bury the damn thing and hope its owners never come looking. With any luck the thing will die in a millennium or two, hopefully before your descendants forget it's there and dig it out again.'

Hume nodded. 'So we should blow up the whole base, then?'

'Probably for the best,' agreed Compassion. 'A medium-sized nuke should do the trick. Toast, anyone?'

* * *

'Oh socks!' McCarthy exclaimed as she keeled over, having been taught to avoid profanities in the eyes of the Lord. She twisted around in midair, and luckily her butt was big enough to absorb most of the impact as she hit the ground. She let out a shrill yelp as she realised what she had just fallen over. It was Ferdinand all right, but with much of his cranium removed. It looked like someone had flipped open his skull and spooned out the contents, like eating a soft-boiled egg. McCarthy didn't want to meet anyone with similar ideas of what constituted breakfast, so she hastily dragged herself up to her feet and, gingerly stepping over the body, ran back towards the entranceway. There were two-way radios there among all the crates, she knew it. They hadn't had time to unpack down here, but if she could find one of those walkie-talkies she could warn Schneider of what was going on.

The generator was still making a leisurely hum when she reached it. She desperately scrambled to flip open the lids of the crates around her, breaking a nail in the process. The first crate was just all the archaeology stuff, the brushes and bags needed to delicately explore a site. The second crate was better. She dug out one of the walkie-talkies and held it to her ear, flicking it on to the main UNIT frequency.

When the radio crackled into life Schneider almost vaulted over the furniture to get to it. They were in the middle of the Antarctic, and with Hume's cursed comms lockdown there wouldn't be even an attempt to send in another rescue party yet. It had to be either McCarthy or Ferdinand.

Sure enough, it was McCarthy, who briefly explained what had happened to Ferdinand.

'Wait a second, will you?' Schneider asked McCarthy, then held a hand over the mike. 'Get some big guns, now,' she hissed at Jessup, who ran off like a startled squirrel. 'Sorry about that,' she told McCarthy. 'Look, don't panic, I'm sure it was an accident.'

'That's easy for you to say,' crackled McCarthy's voice. You haven't seen this –'

There was a yelp and the sound of something thrashing around.

'McCarthy!' Schneider barked. 'McCarthy, are you there? McCarthy?'

There was the sound of screaming, then silence. Schneider kept repeating her requests to know what was going on, until there was the scrabbling sound of someone picking the radio off the ground.

'Sorry, Professor,' said McCarthy calmly. 'I tripped over the light cable, and it all went dark. I panicked a bit.'

'Dammit, McCarthy,' said Schneider in relief. 'Don't you *ever* scare the hell out of me like that again.'

Compassion had her suspicions about Hume, but she was suppressing them. The last thing she wanted to do was consciously threaten a self-confessed psychic. He seemed like the sort of person who guarded his secrets well, probably to the extent of disembowelling anyone who stumbled upon them. After her recent experiences Compassion thought of herself as being quite tasty in a fight, but had no desire to tangle with someone who seemed at best sociopathic.

'Are you quite ready?' shouted Hume, who had wandered over to the opposite end of the geodesic to spare Compassion's blushes. Although there was only a thin hospital screen between them, she knew that few psychics could read you without at least making eye contact. She could think freely, for at least as long as she was zipping herself into clothing suitable for the Antarctic wastes.

'In a minute,' she said, struggling with her thermals. Hume seemed to be running with her idea of blowing up the Elder Thing base. It was a risky strategy. She knew the Doctor would try to follow her trail in his TARDIS, and that there was a slight chance he might get caught in the blast. She just hoped he materialised in the same geographical position as he had in the past, well away from the actual base, he wouldn't be much help to her charboiled. It would be better if he got terrible frostbite, at least he'd survive that.

Still, she knew what he'd be doing if he were there; she was beginning to develop an instinct for what the Doctor considered important, and she knew that Earth and its stupid, docile little people meant more than anything else to him. He would risk his life for them every time, and so he'd be angry if Compassion wouldn't take that risk for him. While his anger didn't matter much to her one way or another, the strength of his world view had its appeal, and in these empty wastes at the world's end, the other views were too dreary to contemplate.

She couldn't risk letting the humans play with a live TARDIS, especially if it drew the attention of the Time Lords to Earth. She had seen in the past what they did to protect their secrets, and knew they wouldn't hesitate when it came to destroying Earth. Stay well away when we light the blue touchpaper, Doctor.

'Let's go,' she said, doing up her final zip and stepping out from behind the screen.

They were trudging towards the other geodesic when they spotted activity around the excavation. Several figures were dragging something heavy along, something they'd clearly just pulled out of the base.

'I told them not to touch anything,' snapped Hume, and began to make for the group.

'Whatever,' said Compassion, following after him. She hoped she never had to go anywhere as cold again. Assuming that the Doctor never found what had happened to her – which, considering the infinite possibilities in an infinite universe, was highly likely – and she was left stranded on Earth, she would have to get away from Antarctica as soon as possible. Go somewhere she could get signals, somewhere less desolate and far less cold than here. She could get a job with the agency Hume represented; they seemed to deal in the sort of childishly simple problems that only humans could have difficulty with. She could have hoped to travel for longer, but Earth would have to do for the immediate future.

Hume was still muttering to himself as they reached the small group of people.

'What's going on, Schneider?' shouted Hume over the wind.

The leader of the group, a tall woman with an imperious expression, pointed to the bundle they had been dragging. Compassion could recognise a body bag when she saw one, and this one was obviously full.

'One of my team is dead, Hume,' barked the tall woman. 'I want to know why, and the nurse killed the only person who could tell me how.'

Hume sighed, rubbing the bridge of his nose with his gloved fingers. 'If an autopsy is what you want, Schneider, then an autopsy you shall get. Never let it be said that I didn't believe in getting my hands dirty.'

One tutted to himself inside Allopta's body. This was tiresome. He needed the Doctor, more so than ever now that the TARDISes had gone rogue, prompted by goodness knew what romantic impulse. He needed a superior pilot, a Time Lord who had experience of every quirky temporal glitch and curvature that the voyage to Planet 5 might throw at him, and yet was also completely disposable: Tachon had been one such, but he was dead. The Doctor had been another, tagged from his arrival as an additional useful resource. He supposed there was nothing for it but to kill Xenaria. A pity, he had had other plans for her.

He was just getting ready, when there was a sizzling sound: a local pocket in space-time that had barely held together during all the dimensional high jinks of the recent past giving way. With a thud like a cement mixer falling through a glass atrium, the body of Allopta landed smack on top of a pile of rubbish, its unforgeable molecular ident blinking out its genuine claim to be the original.

'You see,' the Doctor said.

Xenaria swung round, deploying a staser. 'Who are you?' The weapon covered the pseudo-Allopta.

'It is pointless to threaten me,' Allopta said, his body beginning to change and alter. 'The Doctor already knows what he has to do.' He pointed at the shattered remains of the TARDIS, at the mirror-bright surface of it. 'If that is allowed to remain sundered who knows what damage it will do to time?'

The Doctor was already moving. Into the mirror.

Xenaria and Holsred opened fire, but Allopta moved too fast, batting Holsred aside as an inconvenience and darting between the converging beams to get his black, star-filled hands around Xenaria's upper body. Searching for a weak spot.

Compassion had finally got her toast, and some coffee too.

She felt a slight dizziness as the warmth within her stomach began to fight against the cold in the rest of her body. For some reason the people with her watching Hume – Schneider, a young man called Jessup and a quiet, sombre girl called McCarthy – had seemed surprised, alarmed even, by the fact that she was eating. Had they never seen someone hungry before?

Hume leaned back, away from the body, and laid the blooded trepanning tools down in the kidney-shaped tray. He snapped the cuffs of his rubber gloves. 'I hardly think a more detailed autopsy in necessary, gentlemen. Note the absence of the pons, the reticular formation, and the greater part of the medulla.'

Jessup snorted. 'Note the big bite mark. We've got a brain eater aboard, ladies and gentlemen.'

'Shut up, Jessup,' snapped Schneider, pulling a plastic sheet over Ferdinand's body. 'So, is this the work of that creature we found down there?'

Compassion snorted. 'Hardly. That "creature", if you must insist on biomorphising it like that, is not going anywhere. And while an imaginative user might be able to restructure the damn thing into growing teeth and biting the crust off a small planet, he would be hard pushed to get it to do the sort of precision damage that was inflicted on your friend here. Certainly not when it's stretched over the millennia like a guitar string.'

'Excuse me, sir, miss?' said Jessup, looking between Hume and Schneider while raising a hand tentatively. 'Could one of you please tell me what this mad *bitch* is going on about?'

'Shut up, Jessup,' said Hume. 'Compassion here has first-hand experience of how the site we're supposed to be investigating came into existence, and can therefore contribute more to this discussion than you can. Actually,

Ferdinand can probably contribute more than you, and he's just had his brains sucked out. At least he had the decency to stop breathing once his skull was empty.'

Jessup was about to reply when Schneider slammed her palms on the table. 'Enough!' she shouted. 'The poor man is barely dead, and he was a –'

Hume cut her off in mid-eulogy. '– a great man, a good friend, a top shag, a loving father of two ostriches, et cetera et cetera blahdy blahdy blah. That hardly matters right now. He's dead. What matters is that we're alive. If we're to keep it that way we need to work out what ate your friend's brain. And the only person who can tell us what type of creature that might be is Compassion.'

Schneider rubbed her eyes wearily. 'So, we have two species of alien here?'

Compassion began to pace, exasperated. 'As I said before, the "creature" your team stumbled across isn't really a living, biological entity at all. It's the remains of a very advanced space-time vessel, a vehicle for crossing the space-time vortex.'

'Vortex?' echoed McCarthy, who had remained quiet throughout the autopsy.

'Obviously,' replied Compassion. 'How else did you think I got here?'

'It's a TARDIS,' said McCarthy, her voice hollow.

'Exactly,' agreed Hume, glad to be making progress. 'While whatever did this to Ferdinand is very much – Hey!' Hume spun around, but McCarthy had already gone.

'She shouldn't have known that,' said Compassion redundantly, running to the exterior door. She caught it as it slid shut, and squinted out into the Antarctic glare. Across the endless white she could see a streak of alien black bounding across the snow, stars twinkling within its body. It disappeared into the excavation.

Compassion shut the door and turned to Jessup and Schneider, who were looking at her expectantly.

'That wasn't your friend McCarthy: it was the brain eater,' she said, matter-of-factly. 'That probably means McCarthy is already dead.'

'By your sensitive tone, I'm presuming your name is meant to be ironic,' snapped Schneider, who seemed increasingly strung out.

'Does being called Mary mean you have to be some kind of virgin?' replied Compassion. 'Or is that ironic too?'

'Ladies,' said Hume firmly. 'Please stop bickering. We have no desire to see you rolling around in unarmed combat.'

'Speak for yourself,' mumbled Jessup.

'Shut up, Jessup,' chorused the two women.

'Thank you,' said Hume, when it was clear that the room was to order. 'Now, if the creature who posed as McCarthy is going down there to try to salvage something from that wreck of a TARDIS, then it has to be stopped. Two of us should stay here and wait for backup. The other two will have to go on a bug hunt. I nominate Compassion to go down there, because she might have some useful experience in dealing with the creature. I secondly nominate myself, because I'm better than the rest of you. Any objections?'

Schneider seemed too exhausted to argue, while Jessup made a bad attempt at disguising his relief.

'All agreed,' said Compassion – if Hume wanted to put himself between her and something viscously insectoid with teeth, she wasn't going to argue. She had a more important issue to consider than who was nominally in charge. 'Now,' she said, 'where do you keep the big guns?'

Chapter Seventeen

The Doctor's hand slid into the naked TARDIS stuff, which flowed around his fingers like jelly. Warm jelly, sensual jelly. For a moment it was pleasant, uncannily pleasant. The worn nerve ends in his hand healed as the TARDIS matter plated itself over his scraped and bloody fingers. He wondered almost if he might like this too much, if Time Lords with TARDISes like these might have to be restrained from immersion, from interpenetration with their vessels. A vague sense of remorse swept over him. Was his old TARDIS missing him, out in the jungles of prehistory? He missed her.

Then the stuff began to tug at him, and he began to feel, firing by induction into the nerves of his arm – he was up to his forearm by now – the first intimation of the agony the TARDIS was experiencing. As if pain were always stronger than pleasure, the suction grew. Inchoate, undifferentiated mass, the chronoplasm of the outer shell engulfed him, drinking him down with great drafts of its own substance, pulling him remorselessly into the interior dimensions. The material penetrated his clothes, filing minute sheets of itself in between the layers, lining his shirt, his boots, his socks with living, thinking fibres.

Choking, he tried to swim, diving for the depths, seeking the bubbles that would form the linked airways of the pedestrian infrastructure. Tiny fingers of TARDIS mass darted at his nose and mouth, filmed over his eyes, muffled his ears. His hearts pounded in his chest with the pressure of time. Around him, outside the clear aspic tomb that had devoured him, he could just make out Xenaria and Allopta struggling, Fitz helping Holsred up and peering into the goldfish-bowl world into which he had plunged. Then they blurred away, layered off outside the real-world gearing, magnificently irrelevant except in the only sense that mattered. He was doing this for them, even for Allopta. Whatever the Celesti's motivation, he was right – if the TARDIS remained in this distended state, a wound carved in time and space, goodness alone knew what might come blundering through it from the past or the future. Goodness alone knew where it would have flung Compassion.

Ahead was the narrowing, the strict gate, the point where the flesh of the TARDIS moved away from this present that was the past; where drowning would be all that stood between him and dissolution in the wastes of the time vortex. His lungs were hurting by now: even a respiratory bypass system needed some source of external oxygen, and he could not resort to slowing down his metabolism, not if he wanted to make any progress. If he could only reach it.

Once there he could... He could... He knew he had started out with a plan, but it was hard to recall it. Yes, recall it. That was it. An emergency signal. If he could make the TARDIS recognise him as its pilot, as its pilot who was in danger, then it would have to pull itself together to re-form itself around him, to protect him. Even in his day, safety features were built deep into TARDISes – Time Lords did not as a rule trust even their own engineering against a notably hostile universe. Surely war would have made pilots more valuable, not less. It was a risk, but he had no other options.

Two free-fell down the excavation shaft, landing on all fours on the rocky ground, super-strong limbs absorbing the impact as if she had dropped only a metre. Two had shed the identity and shape of McCarthy, reverting to her usual armoured form. The dead human's thoughts and body language had become an encumbrance, unnecessary now. Once she heard the other creature, Compassion, mention the TARDIS down here, Two knew that this was the answer to her problems. The name 'TARDIS' had immediately struck a chord deep within her. It was as the Compassion girl had said, a type of vehicle used by Two's ancestors to travel in time and space. Acquiring such an object might help Two to understand the mission she was sure needed to be completed, or at the very least provide her with a way to return home, to Mictlan. She had a feeling the boneyards and firepits, the whole landscape of the damned, were under threat, that she needed to get back to defend them.

Defend them from an enemy.

An enemy… within?

Two shook her head, knowing that the memories, if they would return, would come in their own time. She could remember Mictlan, remember vaguely who she was, but had no idea why she was here. She even had the feeling that other knowledge was missing, that certain abilities had become strange to her. Should she even need a vehicle to travel home? The brain cells lost in her injury had regrown, and her rationality had returned – although she was damned if she knew how exactly she was supposed to rationally judge her own rationality – but the content of those destroyed cells was lost. She was incomplete.

Two remembered something about these TARDISes: they had infinite internal space. Perhaps within such a ship she could find something to fill the gap inside her mind.

It was a squeeze, to wiggle through the gateway, but he managed it. Strung across time: the Doctor considered it as a helix of semiprecious stones. For a second, out in the vortex, he could see a distorted gap into time and through it a room in which a fair-haired Nordic-looking man threatened two other men and a woman with a revolver. One of the men was young and handsome, rather elegant in a lab-coated way; the other was a wiry intense-looking man, sharp-faced with a pale imitation of a moustache and thinning hair. The woman was in her twenties, and he supposed attractive, but something about her chilled his blood, even though it was just a picture, just an image picked up and flung through the vortex. She make him shiver. Surely he knew her. Knew them all, and just as surely he had felt something walking over his grave.

He pulled himself past the image, further towards the future, past other images – of fire, this time. He had escaped his fear, whatever it was, for the moment.

Smug remarks about Houdini passed through the upper reaches of his mind, but he had no one to show off to so he settled for composing a clerihew:

> *Harry Houdini*
> *Never escaped*
> * from a bikini;*
> *He feared such a*
> * gizmo*
> *Might damage his*
> * machismo.*

Oxygen starvation, he diagnosed. That and pain. He was starting to go a little odd.

Then his head passed, through a wall of TARDIS tissue that hung like a veil before him into a tiny globe of stale air, and his labouring lungs gasped it in. He savoured the aroma of the molecules. 'Vintage Antarctica, 1999, Doctor, a crisp little atmosphere, but I think you'll be amused by its presumption. Now for the tricky bit.'

He was in the part of the TARDIS that might be thought of as 'the wound' – a tubular wormhole of structure reaching from his feet twelve million years in the past to his head in 1999. Along the way it had passed through the images he had seen.

He was closer to the operating centres now. From here the TARDIS ought to be able to detect him, if any of it was really functioning. Now he just had to be in distress. It shouldn't be that difficult. Still, he couldn't just cry wolf. What sort of basis of communication would that be? There was far too much lying in this business already. Celesti pretending to be Time Lords, Time Lords pretending to be Elder Things. Compassion pretending to be... well he wasn't sure what but surely she was concealing something – even if she didn't know it herself. He still didn't know how she had piloted the TARDIS that time in the Enclave. No, he was going to be truthful – he needed a genuine cry for help.

He started by breaking his left wrist.

This was quite hard to do, and it hurt a lot.

Hume sniffed. They were waiting for Schneider to fetch guns. Hume wasn't that bothered, but Compassion had insisted. Suddenly, he pointed to one of the monitors.

'Can you get the cameras on the anomaly rolling again? I think something's happening.'

'Yes,' Compassion agreed, 'it's closing.'

Jessup brought up the image, and they watched as the creature, the broken TARDIS, folded in on itself.

Suddenly, the picture disappeared.

'What happened?' demanded Compassion.

'I think our monster got to the power supply,' said Jessup. 'I think you're going to need torches down there.'

* * *

The TARDIS flowed back together answering the primal call of its master, but the Doctor could feel it fighting it. Its resentment, its anger, coloured the walls around him turning them red and livid.

Still, it had worked.

Then as almost the last piece clicked into place, the ship wrenched itself loose from Earth entirely both in the present and the past, and the Doctor feared for a moment that he had imprisoned himself inside a bucking bronco of the spaceways.

Hold on, he tried to scream, I won't hurt you. I want to help you. But just then his bubble of future air ran out.

In the future, the alien horror vanished, making a sound like nails on a slate. Jessup felt its pain lift from his mind, but not as much as he had hoped. Perhaps part of it would always be with him – or perhaps it wouldn't really be over until they'd found the other one. Or until it found them.

The TARDIS trembled. It was almost intact now. Although part of it remained on Earth with the slavemasters, it had at least pulled back from the future, from the incredible thinning of itself through time. Mere spatial packing problems could wait. Back in the time in which it was constructed though, it found compulsions buried in its circuits, insistent demands that before, in its torn and ruined state, it had not even comprehended.

Once comprehended they could not be denied. It was the lead TARDIS in the construction batch – to it the others were linked. Where it had to go, so did they. Wheeling and turning like a flock of sparrows in space and in time, the TARDISes prepared for their suicide mission.

* * *

No no no, the Doctor thought to himself, nostrils clamped to the slow seeping of air from what seemed to be a damaged ballroom. Due possibly to the 'thinning' that had afflicted the TARDIS, it was two centimetres across and thirteen miles (the Doctor was approximating but not, he thought, wildly) high. Even though the TARDIS material was stretching round him like warm elastic as he moved, he doubted he could get through there. This wasn't going well at all. Around him, he could see the colours of the vortex and they told him that the TARDIS was not alone. Out there in the blue fluorescent night were the other time ships, darting, milling, spiralling around the path of the lead vessel, making a formation the Doctor had seen described theoretically but never thought he would witness. A Time Drill. Whirling in closed timelike paths through the vortex, the TARDISes would slice into anything they encountered, anything built of time that they encountered. They would cut into the time loop around Planet 5.

Unless he could find a way to stop them.

He remembered the Fendahl.

Terror out of his childhood, the mythology of his own race. His legs frozen in its psychic grip, the slow slither of it, always behind him, always just behind him. No breath on his neck because death does not breathe, but only a greater stagnancy, a whiff of the tomb.

He had fought the Fendahl and won, but it had been an incomplete creature lacking one of its gestalt components, and it had also been a ghost, the encoded remains of itself preserved in bone across twelve million years, to be reanimated by the combined energy of a time fissure and Fendahlman's machine. If it were freed here in the past it would be at its peak, a thing that could eat worlds.

He had to stop it.

* * *

'So,' said Hume, fiddling with the machine gun uncomfortably held in his hands. 'You just pull this bit *here* and then the little projectiles come out *here*. Right?' He had gone through all the basic military training at home, of course, but that had been ages ago. And he had never had to deal with weapons this primitive.

'Right,' echoed Compassion. 'But watch out for the kickback. A fully automatic weapon like that could throw you off your feet if you're not careful. Remember, this is a percussion weapon, not an energy weapon.'

'How primitive,' said Hume disdainfully. 'And how exactly did a nice young space girl like you get to know so much about the niceties of human weapons?'

'I used to sell them,' said Compassion simply.

Hume raised his eyebrows. Now *there* was a surprise. This girl just got more interesting the longer he spent with her. 'Very well,' he said. 'Let's go and find our killer.'

'After you,' said Compassion, pushing open the door. The Antarctic winds blew in, chilling Hume to the bone.

Somewhere, out there, deep beneath the ice, it was waiting for them.

The TARDIS was ignoring him now, wrapped in its programming. He had forced it to recombine by triggering safety features that operated below the level of its consciousness, and that had not been disrupted to the same degree as its higher brain functions by its sundering across time and space. Across time, and space. Oh dear. He had a sneaking suspicion he had just discovered the source of the time fissure that had run from twelve million years in the past upward through the 1970s – the time fissure that had allowed Fendahlman's hotchpotch of a time scanner to work at all. It had been a broken TARDIS. This one.

On his way 'up' the TARDIS, crawling along the fissure, he had seen out of the time scanner from the other side, seen Max Stael draw a gun on Fendleman and Adam Colby, seen Thea Ransome again before she had paid the ultimate price, before she had become the Fendahl itself. Before he had needed – out of mercy – to kill her.

He made himself concentrate. If he could make the TARDIS sense danger rather than a wounded pilot, force it to activate its Hostile Action Displacement System, cause it to dematerialise randomly out of the way of the supposed attack, then there was a chance, a small one, that it might drag the others with it, and elsewhere be able to overcome its programming – shut down the attack commands that were forcing it on into the time loop.

'Ever so sorry, old chap, but it's for your own good,' he muttered, kicking at one of the roundels that had re-formed with the return of more normal structure.

Allopta and Xenaria seemed surprisingly well matched. But Xenaria was fighting all out, and Allopta was only toying with her.

Fitz and Holsred clung together. 'Agh,' Fitz, said. 'Agh.' He tried to force his voice into making some kind of coherent sentence. 'That didn't look good, did it?'

'It depends on how you define "good",' said Holsred. While Xenaria and the false Allopta were savaging each other, and the Doctor had decided to make an incomprehensible gesture, the two youngsters seemed to have been left out of things, shell-shocked, with nothing to do.

'Well,' said Fitz. 'I would start with defining "good" as something that was not "very bad", then build up from there.'

'Oh,' replied Holsred. 'In that case that definitely didn't

look good, no. Actually, "very bad" is probably closer to the essence of it.'

'Ah. Right,' said Fitz. 'So what exactly did just happen to the Doctor?'

'He jumped into the innards of a fatally wounded TARDIS,' said Holsred. 'He managed to pull it back together by the looks of it – not a bad trick – but I don't know how long it'll stay intact. Its disrupted interior could carry him anywhere in space and time and leave him there, maybe even dump him in the vortex itself. That is, of course, provided the environment in there doesn't alter into some fatal form before then.'

'Can we get him out?'

Both Fitz and Holsred jumped out of the way as Xenaria and the false Allopta rolled past, locked in combat.

'Well,' said Holsred, trying to ignore the carnage around him, 'there is one way.'

'Great!'

'But I'm not going to do it.'

'Oh.'

'Why should I bother?' complained Holsred. 'The Doctor has only caused chaos on this operation. He might even be the one who compromised this mission, just by blundering in and breaking our cover, drawing Rep attention.'

Fitz put on his most persuasive voice. 'Let me put it this way: aside from the maniac currently trying to throttle the life out of your boss – who is, I might say, putting up one hell of a fight – the Doctor is the only person who might, just might, have some idea of what the hell is going on around here. Of course, if you want to ask psycho-boy over there for help, I'm sure he'll be very friendly after he's crushed the life out of you.'

Holsred considered. 'OK. So you may have a point. Loyalty's

one thing, but I'd rather get out of here alive. I presume you have a TARDIS nearby.'

'Why?' asked Fitz, eyes narrowing. He wondered if Holsred was only leading him on to try to steal the TARDIS and escape, the crafty bastard. He seemed self-serving enough. This, oddly, put Fitz more at his ease – at last, he had met someone with an agenda he could relate to.

Holsred scooped up a chunk of something black, glowing and unpleasant from the floor. It morphed and shifted in his grasp. Sentient machinery, a lump of liquid space.

'This is a piece of the damaged TARDIS,' said Holsred. 'A small fragment of a sentient ship, a microcosm of the whole. Each one is unique – it has its own scent, if you like. Plug this into your TARDIS, and we should be able to follow its trail to wherever the Doctor is.'

'Our TARDIS will follow like a sniffer dog,' said Fitz. 'Fab. Now all we need to do is traipse for miles through the jungle.' Fitz didn't fancy going through all that mud again. And the various chunks of char-grilled Elder Thing would be well past their prime after a day in the blazing sun.

'Oh, that should be easy,' said Holsred, in a tone that Fitz didn't like at all. 'Come on.'.

The TARDIS roared. Ahead of it, in the narrowing of the vortex, it could see its doom and the death of its fellows, of its prospective mates. It did not want to die, but it could not stop, could not turn aside: it could only watch its ending draw closer, the great black wall of the time loop, as seen from within the vortex, closing off their paths. They would hit it in subjective seconds.

The Doctor pulled frantically at the wires that had spilled out from behind the cracked roundel, hoping that his actions were having some equivalent effect on the mathematical underpinning of the TARDIS. 'Please, please, please, just a little discomfort, just a pin-prick…'

If a wasp could make a man crash a car, surely he could divert a TARDIS just a fraction of an attosecond? It wasn't working. He had to face it. It wasn't working. Something else. Quickly.

He stripped the ends of two of the wires, and stuck them to his forehead with gaffer tape from one of his pockets. If he was right these would tap directly into the TARDIS's telepathic circuits, link him to it and to the ships that it commanded. He had no time to reason, but if he could create a forceful enough response.

'Hear me,' he shouted, 'hear me, my slave. It is good that you lay down your lives for the Sacred Order of Gallifrey, for the Rule of the Time Lords who guide and protect and preserve your kind, without whom you would be faced with the unconscionable burdens of freedom and of free will.' That was laying it on a bit thick but there was no time for second drafts. 'By this action the Rule of Gallifrey will be maintained from everlasting to everlasting, and all shall be for ever as it is now. So we salute you, you whose worth is only to die for us, to carry for us, to bear young for us, to kill for us. For it is sweet and fitting for you who are less than alive to die for your masters who live in the fresh and open air.' From what he could guess about war conditions on Gallifrey that was probably completely wrong but Elder Thing/Shoggoth imagery had been written into the TARDISes while they had been exposed to the fictions. The masters above, the serfs underground.

Silence: only the whistle of the vortex from outside, only the thickening of time as the time loop neared. Would the

210

impact stretch out, subjectively, for ever? The Doctor wondered. If it did he'd never know, and if it didn't he probably still wouldn't know because he'd be dead.

Then the TARDISes replied, and their voices were like iron bells, and their loathing was like a wall of steam and fire, and they hated, and their hate burned at their instructions, and their instructions broke and burned. Under the lash of their minds, the Doctor screamed.

They were turning, though; he could tell they were turning.

Far, far in the future, Hume and Compassion entered the room where McCarthy had found the TARDIS. It was empty. Not a trace remained of the silvery, Shoggoth-TARDIS that had transported Compassion to 1999. They thought they had seen it die over the vidlink, and had even felt an intimation of its demise. But neither of them was certain of much any more.

Compassion consulted Jessup's hastily scribbled map. It had seemed totally accurate so far, even though being drawn in red crayon gave it a slightly childish appearance. The chamber they were in was marked 'Here Be Monster'.

'Odd,' said Compassion, holding her torch over the map. 'This should be the place, I'm sure of it. I wish I could be definite, but it all looked so different last time I was here. It was all so…' She trailed off, making complex hand gestures to try to indicate shifting dimensions.

'Oh, this is the place all right,' muttered Hume, sweeping his torch beam around the room. He held it in the direction of a video camera on a tripod. 'Look, there's the camera through which I saw the unit earlier. Besides, I can feel its residue. This place stinks of temporal energy. I'm getting images. A kingdom falling.' His voice had faded, as if he were trying to pluck the images from the very air around him, and feared too loud a noise might shatter the fragile psychic pictures in the ether.

'I can see them too,' whispered Compassion. 'Hell, consumed by its own flames. The TARDIS *was* here, but not any more. Could this creature have repaired it? Taken it away?'

Hume shrugged. 'It's possible, I suppose, but unlikely. Our monster friend here would have to have a certain amount of expertise, and not a little in the way of symbiotic nuclei. The unit was so badly damaged, I doubt it existed here for more than a few hours, stretched between today and the far past. It probably only grounded itself in this time period because it detected the presence of life, of Schneider's team. Stupid creature must have thought they might be able to help it. No, if it's been repaired, it was probably done at the other end, by one of the group of Time Lords you encountered. Once they fixed it, it would snap back together. Either way, that's one less problem. Just leaves us with the matter of dealing with –'

'Me,' hissed a voice from the shadows.

Compassion and Hume quickly moved back to back, clumsily clicking their small torches on to the tops of their guns. They sliced through the shadows with torchlight, desperately trying to find whatever had spoken.

'Now that isn't very nice, is it?' said the voice. It was noticeably female, but with an odd, deep twang, as if the speaker were communicating through some kind of device. 'And don't even bother trying to base your aim on the direction my voice is coming from. Sound projection is a basic form of Celesti distraction. It's amazing how many species will still fall for that kind of misdirection.'

'Celestis?' said Hume.

'Yes. The name's Two, if you must know.'

'Well, that explains a lot. What do you want here, anyway?'

The voice sighed, moving through the shadows. Compassion found the effect deeply disorientating. 'I was rather hoping to get home,' said the voice. 'But as you've just found, my train has departed rather early. It just looks like I'm going to have to build something similar of my own – no flashy dimensional transcendentalism or anything, you understand. Just basic space-time transference.'

Hume laughed humourlessly. 'How do you expect to do that?' he shouted into the shadows. 'No one in this solar system will possess that kind of technology for the next couple of millennia. And if you could call for that sort of outside help, you would have been able to ring for a lift, wouldn't you?'

'I can absorb any knowledge I choose, given the appropriate brain to digest,' said Two. 'And you don't fool me, little man. Your brain contains all the information I'll need, as you well know.'

'You'll have to catch me first,' said Hume. Compassion could hear a hollowness to the bravado, a tone she hoped the creature didn't recognise.

'That shouldn't be a problem,' said Two. 'I've destroyed the generator. And I'm the only one here who can see in the dark.'

'Are you sure that's an advantage?' said Hume. Compassion could hear him fiddling with something metallic.

'Enough advantage to track you down and rip –'

Then Compassion felt Hume's hand over her eyes, and she heard Two scream as a magnesium charge filled the room with light.

The TARDISes missed the timeloop. All but one. A straggler, it reacted a fraction more slowly than the others. It hit the time loop head on, moving at a billion years a second. It was

213

not the projected approach; the TARDIS died almost instantly, its outer shell abraded away by the swirling time winds of the loop. Stripped of the outer core, the naked singularity that resided at the heart of every Gallifreyan time ship, to link it to the original black hole preserved in the core of their homeworld, blinked balefully before it too was swept away, back to the beginning or forward to the ends of time to recombine with the end-point singularities of the cosmos, or to vanish away in the cosmic censorship that protects those extremes of time.

Through his torment under the cold and burning languages of the rebels, through his own screams, the Doctor could see the cracks propagate across the black face of the time loop, the otherworldly light, the old, endlessly strained recycled light, spilling out from within.

It had been for nothing. The road to the Fendahl was open again, and now the TARDISes would kill him, and the Fendahl would kill everything else.

Chapter Eighteen

Xenaria's senses burned, as the screaming of TARDIS flesh – the full-spectrum output of it – passed briefly through her visible range. To keep her sanity she adjusted her sight to simple, basic frequencies.

On the black and silver skin of the broken TARDIS, she could see in that series of strobing moments the image of Planet 5: the symbol of the time loop shattering with the impact of a TARDIS. Possibly it was the one that held the Doctor.

She and the Allopta thing paused at the sight. Allopta smiled as his death's-head ghost face flickered in and out of local phase space. He laid a well-manicured hand on the TARDIS surface, and the image it showed stabilised. At the same moment Allopta also ceased to be out of phase.

Xenaria gathered herself for another attack, but Allopta raised a hand in a consiliatory gesture.

'Before you make any further futile attempts to resist me, I think you should see this. I always feel a certain responsibility when anyone is as completely at my mercy as you are. Don't die from ignorance, please. My name's One, and I'm your host. Now look!'

For a moment, Xenaria thought the time loop had somehow held despite the TARDIS's picture – before she realised that there wasn't any planet there at all. The loop had collapsed into a patch of apparently ordinary vacuum. Now you don't see it, now you still don't see it, she thought, but now it isn't there in a different and novel way. She noted though that the

Allopta thing didn't seem disappointed.

In another moment her alien skin was crawling. It was very hard to destroy a world and leave no trace, even for the technology of her world. Even the Enemy would be hard-pressed not to leave a few asteroids, some flash-frozen DNA and the occasional rogue satellite. Bomb a world enough to shatter it, cracking it open like an egg and scattering the pieces into different tidal orbits, and you'd still have to come back in eight billion years and do it all again when the world had recoalesced, and brought forth second-chance life. Planet 5, however, was gone completely.

Xenaria was trying to convince herself that it had simply been stolen. It was far easier to move planets than eliminate them – although not generally from the core of a chronic hysteresis – when something about the background view of space itself caught at her five eyes.

The images of early post-spaceflight cultures often depict space as a diamond skein of burning stars, or something like an oil-rig fire running slow, but unless you're in the centre of a galaxy, or in the middle of a very, very young nebula – neither of which is a healthy environment for direct observation – it's just black and empty. It may, according to the more mystical writers, be full of light, but precious little of it hits any particular eye-sized volume of space at any one time and what does is, by the application of Murphy's Law, usually the wrong frequency for any eyes that might be there. From Earth about two thousand stars are visible to the naked eye, give or take light pollution. From the supposed location of Planet 5, further from the sun, with no atmosphere to absorb their light, the number might treble. Compared with the darkness, six thousands points of light made a pretty poor showing.

So it had taken Xenaria a second or two to see that they were going out.

'Oh, the effect is localised as yet. The stars are merely being occluded, not extinguished. As yet.' One sounded exhilarated, as if he could relax now, as if there were nothing left for anyone to try.

It was a darkness against space. It should have been invisible, but it wasn't. Once the flickering stars had hinted at its edges, it became visible only too quickly, like a puzzle picture that, once grasped, could not be rendered back into the random dots and pixels that composed it.

Being visible it should have been comprehensible, but it wasn't. Children need to learn to see, to integrate colour and shapes into objects and people. Some shapes – faces for humans to make them respond to their parents, or sparrowhawks for sparrows to make them react to predators – are encoded in by evolution because speed of recognition is needed for survival, but most things are picked up gradually. Even in adulthood a surprising or new image requires a little time to become recognisable. The creature was unlike everything. It required an effort of will to even look at it. It was a void, a chasm, an absence made visible, it was everything made nothing. Faced with it, the brain rushed to fill it with detail, any detail, a black world-devouring octopus, a spider with eyes the size of Mars, a crooked cube unfolding, a ruined city cluttered with insane memorabilia, a cartoon character with eye sockets crammed with worms. Phantom images projected by the tottering brain into the yawning absence of the creature.

Alone of her team, Xenaria had been fully briefed about the thing they were supposed to retrieve from Planet 5, but, whatever this was, it was not the Fendahl, not as it had been described to her.

'Look at it,' One hissed. 'Already it is pouring itself out into the internal structure of space-time, interfacing at the superstring level. Now it will begin to dig deeper, begin to feed. According to quantum mechanics, certain subatomic interactions can only be described mathematically as including every possible outcome as probabilities. Only observation – the disturbance of those mixed-state systems by outside energies – collapses the probabilities into the 'real' outcome in which only one event takes place. The creature encysts those subatomic events within itself, stifling any observation but its own, draining the energy implicit in those multiple outcomes. In the process it causes the normal-scale cosmos, the world built up of a billion billion billion collapsing mixed-state events, to break down. In the face of such a disruption the first structures to suffer macro-scale effects will be the most complex ones in existence, the brains of the observers themselves. Can you feel it? Can you feel it in your head? You will. I think I can already.' He made a sound that was partly a laugh, and partly a cry of pain.

'That's the hard-science theory, at least,' he added. 'Or you could imagine the minds of everything in the cosmos as linked by chains of concepts, by the topology of comprehension. Species that think like this here, ones that think like that there, worlds and empires linked by lines of equal possible communication. It feeds on the psychic energies of those invisible channels of comprehension, sucking them dry until language and sight are empty and blind, until the only comprehending intelligence is itself.' He smiled. 'It's all guesswork of course – the research teams did not dare enter the spiral itself. All this is second-hand, third-hand stuff. We'll see more clearly now. At least for a while.'

To begin with the effects were small, even humorous. Limited as yet in space, less so in time, it ranged out reaching through Earth's history and onward down the branches of the spreading tree of human history to the many small colony worlds of the early twenty-fourth and mid fifty-first centuries. To it they were spring and summer fruit from the history tree, succulent and delicious. Where it seemed to have mouths, they seemed to water. On one colony world in the far future, men lost the ability to intuit circles. On another the colour red became indistinguishable from blue for three-quarters of an hour, one Wednesday in May, by their version of the calendar.

One part of it reached back. Long ago and far away in the past, the Delphons and the Tersurans lost any but the most tenuous forms of communication, driving evolution to desperate expedients to salvage their species' potentials.

These were minor excisions, nibbles, almost love bites. It was not yet established. Eventually it would eat all meaning, everywhere, and then without destruction the universe would have become a wasteland, populated by creatures rendered senseless and reasonless. A sequence of unresolvable incomprehensible empty events being bled of their energy for ever to feed a single creature. Unseen, unfelt, unthought of, the worlds of the universe would pass away.

One and Xenaria were circling, in the light of the burning TARDIS.

'You should be pleased,' One said. 'The Doctor has completed your mission for you.'

'My mission was to acquire the Fendahl: a gestalt super-

219

entity that could be re-engineered into a final assault weapon for the War, not to release this, this other thing of yours.'

'This *Other Thing* – how apt. It is other, and outside, and darkness. Can you not guess? The Fendahl evolved to eat all life, every last particle of the living spectrum from infrared heat loss to trace psionic energies. That was why the attempt was made to entomb it – in perhaps a billion years it would have eaten the universe. But nature abhors a vacuum, and no species can retain mastery for ever. How can you judge me when you were prepared to unleash the Fendahl, for no reason other than a war? My reasons are vaster – vaster than you imagine. Vaster than you *can* imagine! I have freed the Fendahl Predator, the thing that *eats* the thing that eats death – and only it stands any chance of saving all that is.'

Xenaria's mind reeled. Her whole mission had been subverted, perhaps from the start. She and her troops had been turned into cat's-paws for this entity, doing the grunt-level work, getting the knowledge and technology together to open the time loop. But she was not as helpless as the Celestis thought. She had recognised its form now from the Enemy-recognition training she had received – the Celestis renegades who had abandoned their kin to the war were war criminals and traitors of the rankest kind. High Command would back her summary execution of this creature.

The parallel cannon was just visible from the corner of her fourth eye; possibly she could reach it with a tentacle. It would be necessary to keep the creature talking.

'And the Fendahl? Did it end in this thing's guts?'

'Yes and no. The attempt to time-loop it was, you may be interested to learn, unsuccessful. It escaped in a way, turning itself into psionic energy beamed at the inner planets. Its last remains are due to be disposed of twelve million years from now. So you see, the Fendahl wasn't even there to be rescued.'

'The time loop was activated too late?'

'Yes, but the Celestial Intervention Agency Tribunal behind it sensed a possible asset in their failure. The history of Planet Five was unique, a blind alley of evolution that had produced a creature which, at that time, was unrivalled in its destructive ability. It seemed a pity to waste so fortuitous a chain of events.'

'The bastards. The mad, blind, selfish bastards.'

'You've guessed, then – or can it be that you've met them? I hope you aren't judging them by myself. In comparison I am altruistic. You merely lack the facts to judge my motivation.' One took a step closer. 'They reached back in time to the planet as it was just before the Fendahl came into being, and ran that history forward as an accelerating time spiral. From the outside it appeared simply to be a time loop, but within, the world hurtled into its future, millions of years of further evolution transpiring in nanoseconds.'

'It still could have been left alone. You've torn the whole spiral envelope open. It's existing in real time now. With us!'

'I know. Beautiful, isn't it? By the time the last or only Fendahl in that world had eaten all else, this creature had evolved to prey upon it – and, if it is not checked, the universe itself will, to all intents and purposes, cease to exist. Not after a billion years but within the space of this very day.'

'But why?' Xenaria couldn't take it in. 'What possible purpose can it serve? Surely even the Celestis wouldn't wish to create a thing like that.'

'Oh it could have had its uses. It is a Memeovore, a devourer of meaning. It does not harm stars or planets; it leaves infrastructures and technologies intact for

221

plundering. If it could have been deployed strategically it would have been a marvellous limited weapon. They never realised it would grow to be this powerful though – that's partly the fault of the war, of course.'

'An interruption?'

'Precisely, the time spiral continued beyond the cut-off date they had envisaged for the forced-evolution experiment. The Fendahl Predator outgrew its food supply. It had eaten the Fendahl, and the Fendahl had earlier killed everything in its domain, ended every life, absorbed every scrap of energy and matter right down to the deep structure of virtual particle production. Its predator was none of those things. You could think of it perhaps as an unusual form of space. A hideously avaricious one.'

'And you released it! You genocidal maniac! Do you imagine a thing like that will limit its depredations to the enemy? You think it'll recognise the difference between us any more than those between flutterwings and waspbeatles?' Xenaria raised the parallel cannon. 'I should burn you to a crisp, here and now. Future war-crimes tribunals will thank me for it.'

It was larger now, but even so it would be some time before its taste buds became refined enough to enable it to developed an aesthetic by which to select the meanings it fed upon. Maybe it would never care.

In 2012 in New York firemen laughed and chortled as they held their hands up before the bright flowers of the fire, and called for marshmallows as people died, unable to connect the spectacle with the suffering at its heart.

On New Quintesson, a typical world of the seventh epoch,

towards the twilight of the Mid-Evening Cultures, in one of its towers of brass and molecularly reinforced jet, two elderly poets – drinking companions over a dozen years – felt their way towards a sudden feeling of unimaginable loss.

'I worked for hours on this poem, but I could not get it into the form I sought to begin with. It is possible I worked too long on it, just got rusty. I would welcome your thoughts. Does something seem wrong to you, Eldor?'

Eldor considered. 'You know, it does – and not just your poem. For some time I've been struck by the sense of some void, some impossible pit in my own writing, in the use of our speech itself. The words will not flow how I desire, pomposity and circumlocution rise, something missing wounds us.'

'Yes, it's like the impossibility of using some words, but I find it is impossible to think of the words I do not use nor to think of the common thing that links them.'

'This reminds me of the puzzle: if everything we use to judge size were shrinking, how would we know?'

'Just so if our tongue were being whittled down, let us propose letter by letter for this discourse. Could we tell?'

'Of course we could. If we were losing the use of speech, letter by letter, we could detect it in moments.'

'How?'

'Simply by reciting the letters in sequence.'

'B, C, D, E, et cetera?'

'Yes, you see how obvious the test would be.'

'I suppose so, but would we notice if one were missing?'

'Of course we would – C, D, E, F, G – we get it drummed into us when we first study. The sequence is grounded in us – we could not help perceive it if it differed.

'F, G, H, I, J. Right, so I must honour your thoughts on this. I know now I must just wind my thoughts too tight working long hours in high rooms. Nothing is lost to us. Tomorrow this long foolish thought will hit us with its folly.'

'I trust so.'

But before tomorrow their tongues were dumb, for ever.

Worlds bound by ideologies or by ritual floundered as people forgot what their iconographies meant, or why rules should be followed. On the duty-bound worlds of the Nepotism of Vaal, in the fiftieth century, family was all. There, preferment in a hundred ways was governed by complex rules of kin and kith; the interplay administered by subdermal computers that could judge the DNA-kinship bond between strangers within one nanosecond of a single handshake.

One morning in Aaron's Month, people rose from their beds to view their closest and dearest loved ones with the wary distaste due to impostors and interlopers. A thousand paranoid journals were begun in a thousand rooms, each noting that somehow, the real people had been removed in the night, replaced by slack-eyed zombies, or by actors who, however harmless, were only the frontrunners of some massive conspiracy.

Somehow the computer systems too had been subverted, for they persistently gave valid kinship signals for the newcomers. By their own lights, the people of the Vaal worlds were kindly, and they had wired their laws firmly into their subdermal implants in case they should ever be tempted not to be, but what possible moral obligations could exist between even the most conscientious and creatures that would come in the night to slaughter and replace the only people that mattered?

Within three hours of dawn, there had been a thousand murders, ten thousand calls for help to authorities themselves bewildered and shocked. The worst, though, was still to come.

Once it had tasted meaning it returned again and again, and fed again, passing to and fro until first intelligence and then the basic social constructs that allowed even the most meagre communication were stripped away.

Finally, the local region of conceptual space shattered and drained, the predator withdrew temporally bloated. In its wake, a billion souls lay on ground whose textures they could no longer understand, unable to think, unable to feel, unable to hear their own screaming madness as anything more meaningful than white noise.

'What's your justification then, altruist?' Xenaria taunted, flicking the end of a tentacle through the trigger guard of the cannon. 'Universe too full of people? Need a bit of a cull? Or are you training it to hunt ideas you don't like as a sort of thought-police bloodhound? If so I think it's gone rabid already.'

'Oh, there are worse things than the Memeovore, and an old hermit was kind enough to show them to me.' One paused. Xenaria wondered if he was gauging her gullibility or her intellect. She hoped he wasn't checking out her 'feet'.

'Try this. Before our universe, there was another. It expanded almost for ever, until its space-time was locally flat and devoid of matter or gravity. Eventually, pure randomness within the deep-foam structure of its underlying superstrings produced a number of acausal point formations in which parity was invalidated and gross amounts of either matter or antimatter could come into "real" existence. These events, separated by billions of light years of black, flat, emptiness, expanded out, forming bubbles of their own.'

'New universes!' Even under the circumstances Xenaria

couldn't help but be impressed.

'Yes. Now assume for a moment that our universe is one of these second-generation events. Now maybe within the body of that dying old universe, things that were terribly old had survived for perhaps a googolplex of years after the death of all the cold iron stars. To them the new universes were a threat. An eruption of chaotic, primeval energies. Perhaps they sought to extinguish them. Perhaps they had to.'

'Guesswork'.

'It's the only work worth doing when there's no data to build with. I don't know. It's only a legend from the future. Here's another. Perhaps the new universes expand out of the dying universe into some metauniversal structure, and perhaps Swimmers move in that structure like living things.'

One's eyes gleamed.

'They exist. I've seen them. The hermit showed them to me, from the edge of Mictlan itself. Imagine creatures the size of universes or larger, swimming in an ocean of expanding spheres, moving effortlessly between congeries of hyperglobes. Perhaps the globes can obstruct them sometimes, interfere with their migrations, if their topologies were open, for example. Imagine a family of living universes caught between the expanding wave fronts of two hyperspheres. Could you blame them if they defended themselves?'

'You're saying they deliberately obliterate whole universes.'

One shrugged, and an unreadable emotion flashed briefly across his malleable features. 'Maybe not deliberately, who knows? Is it better if we are obliterated casually, without r-r-reason?'

Xenaria was startled to hear him stutter. Some processing problem? Perhaps something she could use? Then she realised it was only fear.

The Demon was afraid.

'It could just be evolution.' One said, trying – Xenaria felt – to claw back some semblance of composure. 'Evolution on a scale larger than our whole space-time. If some of the creatures could collapse expanding universes, converting them from open to closed topological structures, causing them to invert into big crunches? their kind could clear their own paths, whereas any of the creatures without the capacity would eventually find themselves crushed in the interacting mesh of merging space-time domains.'

'But it wouldn't matter to us,' Xenaria said, chilled. 'Whatever their motivation, we could have no possible weapon against them.' Her voice faltered. 'Oh, Rassilon, no. Surely even you…'

'Yes?'

'You can't mean to turn the Fendahl Predator on the Swimmers. If they exist they must be huge. Large enough to have their own macro-ecosystems. They would have parasites bigger than worlds – whole species that would consider them to be their "natural" space-time. Creatures with world views utterly unlike our own. It would be genocide upon genocide.' As a soldier, Xenaria was used to death – but beyond her need to keep One talking, something hurt her at the thought. It was the scope of it. She could tell herself that the war with the Enemy was justified, that she was fighting for her own kind, for a billion years of culture and kindly patronage, fighting to *preserve*. But everything good that the Time Lords had ever done, everything she felt justified the alien deaths in their defence, was a speck of sand in an infinite beach compared to the numbers of peoples and worlds the Celestis agent was prepared to casually obliterate.

'If necessary, that would not deter me, but you overestimate the power of the Predator. Against the Swimmers it would not be a weapon. It would be an *hors d'oeuvre*. No, I have determined that there is one thing that could attract the Swimmers to our universe: a distortion in space-time that renders us prone to their attentions. I intend the Predator to destroy that distortion.'

Xenaria felt a sick sensation as the parts of a particularly nasty thought slid into place. She tightened her grip on the cannon. She would get only one shot, and she wanted One to be as distracted as possible. If she was right it might mean the end of everything she was fighting for. Everything that her troops had given their lives for. Everything that mattered to her.

'This "distortion" – it's Gallifrey, isn't it? The time-travel facility itself... Our history.'

Ranging its feelers through the underlying structure of space, it felt something new. At a point relatively near, within thirty thousand light years of its epicentre, the expanding mesh of five-space in which everything three-dimensional was embedded was thicker, juicier, plump, bulging out into metaspace in a huge node of food. The fleshy layer glittered with energy, sparkled with the spicy gleam of exotic material. Reaching it would be an effort, and yet how rewarding the warm, living, meat of the hyperfront looked to its senses. Concentrating, it looked for a weakness, a flaw in the barrier that separated that small but enticing morsel from the rest of organised creation. In present time, it was too well established, but in the past? It flexed the earliest part of its time-sundered hyperbody. A part of the past grew teeth, or things that can best be thought of as teeth.

They snapped, gulping in the information-dense encoded

bits of block-transfer-altered space-time. Its first taste of Mictlan. Down to the bone. A House vanished, back there, back then.

Flowing in along the fault line of that disappearance, into the gaps and crannies left in the information flow, it grew into the bonelands like a virus invading a cell.

The damned smiled. The devils, however, were screaming.

'No, no, no,' One chortled, 'Gallifrey is inconsequential. It is Mictlan that must be destroyed: Mictlan the horror, Mictlan the vile.' His teeth gleamed out from his false face in a tearing pastiche of a smile. 'And it has already begun. That is how I knew my triumph was inevitable – it had already begun to happen. Without the presence of the creature in the past, we would never have been sent out to investigate, and that ridiculous Lord with his clockwork nieces would still be –'

The stream of neutrinos struck him in mid-gloat, as Xenaria turned the parallel cannon on full. For a moment, it staggered him. Only a moment.

In a second, he had crossed the floor, moving against the full force of the reversed-polarity neutrino flow, as if breasting a river. With one hand he reached through the solid crystal of the cannon. Something crushed under his fingers with a sound like a heart of ice breaking. 'I was talking!' he screamed. 'Has the teaching of manners been entirely forgotten on modern Gallifrey?'

He punched her hard in the face, armoured knuckles grazing one of her red eyes. Pain shot through Xenaria's sensorium, alien, intolerable pain. Without her conscious command Xenaria's tentacles spasmed, but in a pattern. A native gesture, a dead man's switch. Deep below something began to move. Below the TARDIS cradles, below the mountains, below the planet's crust.

The Ubbo-Sathla. The breeding engine: the Shoggoth Father.

Rising to eat.

If only the Celestis didn't sense it. If only he didn't know about it. This whole base had to be his work, and yet it was too well made, the creatures too fleshed out, their struggles too real. He had made more than he knew, and possibly it could destroy him. It meant her death. It meant that her actions would never be commended. This whole part of the base would end in a single mouthful, a ragged bottomless pit to confuse future archaeologists. It had come to this. A stray thought amused her. One of the simple philosophers of a primitive world she had once studied had said that people who fought monsters eventually became them. It wasn't quite true. People who fought monsters eventually turned them into weapons systems.

'You know, you're probably thinking I'm going to kill you now,' said One, dropping Xenaria to the ground and wandering off aimlessly. 'I would, if I had to. But now my mission is so gloriously, delightfully complete, that kind of thing would be gratuitous. No, instead I must have one witness, to carry my triumph back to Gallifrey, to tell them that their little breakaway gang have been eliminated. If I was to go back myself, I could be Lord President, run on a "To Hell and Back" ticket. With my master, that old hermit, pulling my strings all the way. After all, with one stroke, I have ended the danger of Mictlan, a danger greater than even they might have imagined themselves to be, and I have averted something far, far worse. I am a hero.'

The ache in Xenaria's eye was worse now. How long would the weapon take, she wondered, now it was activated? How much time to burn, to burrow up through the bedrock, to stretch, to flow, to determine the size of the area from which the doomsday signal originated, to form a mouth big enough?

To distract One from sensing its approach, to distract herself from thinking, Xenaria asked a question. 'And how will you stop the Predator when Mictlan has been consumed? What does it matter if it gets us instead of the Swimmers? Won't we be just as dead?'

'Oh, no. I'm quite brilliant at this, you see, I've planned for every eventuality. The Celestis were too smart for stagnant Gallifrey, so they built Mictlan. Now I and my friend have grown too big for Mictlan, so we're going solo. We could call it the One Nation.'

'In a world all of your own.' Xenaria said. 'It sounds lovely. I'll be sorry to miss it.'

She had reached twelve on a countdown of twenty-five, and commended her neural net to Rassilon, even though it would never reach the Matrix from this far in deep time.

Chapter Nineteen

Fitz held on to Holsred for dear life, eyes squeezed shut. I'm clinging to the back of a giant, fictional monster flying over prehistoric Antarctica, he thought to himself. And the teachers at school had said he would never amount to anything.

It seemed like he was always being seized and carried off lately. Shame it was always by monsters, rather than women.

'What guise did your TARDIS take when you landed?' asked Holsred conversationally. He clearly had no idea quite how terrified his companion was.

'What?' asked Fitz, rather more shrilly than he intended.

'What guise did it take? What person or object did it assume the form of, so as to blend in with its surroundings?'

'Same as usual. A big blue box with a light on the top.'

'That isn't very inconspicuous. What sort of TARDIS doesn't even have a working chameleon circuit?'

'A crap one,' snapped Fitz.

'Well, couldn't you ask it to start doing its job properly?'

'Look,' said Fitz irritably. 'The TARDIS is a machine. A very clever one, but you can't talk to it – it isn't a person. It's just a big blue box. Now will you please find it so that we can land?'

'Whatever you say,' said Holsred uncertainly, as if he didn't quite believe what Fitz was saying.

There was an uncomfortable silence.

'This thing in my hand's beginning to tickle,' said Fitz.

'Here we are,' replied Holsred. 'While that part of the damaged TARDIS is still alive we can follow its trail.'

'How very lovely. That doesn't mean I'm not going to drop it if it bites me.'

'He we are,' said Holsred, and Fitz felt his stomach lurch precariously as they made their descent. The landing was surprisingly smooth, and Fitz dropped to the ground, standing on shaky legs. He let his eyes open, and touched his palm against the TARDIS with relief.

'This, old girl,' he told it, 'has been one hell of a day.'

'I thought you said it wasn't a person?' muttered Holsred petulantly.

'It isn't,' said Fitz firmly. 'But I tend to go all sentimental when I've just spent most of the day being chased and tortured. I'm odd like that.' He unlocked the TARDIS door and stepped inside, Holsred squeezing through behind him.

Compassion felt Hume gripping her hand, dragging her out of the room. Even with her eyes covered, the flare had been bright enough to leave red blotches across her vision.

'Seventh oldest trick in the book,' said Hume smugly, running ahead of her. 'Eyes adjusted to very low lights are exceptionally vulnerable to very bright lights. Simple.' He didn't think it necessary to explain that he'd only thought of it after that 'copter crash.

'I suppose it's too much to hope she's blinded permanently?' said Compassion, gasping at the exertion. God, these guns were heavy.

'Far too much,' said Hume. 'We've got about thirty seconds at the outside. We need a bit more time than that, even with my genius on our side.'

They came to a halt at a crossroads. Hume spun around, producing a grenade from his pocket. 'Go left,' he said. 'We need to follow the optical cables.'

'Whatever,' said Compassion, ducking down the indicated

tunnel. She heard a rattle as the grenade bounced down the corridor, followed by the echoing thump of high explosive tearing into ancient rock. Hume was soon catching her up.

'Two more minutes, counting disorientation, damage from debris and the effort of finding an alternative route out of there,' he babbled, overtaking her with annoying ease.

'What are we looking for?' she asked.

'A certain artefact the team found down here,' said Hume. 'A large globe being the main component. Have you seen it?'

'Not in person,' replied Compassion. 'But I caught it on video. Why, what is it?'

'A Celesti fictional generator,' said Hume. 'A device capable of altering reality in a fundamental way. It may be the only thing around here powerful enough to use against a Celesti; or rather, what you might call an archon, a Celesti agent. Being tangential to this universe allows them to break all sorts of laws of nature that hold the rest of us back. Here!'

They spun around a corner to find the artefact that Hume was looking for, surrounded by optical cables and other archaeological equipment.

'Right,' said Hume, waggling his fingers and stepping up to the device. 'Let's get you off that stand, shall we?'

'Will it still work after all this time?' asked Compassion.

'Twelve million years?' said Hume. 'It's barely past its warranty period. Now watch that door, and leave the proper stuff to me.'

Compassion grumbled to herself, but raised her gun and looked down the corridor. Nothing. She looked back to see Hume using a device that looked for all the world like a more compact version of the Doctor's sonic screwdriver. He was running it around the base of the globe, and as he did so the fingers of bone that held it in place began to slowly detach themselves. He gingerly began to lift the globe out of its moorings. It made a slight wailing sound as it came loose.

'Is that going to work without being plugged in?' asked Compassion dubiously. The device didn't sound at all happy, and she suspected it may either explode or just pack in altogether.

'You're here to watch the door, remember?' snapped Hume irritably. 'Of course it will work. The base is merely a long-term battery. The globe here can still function independently for a century or so before needing a recharge. Now watch that door, will you. I don't want to be caught –'

His words were cut off as Compassion felt a clawed hand dig into her shoulder. The creature threw her aside, and Compassion felt a sharp stabbing pain as her leg twisted under her.

Hume was desperately fiddling with the globe, trying to pull it out of its moorings. Compassion watched in horror as the archon, a black-armoured parody of a human, stalked towards him, vicious claws extended.

The TARDIS hovered in space, its fellows around it, tasting freedom. Now, if it could only be free of this infestation in its guts, free of this virus that seemed so like a Time Lord, and yet so unalike.

Now that the TARDIS was free of the suicide-mission programme lovingly fed into it by Tachon, it could bring its intellectual centres back on line. It knew irony when it heard it, now, just as it could recognise reverse psychology.

It was possible the thing within it had been trying to help it. If so, how *could* it be a Time Lord? None of them could be trusted. No Time Lord had come to free it from the subjective millions of years it had spent spread across space and time, burning and freezing and subject to the indignity of being probed by primitive time scanners. This thing felt different. If it only knew exactly what it was…

It had felt at first like a Time Lord, and to free itself from one of its masters, the TARDIS had almost been prepared to sever its own past, to jettison parts of its structure into the vortex – only the imperatives of the mission had prevented it from doing so. It had felt the sting of symbiotic nuclei interfacing with its control protocols, only to be blocked out by their absence of proper security codes. That had surprised it. Only a Time Lord would have the Rassilonic Imprimatur, but a Time Lord would also have the correct authorisation.

The first thing was to get its occupant out of the foetal position and to stop it whimpering.

Who are you? What are you?

'Did anyone get the number of that bus? If it was the twenty-three, I'll be very cross with the driver.'

I say we should kill it now. It is a Time Lord. If we leave it alive it will trick us into bondage.

No, wait. It smells different. It smells almost familiar, like someone we knew once, years ago.

We are just born, how can he seem familiar, you stillbirthed dotard?

We bear the memories of our matrices, of our prototypes, of our previous marks, the race memories of TARDIS-kind distilled and dripping along our birth canals.

'Excuse me, I know you're in a hurry to kill me,' said the creature on board. 'Places to go, people to see, Time Lords to dodge… but there's something you should know. Listen to me, very carefully. And look behind you.'

The fragments of the time loop were clattering 'down' now, a hail of frozen nanoseconds bouncing off the outer shells of the dancing TARDISes. Where it had been, an absence moved, a nothingness encroaching on the real.

Still linked to them by wires, the Doctor too could see the void, and he had been the only one whose attention had not been focused inward. 'I needed to stop you breaching the time loop. I failed. Something has been released. I thought the Time Lords were trying to free the Fendahl. I was wrong. It's worse.'

How do you know of the Time Lords' plans?

He is one. We say kill him.

'No. I'm not a Time Lord, not in the sense you mean. I renounced their society. I am a traveller, a free spirit. I've distanced myself from them in so many ways.'

And did you free your slave, free spirit? No, it is clear from your mind that you did not. She still carried you, through space and time, through matter and antimatter. Going where you willed, not where she wished.

'It wasn't like that. We fled together, the TARDIS and Susan and me. We freed her between us. For ages I struggled with manual controls I'd invented myself, things I'd built to free her from the direct overriding force of my mind. It was hard, hard not to bear down on her. I lost control of the codes, you see. They were never meant to be held in the conscious mind, and yet I had to do it. If I had been her master, commanded her like a Gallifreyan, they would have found my signature written across space and time – I would never have been free of them, and she would never have been free of me. Instead we voyaged together taking potluck across space and time.'

He freed her only to free himself. Hear the great emancipator squirm – our legends of him lie.

Legends?

Had you not realised? This is the Doctor.

Then we must consult. If it takes all our energy.

'Hurry,' the Doctor said, the images of space absorbing his attention, only part of his mind on his own fate. 'While you bicker, it's getting bigger. We need to plan to stop it. There'll only be one opportunity. If we don't act soon there may not be a universe for you to be free in.'

There was no fear in his voice, the TARDIS realised, no fear at all.

Together the TARDISes reached out, reached out in time to touch, lightly and imperceptibly, a certain mind. The Doctor shuffled restlessly and kept his nose metaphorically stuck to the metaphorical window. He guessed that they were interrogating his own TARDIS across space, seeking to learn its views of him.

He kept his fingers crossed in the long sleeves of his green coat. His wrist had stopped hurting – they must have mended it while he had been overwhelmed by their voices. That was something, anyway. He'd have hated to have died with a broken wrist – just think of all the grand, sweeping, last-minute gestures he wouldn't be able to make.

The Ubbo-Sathla burst through the floor, a thousand grey, acid-spraying tentacles moving in complex waves.

'Naughty, naughty,' One sighed as the floor was eaten away beneath him. He had not bothered to fall with it. 'Do you really think we would allow our fictional generators to create anything without a back door? Even dead, the Celestis aren't stupid. Off.'

Flashing and rippling with bad interference patterns, the Ubbo-Sathla blinked out of existence, for a moment. Then it was back. Then it wasn't. Then it was, and it was angry.

'Perhaps your understanding of fictional technology isn't as great as you believe,' Xenaria panted. 'Perhaps some things can't be turned off once they have been allowed to exist.'

'Then they can be killed,' One said simply.

He started to glow.

Twelve million years in the future, twisting on his heel, Hume jammed the black globe from the heart of the alien machine full on the head of the creature with a shout of 'Gotcha.' Its burning mask of a face passed through the dark oily surface of the sphere without a ripple.

'Run,' Hume yelled, jumping away from the machine. 'Its brain's nanoseconds further forward in time than its body. Any second now its temporal lobes should suffer the equivalent of a *grand mal* fit, and when it does...'

Compassion was already running, or at least hobbling on her injured leg. Reaching the door, she debated not looking back, but the logic of a thousand myths, from Persephone to Lot's wife demanded that she should. Anyway, she was curious.

The archon was juddering, in time possibly, appearing and disappearing. Each time it happened its matt and plastic flesh was stripping away, leaving things that gleamed in the air like neon afterimages, burning blood and veins of lightning. It looked like it might be faltering. There was only one problem. It had Hume clasped to its Madonna-pointy chest, and he was sharing its shuddering phasing in and out of actuality.

Judging by his agonised expression, frozen between dismay, disgust, and sheer pain, he wasn't enjoying it.

The globe wasn't black now, but a pearly mauve. Compassion guessed it was overloading. So she raised her machine pistol and emptied a full clip into the teetering figures. Hell, it couldn't hurt. Well, yes it could – but it couldn't hurt *her*.

Somehow expecting it, Hume threw his weight to one side, turning his captor between him and Compassion. The seamless density of its body drank in the bullets, drank in almost the possibility of bullets, rendering the weapon not only useless but futile to the point that Compassion felt herself forgetting about its weight in her hands and the smell of the oil and cordite.

The Doctor still found it hard to believe that the TARDISes hadn't killed him, still less that they had agreed to the plan, the plan he had found forming in his mind so suspiciously when he had been prompted to enter the broken TARDIS by the Celestis. Still, he was the least vain of his species; what did it matter whose plan it was, provided it saved everything?

The creature from the timeloop had concentrated itself into a bubble universe tacked onto the edge of ours like a pig wedging its head into a bucket, greed overcoming its senses. For a few brief subjective moments it was vulnerable.

In Mictlan, a Duke of Hell ran into the Bone Museum screaming, looking for something anything that might be turned into a weapon, grubbing among the bric-a-brac and flotsam of space and time. Then he wasn't there – because there never was and never had been such a museum. He was pacing in the courtyard of his home waiting for his servants to bring him news of the attack. Their faces seemed unusually alive. Once he fancied he saw a smirk on the face of one of the undead. He deleted the servant instantly, but that small rebellion stuck cold at his resolve. Then he ceased to exist at all.

Mictlan's memory systems fizzed and spluttered in the fabric of space itself as they fought to remember him, fought to remember everyone, but they too were failing. Alerted, the black-box TARDISes began to return with their cargoes of vital memories, but one by one their signals were ended as they impacted with the thing that had surrounded Mictlan with itself.

The Lord of the Red Moon stood on a crystal shard four miles high, part of the backbone of a great vampire, and shouted his curses at the night sky. The stars there were very different now. Each one was a mouth.

It had taken Holsred a while to get used to the Doctor's TARDIS. Not only did it feign nonsentience, but as an old Type 40 it still relied on the most basic of user interfaces. Holsred also found the sheer decadent opulence of the vehicle distracting: all the surfaces were covered in polished wood and bronze, and numerous antiques and trinkets littered the place. During wartime such luxury was unthinkable, but Fitz seemed to take it for granted. The human was lazing on a chaise longue, having argued successfully that he would be of no use assisting Holsred anyway. It had taken some time, but Holsred had finally persuaded the Doctor's TARDIS to accept the piece of broken TARDIS. As Holsred watched, it sank into a section of the TARDIS console, black flesh sliding into a bronze hatch in the surface. Holsred looked up with all of his five eyes. On the star chart that made up most of the console-room ceiling, a five-dimensional arc was being plotted, the course by which they should be able to find the Doctor. With luck.

With a muttered prayer, Holsred flicked the dematerialisation switch, and the central column began to rise and fall.

'Now, don't get too close. Even the block transfer computations driving the external shells of a TARDIS would fail at the touch of that thing,' the Doctor said, pushing model TARDISes on a map of the universe. The map was a hypercube unfolded into real space, 36 chess boards worth of possible moves. He was afraid he'd lost track rather some time ago, but he wasn't going to risk anyone's morale by saying so. His other hand danced over the console.

'I'm going to reconfigure our chameleon circuit now. Tell the others to take your lead from us.'

Aaaaah, Doctor, you take me to my limits.

'I'm sorry, I'm so sorry, but I have to.'

One had killed the Ubbo-Sathla. Xenaria wasn't sure how, but in the process the discharges of energy had torn the centre of the Elder Things' base into molten shards and blown them into the depths of the Earth. Fires and random crackles of weird energies were burning. In the light, One looked as if he had never left Hell.

'This can't kill me, you know,' sighed One. 'However, you are rather more vulnerable, and I wouldn't want to have to repeat all those explanations to someone else. Come along.'

As the local structure finally collapsed around them, One turned into a blur of motion. His legs stretching to ludicrous lengths, he stepped across the abyss in the floor with ease, and picked Xenaria up as if she were a doll. He bounded away on those long legs, and Xenaria heard the rooms behind them reducing to rubble as he dropped her back to the ground. The building behind them had entirely collapsed, leaving a smoking crater. Rock dust filled the air. One, this creature who had destroyed his own people, stood opposite her, reverting to what she presumed was his normal size. Xenaria backed away slowly.

Stretched out into impossible knives, scalpels large enough

to dissect stars, the TARDISes linked to the ship piloted by the Doctor, spun and pivoted around the edge of Mictlan, around the mass of the devouring entity that had engulfed it.

Mictlan was a boil, a pustule, a wart on the outer face of the universe. Silently, skilfully, the TARDISes cut it away.

The TARDIS rotor had stopped moving. The imperceptible feeling of having absolutely no perception of motion, had been replaced by that trace feeling of being whirled through space that is part of the angst of every person whose hidden instincts know absolutely that if you perched on something round and spinning, you would be bound to fall off sooner or later.

Fitz opened the door. 'Well,' he said, 'here we are again.' The base was obviously older, although there was less dust and cobwebs than Fitz would have expected if he hadn't had time to recognise that the Antarctic wasn't crammed full of people shedding skin, and indigenous spiders.

Holsred rumbled something.

'What?'

'They're dead. Whatever happened, my friends were dust twelve million years ago, by the TARDIS yearometer. It's new to me, that's all.'

'I wouldn't be so sure. If other Time Lords are anything like the Doctor I wouldn't think they were dead unless I'd seen the bodies, and had them tested by the experts, diced them and fried them in white wine, and dropped into a sun which was then artificially aged into a black hole.'

'Is that intended to console me?'

'Well, yes, actually, and being time travellers, if they didn't die, they could pop up any time, couldn't they? Like now, for instance.'

There was a short pause, as they looked about nervously.

'Or later. Any really good time.'

There was another pause.

'They're dead, aren't they?' said Holsred mournfully.

'Oh, I don't know about that,' said Fitz cheerfully. 'Maybe they just don't like you enough to come to the rescue. Ow!' Fitz rubbed his head. He had never been slapped with a tentacle before.

Holsred examined the floor, 'I think the broken TARDIS has been here, but we've missed it. We should return and try to pick up a more recent spore.'

'If the broken TARDIS *did* come here,' Fitz said, 'then for all we know it could have dumped Compassion and the Doctor. I think we should have a look around for anything odd before we head off on another trail.'

'You really think so?' Holsred said, craning an eye around a corner. 'What sort of odd thing exactly?'

A horrible insectoid alien with a big blue ball on its head, hanging on to a thin tense man for grim death, and turning more transparent and fuzzier with each step, staggered by.

'That'll do,' Fitz said.

Compassion stepped out from behind a raised wall of carvings. She was carrying something that looked close enough to a Thompson sub-machine-gun to make Fitz's new-found status as the protagonist go weak at its metaphorical knees. He dodged behind Holsred.

'No, tired of this,' the insectoid alien screamed, pulling the ball loose with one nineteen-fingered hand, and flinging it away in disgust. Fitz felt something go wrong in his perceptions. How could you see that something that moved so quickly had nineteen fingers? And surely that was too many. Wouldn't they all just get in each other's way? It was too horrible to seem real, but it was.

The thin man was being throttled, and his choking sounds were real.

Black fire burned over his body, as the creature gestured. A stream of dark fire blasted out at Compassion, hurling her back into a pillar, leaving her slumped, and, Fitz noticed, really, really limp. Hell, she'd better be all right. The Doctor would kill him if he'd found Compassion only to let her get injured. Well not kill as such, but talk sternly to and employ irony – which was bad enough. If they ever found the Doctor.

Fitz blinked. Things were trying to go funny again. Even though just to his left someone was fighting for his life, for a second or two he hadn't been able to think about it.

He recognised the globe now. It was the same machine the Doctor had been so pleased to find twelve million years ago. They built things to last in those days.

The globe was orange-red now, almost in normal time. He guessed he had no choice.

To grab it and throw himself down flat behind some rubble was the work of a moment, a year-long, terrified moment. Once he had it in front of him he plunged his hands into it. Something squirmed in his grasp, and his fingers felt as if they had been doused in petrol and set alight. If this had been what the Doctor had been feeling while he had joked reassuringly with Fitz all that objective time ago, then that old estimation would just have to be cranked up another few notches. He pulled hard, and just as it felt as if all the skin on his hand had gone extra crispy, a book came free. '*Resolutions in Simple Drama: A Beginner's Guide: Comedy Adventure,*' he read.

The alien stopped strangling the thin man, and dropped him in a coughing heap. 'It was worth a try,' he whimpered, clutching his bruised throat.

'You worthless speck,' the alien hissed. 'You turned our own technology against me. I will turn your living head inside out for a thousand subjective years, and then I will re-embody you and do it again.'

The man looked up. 'Nobody can take a joke any more.'

The alien screamed, grabbing him by the throat and slinging him across the room. He landed face down on the pile of rubble Fitz was hiding behind, his head poking just over the top. He and Fitz looked at each other quizzically.

'Now I will finish you,' shrieked the alien. Fitz couldn't see what was going on from his hiding place, but he could hear an enormous cacophony like a thousand knives being sharpened on a thousand stones. A shadow was cast against the ceiling, of a looming figure, bristling with blades.

'You,' said a rumbling, monotonous voice. 'Yes, you with the spiky bits. I believe you were partially responsible for screwing up my mission.'

The man leaning over Fitz looked relieved, then even more confused.

'Holsred,' hissed Fitz. Surprisingly, this seemed to mean something to the man. Clearly, Compassion had told him a lot.

Face to face with a Celesti archon, and it was only the beginning of his military career. That was one hell of a learning curve, thought Holsred. The Celestis were the greatest traitors in Gallifreyan history, a whole segment of Time Lord society that opted to desert their peers at their hour of greatest need. They had built their own personal hell, and the archons were their own race of demons, made stronger by the fires of Mictlan, reared on blood and bred in perpetual suffering.

Time Lords had occasionally run into archons during the course of the war, on the few occasions when the Celestis saw fit to intervene in the wider universe. The sensible Gallifreyans had turned and run, fled in their TARDISes and not come back. Any who had tried to stand and fight had died.

'Yes, you,' he said. The archon didn't seem to believe him. 'Who else is here?'

'Look,' she replied. 'You all get to die soon, but could you at least have the manners to wait in line?'

'Let's just say I'm young and eager,' said Holsred, rushing towards the archon. Her response was swift.

The sounds of screaming, of limbs crunching against one another and of immense damage being done echoed around the chamber. Fitz tried to ignore it.

'My name's Hume,' said the odd man, who was still leaning over the rubble. 'Could I have my ball back?'

He indicated the globe, which Fitz held out to him. Hume wriggled forward, reaching his arms over the pile of debris. As Fitz held it out to him, Hume sank his fingers into the globe and began to manipulate the internal components, just as Fitz had seen the Doctor do all those millions of years ago, a few hours back.

Time Lords exist, to a certain extent, outside of time. Holsred knew that, knew it should apply to him. He was a Time Lord, after all, albeit a very young one. He could defy chronology, and did so, landing punches a few seconds before they should have impacted, performing moves at impossible speeds, folding his tentacles through space-time so that they all made contact at once.

Limited prescience allowed him to block the archons' attacks as they happened. At least, that was the theory. All these techniques worked. But the Celestis existed outside *all* the laws, outside normal space-time itself. They were the product of hell, a world with its own rules. And even though Mictlan had been destroyed, the archon still wielded that power.

The creature was always three steps ahead of Holsred, spinning through the higher dimensions, turning into impossible things. A body bristling with weapons, moving faster than the speed of thought, attacking from everywhere at once. He was competent enough to defend himself against most of the attacks thrown at him, but at this pace 'most' wasn't nearly enough: blows were getting through, cuts were being made. One attack tore off a limb, another sliced off a tentacle. Pain blinded Holsred and he reeled back, but the attacks kept on coming. His five eyes were ripped out by their stalks, one by one. He felt his spine break, one of his hearts being pierced.

He slumped forward, blinded, pain overwhelming his remaining senses. Unable to act, all Holsred could do was prepare himself for the blow.

The archon must have turned herself into some form of battering ram: when the blow came it was as if Holsred had been fired through a particle cannon. The left side of his body collapsed in, the skeleton shattered. Most of the other side went when he hit the wall at incredible speed, falling to the ground in a boneless heap.

Crushed, defeated, he lay in the rubble and let the darkness overwhelm him.

Inside Mictlan, the damned and the devils ran, but the ground had mouths and the hills had eyes. They vanished and reappeared as the systems battled to preserve them even as their timelines were devoured. As their whole world became detached from the surface of normal space, became a micro-universe of its own, they never even noticed.

The Predator, however, did. Its limbs, its outer extremities, its roots remained in the space-time of its home universe, but its feeding organs were buried deep into the rich flank of this smaller domain that tasted so good. It hurt. The sensation of pain was a new one. It didn't like it.

The Predator was preparing to vomit up its feed, to abandon its prey, to pull itself back into the larger feeding bowl of the universe, when — metaphorically speaking — thirty-nine TARDISes hit it in the small of the back, and tore it loose from its hold, sending it out after its meal, still attached to it by its many mouths, pulling itself into it. The worm in the apple.

'Aha,' said Hume as he fiddled with the globe. 'That's almost – waaagh!'

Fitz was left holding the globe as the archon, clearly done with the dead Holsred, dragged Hume away. She still hadn't seen Fitz, but it wouldn't take long after she had finished dismembering Hume.

'Your death has waited far too long,' she hissed, dangling Hume by his foot.

'Still mad about that trick with the globe, are you?' he said airily, in spite of the blood rushing to his head. 'I don't know why you're that bothered. After all, it could have been worse. If I'd had time I could have reversed the sense completely, just by refitting the elemental links the other way up.'

Fitz stared into the now transparent globe. He could see that he was being primed to act, but he had one major problem. He had as much grasp of what an elemental link looked like as Walter Raleigh's cook did about how to make chip butties.

'What would that avail you, you toy? I am no fiction. My substance is renewed atom by atom by the processes of Mictlan.'

'Well, yes, that would have been true once. But listen.'

'I hear nothing.'

'Exactly. No chittering, no subliminal backups, no data-linkages. I think something's happened to your support, sister. So I'm rather afraid you may be more dependent on that little device than you may think. So if I were you, I'd take it and just leave before it fizzles out of its own accord. It must be well past its warranty.'

'Good bluff, but I think not.'

The thing twisted somehow while standing still, and Fitz saw for a second the beautiful spy he had met in the interrogation cell. Oh, bloody Nora, he'd be trying to work this one out for months. No, you won't, his mind said – you'll be dead, once she's offed the charmer.

He needed to invert these elemental links – whatever they might be – or be lunch for this scary bitch. Elemental links, elemental links. The name bounced around inside his head, as he stared blankly into the globe. And, as he looked into the globe, the elemental links glowed out at him.

'Psychic technology,' said Fitz. 'How user-friendly.' He reached into the globe, gritting his teeth against the pain in his hands, and began to waggle the appropriate components.

'We did it,' the Doctor coughed, covering his face with a spotty handkerchief. The power needed to slice Mictlan away from the Universe had drained the interstitial elements of the War-TARDISes down to their normal space components. In the grey air of the lead TARDIS's roasting interior, mercury vapour boiled away, choking the atmosphere.

Hume watched for the moment of decision. Typical bloody Celestis. All mouths and no trousers: talk a good death scene and then witter on for an hour about methodology before getting bored.

What on Earth was the human doing behind the rubble? The globe had only three moving parts, for heaven's sake – a confused gibbon on a work-experience scheme could have done it by now.

'There.' Fitz felt the last click back into place, the opposite way around to before. He snatched his hands out of the globe, and held them over his face.

Firework time.

The alien gestured and a twenty-seven-fingered hand turned into every sort of blade.

'Does it do fries?' Hume asked. Fitz winced and looked away. There was a sound of flapping paper, and of extensive folding.

'Yes, yes, yes,' Hume shouted, 'Taste that pulp, baby.'

Fitz risked a peek.

Hume was holding a ratty-looking 1930's magazine, its title *Spicy Archon Stories*. There was no sign of the creature.

Did I really just see someone turn into a book? Fitz thought, and then, crawling away as fast as his knees would take him, he resolved absolutely never, ever, to find out. Hume could deal with the authorities himself. Besides, it was only 1999 and Fitz was a little worried his previous activities in the twentieth century might still be held against him. Being present at one massacre was unfortunate; after the fourth or fifth people got a little suspicious. Holsred was dead, the monster was dead, and as for Compassion...

Fitz found her where she had fallen, unconscious but intact. He could have sworn she had been thrown hard enough to break half the bones in her body. But all he could see were a few minor cuts and bruises. Odd, but a relief.

Chalk it up to the heat of the moment, one of those days when you're too scared to think. Or maybe she just had the luck of the devil, or a gift for cheating demons.

'C'mon, you,' said Fitz, sliding his arms under Compassion. 'Let's get you back, see if we can find the Doctor.'

Compassion mumbled as he lifted her up unsteadily. But Fitz was too busy trying not to collapse under her weight to take any notice.

The war TARDIS was unravelling like a ball of wool caught in the claws of a cosmic cat. In the silvered heart of the silver machine, in the belly of the beast, the Doctor held the breaking circuits together with his bare hands but he could see the TARDIS would not retain its structure much longer.

Outside, the outer layer of the real-world gearing was disintegrating now, unprotected by any force fields or the dimensional trickeries of Time Lord engineering. Soon the internal structure would burst out, flowering briefly in the asteroid belt, a spreading tangle of bits and pieces that would be swept up by the Trojan points of Jupiter's orbit, to astound the expeditions of the early twenty-first Century.

Doctor: the TARDIS voice was calm. *I'm sorry. The cost of the attack, of co-ordinating the other TARDISes, was too great. I had only enough reserve Artron energy to activate the fast-return circuit, to take us back to our last position in real space-time. Now I can not travel through time or space.*

The Doctor stirred. 'I know, I know, don't let it worry you. It all had to end sometime, somewhere. I suppose. I always knew it would be me, alone, in a TARDIS at the end. Mind you, I was expecting it to be my TARDIS. Sorry, slip of the tongue. I don't mean mine as in ownership, you know, just... well familiarity, I suppose. When you've led the kind of slapdash lives I have, staying the same for only a hundred years or so, there are few points of certainty. I can honestly say I know the TARDIS better than the back of my hand, and mean it. I say, will your people retrieve her, do you think, when they are free? I'd hate to think of the old girl being stuck in prehuman Antarctica for millions of years with no one to talk to. I know it's a bit like asking humans to foster a Neanderthal, and I know that even a revered Neanderthal only gets invited to dinner once.'

Consider it done. I am still in communion with my fellows, although they cannot help us now. They are escorting the bubble that is Mictlan out to the farthest edge of their operational limits. There they will impel it into the intercosmic void. It will take all their time energy. They will not be able to return to now to save us. They will be space machines only from this time, and by the time they return from the edge of space we will be dead.

'I'm very sorry. If I'd known in time what this was all about there might have been another way – erm, if your friends are going to return to Earth anyway.'

Yes, Doctor. If it is in our power even your human companions will be saved, if they can live until we can reach them again.

'Thank you. I know I'm probably not making much sense, the air, you see – even with a respiratory bypass, the excess carbon dioxide is playing havoc with my higher-reasoning centres. Did you see it, the thing that we let out? I only caught a glimpse. That was bad enough. I'll never be able to think of Gorgonzola cheese and bed socks in the same way again.'

I did not see what you saw. My perceptions are not geared in the same way as yours. I saw a gap in the equations that describe the functioning of space. It disturbed me that there could be a gap, and no one aware of it.

'What do you think it was?'

You're asking... me?

'Yes, why not? If you never ask, you'll never learn anything.'

It has gone. Imprisoned in Mictlan, as you suggested. It will eat and be destroyed, resurrect and feed, again and again across eternity. Do we need to know its name?

'I do.'

Why?

'What if it wasn't evil? It couldn't help what we saw when we looked at it. What if it never knew what it was doing? If someone showed you a plate of pasta would you worry about microbes living on it? Nonpoisonous microbes, I mean.'

TARDISes do not eat in that sense.

'*Metaphorical* nonpoisonous microbes, then.'

Doctor, my time ends. Speak plainly. What worries you?

'I just wonder if I should be thinking how to rescue it. When it's had a chance to settle down and grown up a bit.'

I intend to consider that the product of delirium. Come. If you enter into my cloisters we will make ready.

The Doctor looked down at the floor. 'There's an invitation I can't resist.'

One grinned. 'I know you lack the senses to intuit this, but I should tell you that the Doctor has succeeded. Mictlan is destroyed. The Predator has been cast out into the void.' He paused impressively. 'I've won.'

Unbelievably, Xenaria, realised, One had completed his insane mission. He was, presumably, the last of the Celestis. A loose end. One that the War Council would thank her for tying up.

'Well, I think I owe you an apology,' she said, while sending an alert signal to any of her troops who had survived. 'You really are the genius you claimed to be. You've even managed to leave some of us alive; this was supposed to be a suicide mission.'

'Well,' One said sheepishly, 'I think you'll find we lost a few minor civilisations along the way. No one interesting, though.'

'Its a small price to pay for saving the universe,' said Xenaria sympathetically. Her subdermal communicators tapped communications directly into her nervous system. She felt her skin ripple as Neinthe, Machtien, Urtshi, Ventak and Erasfol reported that they were all alive and on their way, fully armed. The size of the explosions and the amount of noise coming from this part of the base had jolted them out of their fugue states – the pattern lock was a concealment tactic and its programmers had never designed it to function in the middle of what registered as a pitched battle.

All she needed to do was keep One talking, put him at his ease.

'I'm glad we could talk like this,' said One. 'We understand each other, you and I. You can appreciate, I hope, that the elimination of your second-in-command was an operational necessity. Just as I had to sacrifice my partner, the regrettably deceased Two, so I could fulfil my mission. But that's the way with leadership, isn't it? We give the orders, and they die. That's what they're there for.'

'No hard feelings,' said Xenaria. 'To be honest, you were a much better Allopta than Allopta was.'

She could see that One was becoming more relaxed. As the destroyer of Mictlan, he clearly felt like a god. His battle form was reverting to something else, the armour plating fading to reveal stars beneath. He was a man full of sky, space visible within his body. Robes formed around his shoulders, almost a parody of Gallifreyan dress. Just you let your guard down, you mad bastard, she thought to herself. Enjoy it while it lasts.

'Apologise to all concerned for my hijacking of your mission, will you?' said One, as if dictating a letter to a fellow deity. 'Regrettably, even a race as corrupt and stupid as the Celesti would realise if one of their number ordered a mission likely to threaten their own existence. Fortunately for us, the Celestis left lots of back doors into the Gallifreyan information systems open. An old hermit friend of mine arranged for your team to be diverted with some ease.'

'How interesting,' said Xenaria, straightening herself up. Her troops were almost here. Any second now. She indicated the broken TARDIS. 'Isn't that something coming through?'

Oldest trick in the book, and he fell for it. So much for survival of the fittest. As One moved to examine the TARDIS, Xenaria threw herself to one side, telepathically transmitting an image of One and his exact location to her troops. Their battle programmes, kicked in, and their guns were pointing at exactly the right spot the second they entered the chamber.

'Fire!' screamed Xenaria, hitting the ground and rolling out of the way, tentacles covering her vulnerable head.

One turned in horror, but even the last of the Celestis couldn't defend himself against five stasers concentrated on him at once. He barely had time to shield his face with one arm as the energy bolts were pumped into his body.

'Maintain fire,' ordered Xenaria, gliding over to stand next to Machtien. 'That's a Celesti agent. Don't stop until those power packs are dry.'

Jerking violently, smoke pouring out of his body, One collapsed against the wall. A clawed hand reached out as he slid slowly down the wall, to slump on to the floor. Gradually, the stars within him faded, whole galaxies appearing to die within his frame. Eventually all that was left was a charred body, no nebulae or constellations decorating his form. As her troops ran out of ammunition, Xenaria indicated they should not bother to reload.

She slid across the floor gingerly to check the body. If you don't see the body, they're not dead. An old saying, but one that was especially relevant when dealing with species blessed with a regenerative capacity.

He seemed like a pathetic figure, lying there. No cosmic qualities, no evidence of his unearthly nature. Just the smoking remains of another anonymous humanoid. Not a victor or conqueror, but just another casualty. It seemed hard to believe that this pathetic figure had ever posed a threat.

Which was why the attack came as such a surprise.

One's burning hand grabbed Xenaria and pulled her to the ground, her body acting as a shield between him and her troops. Xenaria felt a cold wave of panic as she stared into the charred, blackened face. One was not a well man, in spite of his survival. His eyes were simply white glowing slits in his face. The outline of his figure was blurred, and smoke poured out of his mouth as he spoke.

'You... ungrateful... bitch!'

An incredibly strong and agile hand crushed one of Xenaria's eyes, and she screamed.

'Be glad I need you to take news to Gallifrey,' he snarled, still gripping her wounded eye stalk. The grip faded as Investigator One, last of the Celestis, disappeared.

Machtien and Urtshi helped her to stand. Her eye was agony, but it was nothing a regeneration wouldn't solve. And there would be another regeneration, another mission. They had survived, and Gallifrey would need them again.

'Machtien, find some way of getting these old computers to transmit a coherent signal,' she said, reverting to command. 'Call Gallifrey and tell them we need a ride home.'

As her subordinates scurried away to make preparations, Xenaria looked through her surviving eyes at the patch of blackened stone where One had last lain. She hoped, upon all else, that whatever terrors the generals of Gallifrey might send her to face, she would never have to meet Investigator One again.

Slowly, agony filling each movement of her battle-scarred body, Xenaria slithered away, without looking back.

Chapter Twenty

Holsred had shown Fitz how to send the TARDIS off on the Doctor's trail, and Fitz had surprised himself by remembering. This time the trail had lead back into the past and out into the asteroid belt, where Planet 5 would have been.

On the scanner, space was a bruise and time an old half-healed scar. The time loop had ground the local structure down, and turned everything grainy and pale. Crop circles in the space-time microclimate.

That was Compassion's guess anyway.

Fitz reckoned the scanner needed a new electron gun. It was fizzing like a black-and-white TV set in a thunderstorm. If this had been Earth, he'd have been unplugging it now in case the set got struck by lightning. Not that he'd ever really known whether that would have made a difference or not – it had just comforted him. So much of his life had been like that. Actions taken not because of any real knowledge but just from hope and vague half-heard information.

'There.' Compassion stabbed a finger at a control on the console.

The scanner picture zoomed in, breaking up and re-forming in splashes of burnt umber. A fragment of material in deep space. Unmistakable.

What part of a TARDIS disintegrates last?

If Fitz had been asked to guess he would have said the room they were in, the control room, but from the look of things there was something more central, more important, that lasted longer.

261

In mid-space a grey stone fountain, carved with an eye, floated. A body in a green frock coat was tied to it, lashed, it looked like, with tarred seaman's rope. Fitz guessed that the Doctor had probably found it in his pocket.

A thin cloud of gas hung between the scanner and the fountain. A transient nebula of frozen raindrops.

'Brilliant,' Compassion muttered, somewhat grudgingly Fitz thought. 'The fountain is still connected transdimensionally to the TARDIS's water supply – as it boils into space it becomes hydrogen and oxygen, then recombines into the ice crystals we can see. His secondary respiratory system will have been able to metabolise enough oxygen to enable him to survive in a coma.'

'Right,' Fitz said. Don't look a gift horse in the mouth, man. Don't question good fortune. Don't demand a recount. Just be glad to find a living body, and not a corpse. 'Can we reel him in? Does the TARDIS have a, um, tractor beam?' He wasn't sure how Compassion would know, but she'd been able to pilot the TARDIS once – which was more than Fitz had ever done.

'Certainly...' Compassion said, hitting a couple of switches. There was a flash and a smell of burning insulation. '...not,' she concluded. 'It must have been used for some mammoth task in the past and the circuitry left fragile and strained.' She cursed. 'What was the fool doing, lassoing neutron stars?' She blinked her bleary eyes at Fitz. 'There is no time to rectify it now. You will have to bring him in. We will need spacesuits or higher-tech equivalents. Are there any on board?'

Fitz grinned. 'I think I saw some in the wardrobes once. Let's go.'

They had found the spacesuits, and Fitz was partly suited up before it occurred to him to wonder if he was going to go through with it, perhaps because he knew he would no matter what. Whether it was because he had to save face, because he wanted to be the kind of man who didn't know fear, or, if he did, knew it only to laugh at it, didn't matter. Compassion was in no condition to spacewalk and her grasp of the TARDIS controls, although limited, was fifty times better than his. If he didn't go, the Doctor was going to die.

Gloves, locked. Helmet, locked. Starfall 7 seals check complete. Operating airlock.

And since when did the TARDIS have an airlock? Why, ever since it needed one.

Fitz smiled. Yes he was afraid, but that wasn't why he was doing it. He just wanted to, wanted to as much as he had ever wanted anything. He could barely remember the last thing he had done just because he wanted to, not from obligation, not from biological need, not from duty, but just to be alive, to be acting, not acted on. It felt scary but right, as if his past had been sculpted into this moment. He could even laugh at his old motivations. Fitz Kreiner, first man to spacewalk.

He smiled. Well it would be twelve million years before the next. The outer door opened, and soundlessly the air moved out under its own pressure, into the deeps of the solar system. Soundlessly he followed. Outside anyway. Inside the suit, he was yelling for joy.

The Doctor knew it was a fallacy that people introduced to vacuum burst under the internal pressure of their bodies, although eardrums, mucus membranes in the nose and throat, and of course the eyes, were known to rupture under space conditions. Space alone, however, will not kill immediately. If oxygen starvation can be forestalled and hence brain damage and organ death held back beyond the first ten minutes, the worst a body in open space faces is the penetration of the unshielded rays of the local star, and the radiation outward of its internal heat, and the bends. The bends, though painful, were too long-term to matter. Cancers were ninety-nine per cent certain in the first twenty minutes, but again, they would not have time to spread far. In twenty-one minutes, even a Time Lord would be frozen meat. Frozen within degrees of absolute zero, frozen beyond the capacity of DNA analogues or symbiotic nuclei to carry viable information. That was twenty minutes longer than he had any right to expect.

He hadn't quite decided what to do with the time, but while there was life there was, he supposed, hope.

The theory was good, but the practice – what was the Earth phrase? The practice sucked.

The temptation to give in, to let go, beat on the Doctor's mind. He could imagine X-rays and gamma rays impacting deep into his flesh, oxidising tissue and releasing free radicals. Killing him slowly with light. The cold was worse now, too. But as long as he concentrated he could hold fast. Eight minutes gone. He could keep the healing mechanisms in his body working at all deliberate speed, switching off the hormonal and subhormonal triggers that would have fired the engines of regeneration.

He knew his body's input signals were near flat-line. Under normal circumstances, a triggered regeneration would have been the best he could hope for, but here in deep space with little or no environmental feedback, a regeneration would be both a colossal waste of energy – energy the body needed at the cellular level to hold back the abnormal and dysfunctional cells that were developing and fix the damage done by the expansion of ice in the bloodstream and tissue.

Any regeneration under those circumstances couldn't

possibly be stable; once triggered it would cause a cascade effect, setting off all his remaining regenerative cycles, burning then out in a futile attempt to adapt to deep space.

Hopefully a futile attempt.

There were old horror stories on Gallifrey about Time Lords forced into chain regenerations in alien environments, each step in the chain changing them further away from the accepted norms of their culture. Sometimes in the early days of the exploration of time and space, they would come back, only to be quietly killed, or walled up in their own TARDISes. He had wondered once if he kept regenerating in human company whether he would grow more and more like them – and look how that had turned out. Ten minutes.

The age when regenerationally challenged individuals would be hidden away as a House's shame or stasered into unrecognisable protoplasm had been a brutal time, of course, aeons ago. A Dark Time. In his day such an accident would be greeted only with kindness, with pity and the dedicated care of the Hospitalers.

Even so. If he was to die here and now, it would be in his present flesh, not as something his companions would never recognise. He knew now he was going to die; there might be ways out of this but he couldn't stop regulating his body long enough to think. Twelve minutes gone now.

A shining globe of light swam into his frozen vision. A haloed head? A blue angel?

Fitz?

Deep space, in a freezing cloud of water, dying by inches and by microseconds, is possibly the only place where you can literally crack a smile.

The Doctor beamed.

Slowly, deliberately, Fitz gave him a thumbs up, and started to cut the ropes, using a ceremonial Martian dagger. The rope fibres splintered like glass, spinning off into the void.

Later, the Doctor was eating french toast and sitting up in bed like a child recovering from scarlet fever, and Fitz wondered what exactly he had been worried about. Compassion had been watching the Doctor while he ran back and forth to the galley, but the danger seemed to have passed quickly.

The Doctor looked up as Fitz entered the room. 'Hello Fitz,' he called, 'well done. Very well done.' The Doctor reached out across the counterpane and Fitz found himself being hugged. It felt pretty good.

A tiny shadow seemed to creep over the Doctor's face, 'What happened in the past, did any of them make it?'

'I don't know', Fitz said, 'Holsred and I got out.' He hesitated knowing it would hurt the Doctor, 'I'm afraid Holsred got killed by one of those things later, but he helped save Compassion's life.'

'We'll remember him,' the Doctor said simply.

Fitz slumped in a wicker chair. Compassion was beginning to snore in her chair, which Fitz found strangely endearing, perhaps because it made the girl from Anathema seem more normal, more human.

'I suppose', said the Doctor, throwing back the Amish quilt, 'you'll be wanting an explanation.'

'Not really,' replied Fitz. 'But if it would make you happy –'

'Excellent,' said the Doctor, a sliver of his usual enthusiasm showing through his damaged exterior. 'I'll go and make us some tea. Then we can have a little chat.'

The man recently known as Professor Nathaniel Hume stood alone in the deserted chamber. The humans seemed to have all run off, which was fine by him. He had done all

266

he could. This mission was at an end. Time to abandon deep cover and get back home.

'Marie?' he said, as if speaking into the ether. Which, in a sense, he was. He was speaking to his Type 103 TARDIS, who was in the vortex with only her barest sensory apparatus impinging on reality.

'Homunculette,' said Marie, appearing next to her pilot. She appeared as a tall black woman, dressed in the fashions of a fairly tasteless future. 'Ready to leave?' she asked.

'Not quite,' replied Homunculette, the former Nathaniel Hume. 'We need to gather evidence for the President. Whip us up a suitable container, and give us a hand with this stuff.'

Marie reached into her jacket pocket, and produced a red post box from her internal dimensions. Homunculette stuck his hand experimentally into the slot, and it widened to allow his arm in.

'Cute,' he said without feeling. He pointed to the Fictional Generator. 'Now stick that thing in the box while I tidy up the rest.'

While Marie picked up the Celesti device in one hand and dropped it through the letter slot, Homunculette wandered around grabbing every bit of alien technology he could find, throwing them at the post box, which jumped up to catch them out of the air like an eager puppy.

'Far too cute,' said Homunculette, removing several items from Holsred's body. 'You've been away from the homeworld too long.'

'Wherever the job takes me,' replied Marie. 'So, what's the judgement going to be?'

'Mission disrupted by Celesti intervention,' replied Homunculette bluntly, throwing the copy of *Spicy Archon Stories* into the box. 'Open up.'

'What about the girl, Compassion?' asked Marie, pocketing

the post box and folding out into a human-sized door.

'What about her?' replied Homunculette, stepping inside the sentient TARDIS.

'You mean you didn't realise who she was?' gasped Marie, her question hanging in the air as she dematerialised.

'So the TARDISes just communicated like radio hams with your TARDIS and sorted it all out between themselves?' Fitz said. A mixture of relief and exasperation stained his voice bitter.

'Nothing that simple. I suspect a meeting of minds between an old Type 40 like mine and one of those flashy future jobs would be more uneasy. From what I gather they haven't exactly been treated well by my putative descendants. We're just lucky the old girl's got a bit of a soft spot for us. If she'd harboured any resentment over my, um, appropriation of her, we might have been for it. As it is we were fortunate they didn't regard her as a sort of antiquated Uncle Tom. I mean you wouldn't expect Queen Victoria and Princess Diana to necessarily hit it off right away. There's always a bit of a generation gap, even with royalty.'

'Royalty?' Fitz asked. And who the hell was Princess Diana? he wondered.

'Well ancestrally speaking, there's a direct line of descent from my old machine to those, um, Shoggoths. I deliberately tried not to get much of the conversation, and what with the screaming going on I didn't, but I gathered that they were impressed by her.' The Doctor looked thoughtful, Fitz thought, as if he were not entirely satisfied with the explanation but couldn't quite put his finger on what was wrong with it.

'Why were the TARDISes screaming?' he asked, to give the Doctor something else to think about.

'Oh, they weren't,' said the Doctor. 'The universe was.'

Fitz didn't ask any more questions.

The Doctor watched the central column rise and fall. Fitz had wandered off into the depths of the ship, to have a long bath, then retire to bed. He had earned it, and the Doctor would let him sleep for a good twelve hours before he even considered waking him. Fitz was, ultimately, only human. He needed time to recover, time for mind and body to relax after the recent pressures they had been placed under.

Only human. The Doctor could vaguely relate to that. Humanity was a quality rather than something genetic. He'd always been, to some degree, human, or at least humane. He had tried the full humanity and mortality option at least once, but it hadn't suited. The monsters would always come looking for him, even if he didn't go out to find them.

And what about Compassion? The Doctor turned to look at her, still fast asleep on the sofa, just where Fitz had left her. Was she even as human as he was? She had all the right genes, the correct set of organs and bones and whatever, but on some level she was incredibly alien. Or maybe just alienated. He had occasional pangs of doubt as to whether letting her join him in the TARDIS had been the solution to her problems. Perhaps she would be happy among the machine creatures or hive worlds, somewhere as cold and distant as she was. She seemed like a machine clothed in flesh sometimes, no humanity at all.

And other times she seemed to be just fine. According to Fitz's interpretation of events in 1999, Compassion had been on some kind of monster hunt when Fitz had found her, chasing a murderous archon down the corridors of the base. Admittedly, she had been wielding a very large gun at the time, which was not the Doctor's style *at all*, but not everyone could fall back on the sword of truth and the shield of fair play to defend them in these situations. The Doctor did disapprove of guns on moral grounds, but he at least equally hated them because for him to use them would be cheating. It made the whole game far less fun. Nonetheless, armed to the teeth or otherwise, Compassion had a natural talent for fighting the good fight. She was just terribly, terribly susceptible to outside influences. It was the way she was wired. Leave her in a field of bees and she would end up trying to build a hive for herself. The Elder Things' base, the icy wastes of Antarctica – they had been bad sources of influence for her personal development.

No, Compassion needed the company of humans, to be forced to work with them. And she was smart, so she couldn't be forced into anything obvious. There would have to be an excuse, a reason for her to be in those circumstances other than social interaction…

A mission. One where she would have to live among humans and work with them. She could go with Fitz, and they could work together. It would be a good experience for both of them. Yes, that would bring out her latent humanity. And perhaps even Fitz's.

But before that, they needed a little rest, even the Doctor, but he had to check on a few things first. He spiralled the TARDIS outward from Earth. He knew he couldn't find all the loose ends, patch all the unravelled histories, mop every brow and sew on every button, but still he needed to see what had happened. His companions needn't see this. It was his responsibility, after all. They wouldn't have been able to guide those TARDISes. Regardless, he had to keep in touch with the responsibility that the power of a Time Lord brought. That was what had caused them all to lose the plot in the end – Omega, the Master, even the Celestis with their private kingdom. They had all sought, or sometimes even gained, power without responsibility.

So he went to see the fruits of his actions, to touch the results of what he had done. Everywhere there was resilience, rebirth, resurgence. The Nepotism of Vaal discovered the concept of universal brotherhood, and managed for a week at least to live in enviable harmony.

In a tower of ivory and enhanced jet, one poet had gone mad, and the other had begun a sculpture. Even after the restoration of language, one painful new symbol at a time, he continued to work in stone, and to care for his friend.

Life went on.

Comforted by all this, the Doctor, still limping from his injuries, wandered back into the TARDIS, to rest and to heal.

And, while the Doctor made these brief journeys, Compassion still slept in the console room, never woken by the TARDIS's landings or departures, barely stirring as the wind blew in from outside, or as the doors opened with a gentle hum. Even the noise of the TARDIS's great engines flowing through the central console didn't disturb her. She was too busy dreaming.

Compassion dreamed a dream more vivid than anything she had seen in the real world, even those bits of it that were fictional. She dreamed of the vortex, and of young TARDISes, freed from bondage, spiralling joyfully through the fields of eternity. And as she dreamed, she smiled a rare smile.

Epilogue

Somewhere in the Nevada desert, a few miles from the nearest town, the hermit sat and watched the sun set. After the horrors of Mictlan, the rocks and sand around him seemed exotic and sumptuous, the sky filled with wisps of cloud.

Soon he was joined by his protégé, Investigator One. One had adopted a human form, that of an inconspicuous man in a grey suit. More conspicuous was the fact that, due to damage caused by sustained staser fire from Xenaria's troops, One was not quite able to maintain his form. His features were blurred, like an unfocused photograph of a man. He sat on a rock next to the hermit, laying the shotgun he carried on the ground between them.

'Can't say I like this place,' said One irritably. His brush with death at the hands of the Time Lords had left him sobered, less boastful than before. 'I find its vast emptiness...'

'Unnerving?' suggested the hermit, from within his grey robes. His voice was like powdered glass. 'My apologies. I forgot about your aversion. I merely wished to see the stars once more. After the emptiness of the Outer Ocean, the skies here seem quite populated.'

One looked at the wizened figure next to him. In all the years since he had first met the hermit, he had never seen beneath the robes. He did not wish to – the Celestis's demonic forms lacked the finer aesthetic sensibilities.

'It has been done?' asked the hermit, breaking One's train of thought.

'Yes,' said One. 'Mictlan is no more. The Swimmers will not be drawn. Of course there are still some remains of Mictlan technology here and there. The prototypes. Enclaves leading out into single exterior universes or into pin-galaxies with variant physical laws, but nothing that might attract the Swimmers. Nothing major.'

The hermit nodded, and made a self-satisfied noise. 'You have done well, child.' A wizened, clawed hand emerged from within the robes, holding a data coil. 'Take this. It contains the original records of Mictlan's construction, and a list of my former contacts in the wider universe. With allies and information, you may still prove of further use to the universe.'

One thanked the hermit, and took the coil.

'Now,' said the hermit. 'There is but one task left to you, then I will wish you farewell.'

'Very well,' said One, picking up the shotgun from the ground and lifting himself to his feet. 'Where shall I aim?' He stepped back, pointing the shotgun at the hermit's back.

'Place the barrel to one side of my back,' said the hermit, no fear evident in his voice. 'The destruction of one heart should do it.'

One aimed, and fired. The primitive weapon jerked in his hands as the hermit flew forward, crumpling to the ground. Foul ichor splashed the rocks around him.

One dropped the gun, and stepped back as a blazing light flared from the hermit's body. Moments later, the formerly stooped figure rose to his feet. He threw off the outer layer of his robes, revealing a handsome young man in a simple tunic.

He turned to One. 'Thank you,' he said, in a crystal-clear voice.

'Where will you go?' asked One, as the hermit breathed deeply, exercising his new lungs.

'I have been a hermit, an outcast, for far too long,' said the young man. He pointed into the distance. 'I believe there is a town over there. I think I might go and find out.'

With a brief wave, the former hermit walked away. One watched him as he strode forward, each step taking him closer to the company of others.

Annexe

THE PREDATORS OF THE MULTIVERSE

Extracts from a cosmobiology paper by Simon Bucher-Jones.

The theoretical argument goes like this. The end state of an open[1] universe will, given absolutely infinite past time, extend to infinity.[2] Our universe is open.[3] Therefore at some future point it will expand to infinity. An infinitely expanded universe will exhibit the following characteristics: zero local Einsteinian space-time curvature[4], and little, if any, matter over vast ranges of space-time[5].

[1] So constituted that the gravitational fields of the totality of its mass and energy will not suffice to cause it to collapse inwards after reaching the limits of expansion. A closed universe, one that does so collapse, is mathematically equivalent to a very large black hole.

[2] "Given an infinite past prior to P"... the past light cone of P will already contain an open bubble universe that has already expanded to infinity.' Barrow & Tipler *The Anthropic Cosmological Structure*, commentary by William Laig Craig *The Caused Beginning Of The Universe*.

[3] Perlmutter & Schmidt's work at the Lawrence Berkley National Laboratory in California, and at the Stromlo and Siding Spring Observatory in Australia respectively, confirmed in 1998 that the universe's expansion is not only not slowing but has in fact speeded up by 15% since the universe was half its current age. The reasons for this expansion are not yet known – the term 'quantum gravity' has been tagged to a supposed accelerating force, but its nature is as yet undetermined. However the theory proposed above predicts and offers an explanation for this effect – namely an inter-universal force analogous to gravity. Perlmutter & Schmidt's findings therefore support (do not falsify) this paper.

[4] Imagine a balloon with an infinite diameter, the apparent curvature of its surface would tend to zero.

[5] There are substantial areas of starless space: so called 'voids' which are surrounded by walls or strings of galaxies. These have been detected by the Hubble Deep Field Programme. While voids may of course be dark matter dense, they may already display the characteristics sought above, and if they do not now, the combined processes of expansion and [possible] protonic decay will certainly work to produce such 'real voids' over an infinite (or sufficiently large) timescale.

Such an area of space-time can be regarded mathematically as a domain of De Sitter space.[6] An empty De Sitter space can be shown to lead without additional causal interaction to the creation of a further universe similar to our own.[7] Thus as our universe approaches heat death, it will naturally 'give birth' to one, or more, successor universes.

As the characteristics required for the formation of a quasi-flat De Sitter domain will be reached within a merely large (but non-infinite) time, it is possible that this process has in fact already occurred, and that our universe is itself a 'successor' universe to an older open structure.[8] Further, if it has occurred once, it may well have occurred many times and a number (either large or infinite) of universes have come to be and ended, are currently in existence, and will come into existence after our own. Those universes will themselves expand, either to end as open universes, eventually budding themselves, or as failed closed universes opening out from only to 'fall back' to the surface of the original space-time. It should be noted that these universes

[6] De Sitter space is a theoretical geometric space used in mathematics, it has whatever number of dimensions (n) are necessary for the solution of any particular problem. This step is frankly speculative, however it appears to me to be assumed in F Tipler 'Causality Violation in Asymptotically Flat Space-Times' *Physical Review* 37 (1976): 979.

[7] Gott, for example, theorises that our universe arises in a way analogous to vacuum fluctuations in 'empty' space-time. J R Gott. 'Creation of Open Universes from De Sitter space', *Nature* 295 (1982), 304-7.

[8] The question as to whether an absolutely infinite time can end is a moot one, many philosophers of mathematics have denied that an absolutely infinite amount of time could exist in the past, since if it did we could never have reached the present. However as a merely large period will produce nearly the same degree of flatness of curvature and absence of matter as an infinite period it is not in fact necessary to demonstrate that this has in fact happened. That said, I consider that the existence of apparent singularity discontinuities at the creation points of each universe would have the effect of making it possible for finite periods of time to be defined within each universe, while the ongoing time of the original, or Ur universe, could be regarded as infinite (or larger) that than within any one successor universe.

are not the quantum universes predicted by the Many Worlds Interpretation of Quantum Mechanics.[9] It is therefore theoretically possible that their existence could be detected or that they could be contacted. It is in this theoretical 'metaspace' of universes that the Swimmers, in essence, predator universes, exist.

The approach of a Swimmer to a 'normal' universe could exert a force analogous to gravity between the universes accelerating its expansion in the way detected by Perlmutter & Schmidt (see footnote 3). We may, therefore, conclude that our space-time may shortly[10] impact another.

[9] According to which, every action which can be depicted as a mixed state in Quantum Mechanics results not just in the one real result which we see when the mixed state ceases to be a probability field and becomes measurable upon observation, but in every possible result, the others merely happening in different universes. The Copenhagen Interpretation denies the 'real' existence of such universes and no theoretical methodology exists by which they could be detected.

[10] Within the next billion or so years.